# SUMMER BREEZE

## WILDFLOWER

### JILL SANDERS

GRAYTON

Printed in the United States of America



Published by Grayton Press

DIGITAL ISBN-13: 978-1-945100-60-4

PAPERBACK ISBN: 979-8-831930-92-4

Paperback: 978-1-945100-75-8

# SUMMARY

*The best place for a summer fling?*
*A ritzy adult summer camp.*

The moment Julie laid eyes on Damion five years ago, she'd fallen hard for him. Unfortunately, it was obvious to her that he'd put her in the friend zone. But after a spontaneous weekend sail turns their relationship into something more, the fight for the life that they want together may just turn deadly.

Damion loves his job at the classy camp for snowbirds. Being dubbed the hot pool boy has a few perks, especially with the ladies, even if he's far more than just that. Now that he's finally worked up enough courage to make his move on Jules, he has to deal with some crazy guests accusing him of harassment. Can their love stand the tidal wave of hate aimed directly at them?

# PROLOGUE

Ten-year-old Damion Wells was content with being an outsider. The reason he felt that he stuck out from all the other ten-year-old kids that he knew wasn't because he was the only black kid in the small town of Pelican Point, Florida. Or because he had a black mother and a half-white, half–American Indian father. It wasn't even due to the fact that he lived in a massive house with his great-great-grandmother and both sets of his grandparents.

No, the real reason Damion Wells was an outsider was because, unlike all the other kids around him, he knew exactly what he wanted to do when he grew up.

While all the other kids were boasting about wanting to be pilots, astronauts, or doctors, and days later changing their minds, Damion was certain that someday he was going to be captain of his very own boat.

No matter how much he begged to go out in their small fishing boat, he was lucky if his dad or one of his grandpas took him out once a week. Twice if it was summer and his dad hadn't been out on a military assignment.

To his family, fishing and boating were hobbies or something they did when they wanted to relax. To Damion, it was his life's goal, all he ever wanted. He dreamed of it at night and daydreamed about it when he was awake. All of the time.

When he grew up, he planned on being a captain of his very own sailboat. That way he could spend every day out on the water where he couldn't hear all the mean and hateful things that everyone said to him.

He would allow a few of his friends to come with him. After all, there were a handful of people who stood up for him. Some had even fought off a couple of older bullies that tried to drag him into the ditch where they swore that they had seen a ten-foot alligator the day before.

Aiden Stark and Brett Jewel were both just two years older than he was, but where Damion was skin and bones, both the older boys had muscles already, mainly due to the sports that they both played.

Not that Damion didn't play sports. He liked soccer just fine. But there was far too much running. He couldn't wait until he got into junior high, where he could join the basketball team. There was plenty of running in basketball, but it was inside instead of out in the Florida heat, so that didn't really count.

Besides, he knew that Leif was far too short to play basketball. Leif Harris was one of the town's biggest bullies and the star of the soccer team, along with his best friends Robbie Dixon Jr. and Larry Ryan, two other bullies. Damion made sure to avoid the trio at all costs.

Which is why he absolutely loved the water so much. Out there, the bullies couldn't get to him. Out there, he was in command. Out there, he no longer felt like an outsider.

## CHAPTER ONE

There was a point in everyone's life where you had to stand up for a completely different path than the one everyone else expected from you. Taking the job at River Camps was that break in stride that Damion had needed. Over five years later, he still didn't regret breaking away.

Even though he'd attended college for the first few years out of high school like his parents had wanted him to, he'd still felt that strong pull to the water. He never felt that way taking the business classes that he'd signed up for because his parents had nagged him about college.

At first, his parents and his surviving grandparents—his grandmother on his dad's side and his grandfather on his mother's side—had tried to talk him out of working at the swanky adult summer camp.

But then he'd convinced Elle and the rest of her Wildflower gang to let his family spend a week at the resort before the doors officially opened. After their first day there, his family stopped complaining about his job. Now, they paid Elle and her friends yearly for access to the pools and the fun activities and events they held each week.

His parents had learned how to ballroom dance at the camp, along with zip lining and yoga, and his mother was even taking self-defense classes taught by Aubrey.

There wasn't a week that went by where his parents didn't have massages booked with the camp's masseuse, Andrea, a woman his mother claimed he should marry right away. Damion was pretty sure his mother was saying that just so Andrea would give her free massages.

Still, the camp had a lot to offer him in the dating field. In the five years he'd worked there, he'd never been bored. The camp boasted plenty of local hotties to pick from. And over the five years, he had gone out on dates with most of them. All but one.

He was currently hanging out around the front desk, waiting for Julie—or as he called her, Jules—to get off the phone. Jules was by far the prettiest and smartest woman he'd ever met. She was funny to the point that even thinking about her had him busting a smile.

There wasn't a day that went by when he didn't enjoy being around her or think about asking her out.

The only problem?

She'd put him in the dreaded friend zone. Actually, in the five years they had both worked at the camp, she'd put every man he knew in that same zone.

That had never happened to him before and he wasn't quite sure what to do to get out of it. Or if it was even possible.

At first, he hadn't even known how to act around Jules. It had been going on so long now that he pushed it to the back of his mind whenever he was around her. He had grown so comfortable around her that their relationship had changed over the years, and he found himself starting to flirt more and more openly.

They had slid into a flirty-friend comfort zone that he had never experienced before. Nor had anyone else he knew.

Julie Kahala was a lot like him in many ways. Her Hawaiian descent made her a target for the haters that filled the backwoods zone they lived in. He knew that she lived with her parents and her grandmother. Her father's mother wanted to be called Tutu, which he had found out was a Hawaiian thing that grandparents were called. The name suited the woman. She was as spunky and energetic as his own grand-mother was.

The other thing they had in common was how much she loved her job. It was so obvious to everyone around her. She practically glowed each morning when she showed up for work.

He knew that she'd attended some online classes after grad-uating from high school in Panama City, which wasn't too far from the camp.

Besides all that, she looked pretty amazing in the summer dresses she was always wearing. Like the pretty white and red one she was wearing today. She'd bleached her long dark hair recently. Normally there was a slight curl to the long tresses, but today it was straight. She'd pulled the top part up and had one of the pretty flowers she normally wore just above her left ear.

"Hey, girl," he said the moment she hung up.

Jules's smile grew. "Look at you." She ran her eyes over him.

Yeah, she'd caught on and had started flirting back almost a full year back. Now, it was a game, one that excited him more than if he'd just straight up asked her out.

"You clean up nicely," she finished after taking in his button-up shirt, black slacks, and matching tie. "Hot date?"

He laughed. "I wish. They're shorthanded tonight, and I agreed to lend a hand."

Jules leaned her elbow on the countertop and rested her chin in her hand with a sigh. "It's a Summer to Remember night."

He nodded. Once a week, the camp held themed dinner-dance events. Most nights there was something fun going on—live music, karaoke, ballroom dancing—but once a week, there was a real big shindig, as the Wildflowers called them.

The Wildflowers were the five best friends who owned the River Camps. They consisted of Elle, Hannah, Aubrey, and sisters Zoey and Scarlett.

The Wildflowers had met at the camp back when Elle's grandfather owned it. They'd all been in the same cabin and they'd chosen the name Wildflowers for their group. They had remained friends outside of camp, and the name had stuck with them their entire lives. They even had their own cheer, and it was quite funny to watch a group of grown women, two of which were currently pregnant, jumping around like teenagers.

Zoey was already a new mom. Her and her husband Dylan's daughter Paige had been born last year. Now both Elle and Hannah were expecting kids. Which is why they were short-staffed.

"Don't you usually work at these events too?" he asked Jules.

"Sometimes." She shrugged, her eyes still running over him.

Normally, he was dressed in boardshorts, flip-flops, and a camp T-shirt or tank top. He'd had to dress up to help out at these events on several other occasions, but this was the first time Jules had taken so much notice.

"I'm sorry." She straightened suddenly. "Did you need something from me?"

He smiled. "My mother said she left me something up here?"

Her smile doubled. "Yes." She disappeared into the back room and came back holding a large, covered pan.

He instantly felt his stomach grumble at the thought of his mother's homemade brownies.

"Is it your birthday or something?" Jules asked as she set the pan down in front of him.

"Nope," he said as he lifted the lid and smiled at the chocolate frosting. He opened the note his mother had left him and scanned it quickly.

*"An offering and an excuse for you to ask the girl out finally. Give her a damn brownie too. Love, the woman who birthed you."*

Okay, so maybe another reason he hadn't asked Jules out was that his family loved her like she was already part of it. In the past year, Jules had attended more of his family functions than he had. His parents and even his grandparents made a point to invite her to everything. The crazy thing was, she always went and appeared to enjoy herself. She'd even brought along her folks a few times.

There wouldn't be a quick summer fling with Jules. His family, and maybe their friendship, wouldn't survive the outcome if things turned... bad.

"I guess it's just my lucky day," he said after tucking the card in his pocket.

"It must be." Jules eyed the pan.

"Want one?" he asked, pushing the pan towards her.

"No." She shook her head and put her hands out. "I'm watching my figure."

"Why?" he asked, running his eyes over her perfect form. "You're perfect the way you are."

She laughed, the way most women did when they didn't really believe a compliment.

It was true that Jules didn't fit the mold of the skinny women running around that seemed to be the US standard. She was shorter, probably only five-four, and her skin was a soft taupe color, naturally. She was lush in ways that others looked at negatively, but all he could see was beauty. He dreamed of exploring those curves.

"I'm serious," he said, getting her attention.

"Thanks, but I'll pass. The last time I enjoyed one of your mother's brownies, I had to attend Elle's yoga classes for two weeks to burn off the calories," she joked. "I don't know how you can eat stuff like that and stay looking like you do." She shook her head slightly as she ran her eyes over his suit and tie again.

He shrugged. "I burn a lot of calories sailing and swimming," he explained. "I'd better save these for after the dinner." He shut the lid and slid the container back towards her. "Save them for me back here?" he asked, knowing it would be another excuse to see her later.

She smiled and nodded. "Sure thing. You'd better head on in."

He glanced down the hall where large double doors led to the main dining area. He could hear voices starting to gather inside.

The guests would arrive for the event via the outside doors off a large patio area that held more dining tables and overlooked the camp's lush green lawn. The waters of the Gulf of Mexico were just beyond.

"Aren't you heading in?" he asked her.

"I have a few things to finish up here first. Then I plan on grabbing some of the dinner and taking it home with me."

One of the perks of working there was that employees had

access to one of the best chefs in the States. Celebrity chef Isaac Andrews had run the kitchens at the camp since the doors had reopened.

"Smart move," Damion said. "Well, if you want, grab a brownie on your way out." He shook his head. "Otherwise, I'll be eating brownies for breakfast, lunch, and dinner all week."

"I might take you up on that offer." She turned to go back to her computer.

He started to walk away, but then on a whim turned back to her. He'd been wanting to ask her the question all week but kept putting it off. Now was his chance.

"I'm going sailing next weekend. I have the entire weekend off and was planning on a quick trip down to St. George," he said quickly.

"Oh?" Jules looked up from her computer.

He moved closer. "I overheard you telling Andrea you had that weekend off. Want to tag along for the ride?"

He watched her face closely. He'd been thinking about asking her along on one of his trips for a while now. But this was the first time he'd gotten the nerve to. He supposed it was his mother's brownies and his conversation with Tutu that pushed him over the edge this time.

"I... can I let you know later this week?" she asked.

"Oh, sure, yeah." He started backing up and stopped when he bumped into the trashcan and almost knocked it over. Thankfully, he was quick enough to stop it from dumping a full day's worth of trash onto the lobby floor. He turned to leave quickly and bumped solidly into the doorway. He heard Jules chuckle at him, and he quickly turned around and rushed from the room.

He was a complete idiot. He shouldn't have asked her. He should have been ... smoother. He normally was a hell of a lot better at this than that. Why couldn't he get his shit together around her?

He stepped into the massive room and instantly fought the urge to turn around and head back out to spend more time with Jules. Instead, he lifted his chin and went to find out what he could do to help get things ready for the guests.

Almost five hours later, he was in the middle of helping a couple move some chairs to their table when he glanced over and saw Jules stroll in, looking as if she was searching the room for someone. When her eyes landed on him, she smiled and started heading his way.

"There you are," he told the older couple.

"Thank you, young man." The woman sat down. "These old bones of mine don't like standing for too long anymore."

"Enjoy," he said just as Jules stopped beside him. "Hi," he said to Jules. "Taking off for the night finally?"

"Yeah. I wanted to just say thanks again." She motioned to a plate of brownies she was holding along with a container of food from the kitchens.

"Any time," he said.

"Oh, what a lovely couple you two make," the woman who had just sat down said to them.

"We're..." he started to say, but Jules laid a hand on his arm and quickly said, "Thank you."

"Look, Charles, don't they remind you of us at that age?" the old woman said.

Damion wanted to laugh. First off, the couple was as white as could be. Actually, since they were from Minnesota and it was early spring, they were paler than white. They were down-right ghostly. Still, they were nice, so he didn't say anything. He just nodded and took Jules's hand and stepped away from the table.

"I bet they were just adorable when they were younger," Jules said softly.

"Take some air with me?" he asked suddenly, needing the cool of the spring air outside.

"Sure." She followed him through the crowd to the wall of French doors.

The moment he stepped out on the patio with her by his side, he felt more at ease. He hadn't realized how stuffy the massive room had gotten.

"Better?" Jules asked as he stepped to the low banister at the edge of the patio. It was dark, but the pool lights in the distance showcased that there were still guests enjoying the larger pool. Beyond that, he could just make out the lights at the docks where his sailboat, the *Wind Chaser*, was harbored.

"Much." He glanced over as she leaned against the railing and looked out over the darkness beyond.

"It gets stuffy in there with so many bodies," Jules said as she set her dinner down on the balcony.

"It can," he agreed. "I didn't mean to keep you from your dinner." He motioned to the food.

"It's fine." She sighed and then turned suddenly. "Maybe I'll just enjoy it out here before heading home?" she suggested with a giggle.

"You should. I might sneak some food away for myself and join you."

"Oh, do," she said quickly. "Eating alone is so..."

"Depressing?" he asked.

"Lonely," she corrected.

# CHAPTER TWO

Jules should just shut up. She was allowing her mouth to rattle on unchecked, something her mother always claimed would get her in trouble.

Out of the grace of his kindness, Damion agreed to grab some food and enjoy it out on the veranda with her so that she wouldn't be lonely. Her words, not his.

Now she was going on about... God, she didn't even know what she was talking about.

"And that's why the book was better than the movie," she heard herself finishing up.

"I'll keep that in mind when I pick out the next book to read," Damion joked.

"I think we both know that you probably don't spend a lot of time reading," she said and felt mortified at her words. She really should shut up soon.

"You'd be surprised," he replied with a smile.

Over the years, she'd come to learn each of Damion's moods. Right now, he wasn't acting offended or bored. Then again, she hadn't stopped talking or gained control over her mouth yet.

No matter how much she tried, she just couldn't stop herself from babbling around him. It was probably due to the fact that her heart rate was always elevated when he was around.

She knew from her online first aid classes that that meant her brain was flooding with endorphins, causing the nerves, and her mouth, to go on a rampage.

"You must not have been that hungry," Damion pointed out.

"Hm?" she asked, trying to physically bite her lips and hold them together.

"All you've had of that chicken salad is two bites," he pointed out.

"Oh." She looked down at her forgotten food. "Right." He was politely telling her to shut up and eat. She took a few more bites. And then he did something stupid. He asked her another question.

"How are those online classes coming?"

"Good," she said, telling herself to leave it at that.

"You were taking first aid and..." he asked, waiting.

"Graphic design."

He smiled. "Okay."

"First aid is just the refresher course I take each year. I get my CPR and CERT trainings out of the way. I started taking the classes when Elle said the camp would pay for the training for any employee who wanted it."

"Yeah, I take it too. It's always good to know what to do in case of an emergency." He frowned slightly. "Your dad is a fireman, right?"

She nodded. "Retired. He still volunteers every now and then when needed."

He nodded. "Your mother? What did she do?"

"School nurse. Still is at the high school. She keeps threatening to retire but says she wouldn't know what to do with her time."

"Cool." He nodded. "And the graphic design classes?"

"I wanted to see if I could help out a little more around the camp. I figured that if I knew a little bit about design work then I could lend a hand with some basic marketing," she answered. "I helped create last year's flyer and had fun doing so. I wanted to be able to learn how to do more with the design programs they have. Plus, it helps fill the downtime I have sitting behind the desk," she added with a shrug.

"That's cool," he said, but his eyes returned to the dark water beyond. "From what I've seen, you've always been very busy."

She was boring him. Oh god. This was worse than the nightmares she'd had of their first date together, where she'd opened the door wearing her softest and most comfortable pajamas, the ones with the pink stars and purple moons on them. She'd also been wearing the retainer she'd worn in high school and her glasses instead of her contact lenses.

Being dubbed the ugly duckling of the school had left her marked for life and with extremely low self-esteem. She'd spent most of her adult life trying to push beyond it.

This job here at the camp had helped her achieve that. Until Damion had started flirting with her. Then everything had changed.

"Oh, normally I am. But there are slow times. I'm sure you have a lot of downtime too," she answered.

He smiled. "Not as much as I'd hoped."

"Still, our jobs aren't as difficult as some. Before working here, I was an office assistant at a chiropractic place in Destin." She rolled her eyes. "Worst job ever."

He nodded and was quiet for a moment. "Yeah, I don't know what I would have done if this hadn't opened up for me."

"It must be amazing to get to go on sails whenever you want." She sighed. She'd gotten to go on one a few months ago during the slow season. It had been cool, since it was in the middle of winter, but it had been amazing.

"You seemed to enjoy it last time you went out," he said.

The fact that he'd taken note of her and remembered that she'd enjoyed herself back then made her smile.

"I love sailing," she admitted. "I don't get to go as often as I want."

"Have you thought about coming with me in a week?" he asked.

"I... have." She nodded. She had done nothing but think about it. She did love sailing, but she'd only been on short trips. The longest she'd been out on the water had been for that sunset tour.

The thought of sailing down the coast to St. George had her scared. Not that she didn't trust Damion. She did without a doubt. Over the past five years, she knew for a fact that he'd taken the same trip at least three times a year.

She knew that he had a place down there that was owned by his family or something. She didn't know the details, but he often talked about staying at the house when he sailed there.

"In truth," she said, feeling stupid but knowing she had to give him an answer, "I've never sailed that far."

"Afraid?" he asked, and she knew he was teasing.

"Yes." She laughed. "Weren't you the first time you sailed alone?"

"You won't be alone," he said calmly.

"No, I suppose I won't. Still, it's pretty far. I don't even know how long it takes you to get down there."

"About four hours if the wind is good."

"What about weather?" she asked. "We get afternoon storms sometimes."

He smiled. "The sailboat still works in the rain."

"Lightning?" she asked, her mind playing over the possibilities.

"The mast allows the lighting to pass through without harming any of the instruments or the boat. You'd be safe. You have my word," he added softly. "It's a nice short trip. The sunset tour you went on was about half the time we would be spending on the water. Although most of that time was spent sitting still in the water so that the guests could enjoy the sunset." She was quiet for a moment. "Take your time deciding. We have a week and a half before I leave." He smiled at her. "I'd better..." He motioned to the doors. Several people had come outside in the past few moments, which meant things were winding down. She knew that most crew who worked at the event helped clean up after.

"Yeah, thanks for spending your break with me." She shoved the rest of her food back into the container. She hadn't eaten much, but figured that when she got home, she'd probably finish it. Along with the brownie.

"Thank *you*," he said, standing up. "It was a nice break."

He started to turn and leave, but then stopped. "I hope you do come. On the trip. I think we would have a great time together."

With that, he turned around and stepped back inside, leaving her on the patio in the cooler spring night.

It was a short walk from the main building to the parking lot. The entire time she drove home, she berated herself and ran through the pros and cons of going on the trip with Damion.

As she let herself into her small apartment, which sat next to the local laundromat in town, she realized that the pros far outweighed the cons. She had to jump. Just had to. If she didn't, Damion might not ever invite her on another trip with him.

She pulled off her shoes and sat on her sofa to send him a text message.

"I've thought about it. Count me in."

She didn't have to wait long for his response.

"Cool. I think you'll have fun. I promise we'll be safe. We can talk more tomorrow. Night."

She drifted off to sleep that night dreaming of sailing into the sunset with Damion. How many times had she had the same dream over the past five years? Too many to count.

The following morning, as she sat around a large round table and listened to Elle hold a brief employee meeting, she started having second thoughts.

Why had Damion invited only her? Not that she was complaining, but... why? Over the years, she'd watched him hit on so many women. She knew for a fact that he'd gone on a lot of dates. Far more than the measly two dates she'd gone on in the past year. Both of them ended up in nothing but disappointment.

She knew that he hadn't been with anyone longer than just a few dates, had heard through the rumor mill that he was a player. But having known him during all this time, she still doubted it.

She'd known players before and had even dated one before and promised herself never again. What if things changed between her and Damion? Would she be prepared to let his friendship go if things turned bad?

What was she thinking? Of course, Damion had only invited her on the trip as a friend. She pushed all other thoughts aside and focused on her work.

Each day, she welcomed new guests and arranged for a

welcome committee member to show them to their individual cabins. Sometimes she took them out to the many cabins herself.

There were thirty-eight small cabins now scattered around the massive property, which meant that at any given point there were close to a hundred guests on site.

Each of the unique cabins had distinctive names. Besides the cabins, there was the main building, which housed the welcome center, front desk area, gift shop, main dining hall and ballroom, employee's offices and dining room, and first aid office on the main floor. The second floor had more than twenty employee housing rooms, little apartments for employees who wanted to rent them out instead of finding housing of their own. The top floor was a private residence where the Wild-flowers stayed when they needed to. All of them had other full-time residences, but sometimes if they worked late, they would just head upstairs instead.

Zoey and Dylan had built a home on the edge of the camp's land. Elle and Liam lived in an actual tree house on the grounds. With her being pregnant, however, they spent more and more time upstairs in the apartment and had plans to build their own home next to Zoey and Dylan's.

Hannah and Owen owned a huge house just outside Pelican Point.

Scarlett and Levi lived in town in his home, which they were remodeling. Aubrey and Aiden lived in their place on the other edge of the campgrounds. Still, at least one night a week, the five best friends gathered upstairs together.

She'd been invited to a couple of those special nights over the years and had been to each and everyone's weddings and bridal and baby showers. They had even given her and Dr. Lea Val titles of honorary Wildflower members.

It was so nice working with a group of women she consid

ered close friends. Maybe it was one of the reasons she'd stuck around so long. That and she really loved what she did. She loved greeting the new guests. Showing them the beautiful grounds and all the exciting, adventurous things there were to do on the grounds.

Besides amazing food, there were three swimming pools, horseback riding, zip lining, sailing, kayaking, fishing, volleyball, and newly built pickleball courts, just to name a few things.

There were two full-time massage therapists, Andrea and Kara, whom she had occasionally enjoyed massages from herself. She'd even purchased sessions for her parents for their anniversary last year.

All in all, River Camps really was a wonderful place that had it all, except for being kid friendly. Only adults were allowed as guests, something that she, as the main person answering the phone, had heard complaints about over and over.

It was right there all over the brochure and website—an adults-only summer camp experience.

It wasn't as if there weren't plenty of places nearby that catered to families. There were tons of them. But, still, people liked to complain.

They had actually had several people try and sneak kids in in the last year. How they expected the kids not to be noticed at the swimming pools or other activities was beyond her.

Thankfully, she hadn't been the one being yelled at when she'd had to tell them they had to leave. Elle had always taken that bullet for her.

Elle Costas had grown up living at the camp and in a home she still owned in Pelican Point. Her grandfather had owned the elite summer camp for young girls and, after his death, the five friends had inherited the place and turned it into what it was today.

It was just after lunchtime when Damion walked through the front doors. Her entire body responded when she heard his laughter.

He was chatting with Carter, the employee who handled the horses and horseback rides. The man only worked at the camp a few hours each day. He was an actual veterinarian who worked at a local sanctuary in town but since he was friends with the Wildflowers, he'd agreed to help out when he could.

But everyone knew that he absolutely loved working at the camp. She didn't know why she hadn't ever had a crush on Carter. The man was a very attractive package. He was not only one of the nicest guys she knew but was damn sexy to boot.

The fact that he was a vet and loved animals just added extra bonus points.

Actually, there were several guys who worked at the camp that she should feel attraction towards. But all of them paled in comparison to Damion, so there was no point in wasting her time. How was it that they hadn't ever gone on a date? Somehow in her heart, she knew that he was the one. So many times, she'd dreamed of what it would be like to be with him.

On the two dates she'd gone out on in the past year, she'd spent the entire evening comparing the men to him.

Damion laughed at something Carter said, then the men slapped each other on the shoulder and did that bro-bump guys do before parting ways. Carter disappeared into the dining hall, and Damion walked towards her.

CHAPTER THREE

Damion leaned on the counter and ran his eyes over Jules. She was wearing one of those cotton summer dresses she always wore. The kind that made her look like a summer goddess, a tropical dream. Today's dress was bright yellow and had green flowers all over it. Her long hair was tied in a braid that hung over her shoulder, and she had a white flower tucked just above her ear. She looked every bit Hawaiian, and he found it more appealing than he wanted to think about at the moment.

"So," he said as he gave her a smile.

"So?" She smiled back at him.

"There's this couple." He motioned to the front doors. "They're about a hundred years old. He's even in one of those electric chairs. And Carter just caught them having sex on the pathway."

"Seriously?" She chuckled as she shook her head. "Old people like sex too. I just never knew how much until I started working here. I've had my share of..."

"Run-ins?" he suggested. "That's what everyone calls them."

"Yes." She laughed.

Every staff member had their own stories of run-ins. There had been stories of orgies and crazy parties at the pools or in the cabins since the camp opened.

"How many guests am I taking out for the sunset sail tonight?" he asked her.

She glanced at her screen and checked the scheduling app they used. He could have logged into the app on his phone, but then he wouldn't have had the excuse to talk to her.

"Six couples," she answered after looking. "Zoey's going with you tonight."

"Yeah." He nodded. "She's been begging to go out again. I think she loves sailing almost as much as I do. What about you?" Damion asked her, leaning a little more on the counter.

"Me?" she asked, trying to search his eyes.

"What sort of hobbies or things do you love?" He had learned a lot about her over the years but felt as if he was still missing things.

She shrugged. "I don't have a lot of time for hobbies."

He chuckled and shook his head. "I've heard you singing karaoke. Girl, you got some pipes on you."

He watched her cheeks turn pink. "Thanks."

"Did you train?" he asked her.

"No, just... Both of my parents are musical. I grew up singing with them." She glanced over his shoulder as a couple stepped through the front doors and headed towards the desk.

He knew he'd have to let her get back to work. He wanted to hang around until after she answered the couple's questions, but then he spotted Elle walking towards him. She had that look in her eyes, the one she always got when she needed to ask him a favor.

Leaving the front desk area, he met Elle in front of the large staircase.

"What do you need me to do this time?" he asked as she stopped in front of him. He noticed that her hands covered her growing belly.

Hannah was a few months more pregnant than Elle, but their belly sizes were almost identical. Maybe because Hannah was like five-six and Elle was almost as tall as he was?

Elle smiled at him. "I was hoping you'd help me." She grabbed his arm and dragged him towards her office.

He was a sucker for her and the rest of the Wildflowers. To be honest, if it wasn't for them, he'd probably be stuck in a job in an office or worse. His soul yearned to be on the water. Thrived there.

He was pretty sure that it would shrivel up and die if it didn't have a daily dose of wind and waves.

He couldn't wait until both she and Hannah had their kids. Most of the time they wanted him to lift things or get things down off of high shelves.

He didn't mind, but today it was eating into his flirting time with Jules.

"When are those babies due again?" he asked as they stepped into her office.

She stopped dead and looked at him. Her eyes going big.

"How did you know?" she asked as she bit her bottom lip.

"Know?" he asked, his eyes going down to her large belly. Then it hit him. He suddenly understood why she was the same size as Hannah even though her due date was three months behind her friends. "Holy shit," he said, covering his mouth and then doing a little dance around Elle. "Twins," he sang as he twirled her in his arms.

"Shh!" She laughed and reached over to shut her door. "I

thought…" She narrowed her eyes. "You meant Hannah's baby and mine, didn't you?"

He nodded. "Yeah, but now." He wiggled his eyebrows. "Twins."

"Shh!" she said again. "No one knows yet. Liam and I want to keep it a secret until the gender reveal this week."

"Okay, okay, I gotcha." He nodded and then pulled her into his arms. Then he drew back. "Hey, I thought you weren't supposed to know the sex of the baby until the big gender reveals this weekend?"

"We don't know the sex, or sexes." She smiled. "But we knew early on there were two of them." She rubbed her hands over her belly. "During the doctor's appointment, we heard both heartbeats."

"Congrats, mama." He hugged her again.

Just then the office door opened, and Liam stepped in. The man's eyes narrowed for a second then he smiled at them. "Should I be worried?" he asked playfully.

Damion dropped his arms and then walked over and slapped Liam on the shoulder. "Just heard your good news is doubled."

Liam frowned and looked over at Elle.

"My misunderstanding," she said with a roll of her eyes. "He asked when the babies were due." She shook her head. "Pregnancy fog had me believing he meant"—she pointed to her stomach with both of her thumbs— "instead of me and Hannah."

Liam chuckled and shut the door behind him. "I told you we wouldn't be able to keep it a secret for much longer." Liam walked over and hugged Elle. "You're getting too big."

"Me?" She glanced down at her belly.

"You're bigger than Hannah," Damion chimed in. The pair of them turned towards him. "Don't worry." He held up his hands, then pretended to zip his lips together and toss the imaginary key over his shoulder before crossing his heart.

"How old are you?" Elle chuckled as she walked over and hugged him. "Thanks," she said softly.

"Elle really wanted to surprise everyone at the gender reveal this weekend."

"Boy, are they going to be surprised," he added. "What did you need me to get down for you?" he asked, looking around the room. "Or lift?"

Elle sighed. "Nothing, I... overheard Jules telling Zoey that she was going on your little trip next weekend."

He held in a groan. "We're friends. I've taken loads of friends..." The look she gave him had him shutting his mouth.

"On that note..." Liam made a move towards the door, but Elle took his arm and stopped him.

"Say something to him," Elle said, motioning between them.

"Like what? It's about damn time he made a move?" Liam joked, earning a pinch on his arm from Elle.

"He can't break her heart. We won't let him," Elle added.

"What makes you think I'll break her heart?" Damion asked.

This time both of them turned and looked at him, causing him to roll his eyes.

"I won't. If anything..." He thought about it and a sinking feeling had his heartbeat skipping. "She's the one that will be doing the breaking. That is, if anything happens. I fully intend for the weekend to be nothing more than two friends going on a nice peaceful trip. Jules's Tutu happened to mention to me last week during our lunch how stressed Jules has been lately."

"Not about work, I hope?" Elle asked, taking a step towards him.

"No, apparently... it's a family thing." Her grandmother

had confided in him about her father's health and how his latest doctor's visits had brought up the possibility of the early stages of Alzheimer's.

"Right." Elle seemed to relax. "Okay," she said, then her eyes narrowed. "Friends?"

He nodded. "I promise." He held up his fingers.

"You were never a Boy Scout," Elle said, walking over and taking his hand in hers. "I trust you." She leaned up and placed a kiss on his check. "I've known you too long not too. Just... enjoy. Everyone knows the two of you have been dancing around each other for a long time now. I'm not opposed to... whatever, just... don't hurt her and don't get hurt. I'd hate to see it."

He nodded and then decided to change the subject. "Twins." He looked down at her belly. "Going to name one after me?"

Liam laughed. "Hell no."

He smiled. "It was worth a shot." He shrugged.

Since his time was short after the interruption, he headed down to the docks directly after leaving Elle's office.

There were four couples already lined up on the dock waiting for him.

"Evening," he said as he walked over to the *Wind Chaser*. After stepping onboard, he held out his hand to help the first guest step on board. "Who is ready for some fun?"

The couples cheered and happily stepped on board.

They waited for the rest of the group as the guests settled on board and he prepared to head out to the Gulf. Since he kept an eagle eye on the weather, he knew that it would be a perfect night for the sunset tour.

He'd already restocked the champagne, wine, and beer, along with plenty of complementary souvenir refillable water bottles with the camp's logo.

Normally, one of the other staff members worked with him for each sunset tour. Tonight, Zoey rushed to the sailboat just before the last couple arrived.

"Sorry I'm late," she said, helping the last couple on board. "Paige fell asleep in my arms, and I lost track of time." She smiled.

"I'd say it was perfect timing." He shrugged. "But you can ask my boss if you want?"

Zoey laughed. "All aboard?" she asked looking around.

"Six couples." He nodded. "Ready to head out."

This was the part of the evening he loved. The first few moments heading out to open water. For the first half hour, Zoey filled everyone's drink orders while he navigated them out of the narrow canal and headed out to the bay and then into the Gulf's crystal-clear waters. Once they were in open water, he shut off the onboard motor, and Zoey helped him raise the sails.

He let several couples take pictures of themselves standing behind the wheel with the sunset behind them before someone spotted the first dolphin. After that, everyone was glued to the water, looking for more.

Zoey made her way towards him and lowered her voice.

"Not to raise any alarms, but I'm going to suggest that we not allow the Steins to return." She motioned to the middle-aged couple staring out at the water with sour looks on their faces.

He hadn't known the couple's names or, for that matter, cared too much. It wasn't as if he normally got close to any of the guests. Sometimes, there were those who had extended stays or had booked him for private trips, and he grew familiar with them.

"Okay," he said slowly.

"Just a heads-up, I doubt you'll be getting a tip from them."

Zoey sighed heavily. "Honestly, if we weren't in the middle of the Gulf, I'd kick them off the boat right now."

He turned to her and for the first time since she'd started talking, noticed the anger in her eyes.

"Did they say something to you?" he asked, immediately going on guard.

He understood that not all guests were cordial. Since opening the gates, they'd had a few run-ins with guests. Some had to be asked to leave, while a couple others had to be hauled away by the police.

Zoey moved closer and lowered her voice even more. "Since stepping foot on your boat, they've complained constantly about you."

"Me?" He frowned and glanced over at the couple again. Hell, he couldn't remember saying two words to them. What would they have to... He saw it then in the man's eyes as he glanced his way. Utter disgust. Not at anything Damion had done or said, but at who he was.

It wasn't the first time he'd seen that look in someone's eyes, nor would it be the last.

"Don't worry about it," he told Zoey, giving the couple no more of his attention. After all, that's what haters wanted. Attention. To spread the way that they felt like a disease. He'd learned long ago that the best way to win was to ignore them when you could. "They'll soon be on their way and off my boat."

"I just can't fathom that in this age there are still those out there thinking they are better because of the pigment of their skin," Zoey said, sitting beside him.

"It's not the first time I or others of darker skin have had to deal with people like that." He motioned. "Remember what happened to Lea?"

"Yes, which is why the moment we dock, I'm having security escort them off the campgrounds. River Camps does not condone that sort of behavior."

"They haven't harmed anyone," he pointed out, not sure why he was defending the couple. Then again, he hadn't heard what they'd said. "On a scale of one to ten, how bad was what they said?"

Zoey seemed to think about it. "Five."

"Let's see how the rest of the trip pans out," he suggested. "We don't want to spoil anyone else's good time." He motioned to the rest of the group having fun taking pictures and sipping their drinks.

"Fine, it's up to you. But if you want, I can have them off the grounds tonight." Zoey went over to refill someone else's wine.

Most of the time, people like the couple tended to grumble but rarely said anything in situations like this to cause attention from anyone other than the person they were hating on. This couple seemed to fit that bill perfectly. Even though looks were aimed at him, not once did they say anything directly to him.

He was pretty sure Zoey had overheard the man saying something to his wife, since neither of them talked to anyone else during the entire trip.

By the time they docked, Zoey had calmed down and had agreed not to take any action against the couple. At least for now.

Zoey had been correct—he hadn't received a tip from the Steins. Not that he lived off tips alone. The camp paid him well enough to keep him in comfort. Besides, he really loved what he did for a living.

He enjoyed waking up in the early hours to make sure all three of the swimming pools were cleaned. He added any chemicals needed, cleaned the filters, and scooped out leaves. Then he headed down to the boathouse and helped guests check out paddle boards, kayaks, and canoes. Occasionally, a couple would book a special day sail, and at least twice a week there were enough to take out for the sunset tour.

Since he was a camp employee, he got two free meals in the employee lounge a day and discounts on all the services, such as massages, horseback rides, zip lining, and other events. He was also occasionally called on to help out at one of the weekly dinner events, where he earned plenty of tips.

All in all, his life was like one big party filled with fun people, events, and things he enjoyed.

Even if he had to deal with an occasional jerk, the perks far outweighed everything else.

"I'm sorry," Zoey said as she helped Damion clean up the deck of the sailboat.

"For?" he asked, tossing the bags of trash over his shoulder. There were large bins for trash at the edge of the parking area.

"It just gets to me. Hearing that shit." Zoey shook her head. "You know, I don't mind gossip, name calling, or someone being rude because they're just assholes, but racism is a whole different ballpark. After what Lea went through last year, I guess you can say my eyes are opened to it a lot more."

"That's because, and don't take offense, it never directly affected you," he pointed out.

"You're right." She nodded. "After the sensitivity training we all went through after what happened, I realized that. Still, it really sucks."

He set the trash bags down and walked over to hug Zoey. "Go home to your family." He kissed the top of her head. "Thanks for being woke," he added with a chuckle.

She pinched his arm playfully. "Thanks for letting me go out tonight. I know Reece was supposed to. He told me you rearranged things for me. I needed a night out on the water."

"Having a kid can drive you crazy," he said as he picked up

the trash again. She followed him off the boat and they made their way towards the parking area.

"Oh, but so worth it. We're already planning our next one," Zoey said with a smile.

"Seriously?" He shook his head. "You and your friends are going to have to make this place a kid-friendly zone soon."

Zoey laughed at that. "I hear you and Jules are going out next weekend?" she asked. "Taking her to your place down the coast?"

"Yeah, she hasn't been there, and I made a promise..." He dropped off.

"What?" Zoey asked, stopping on the trail to look at him.

"Nothing." He shook his head. But Zoey gave him a look, and he knew he wasn't going to be able to get out of telling her. "Okay, just don't... tell anyone. Not even the rest of the Wildflowers. Promise?"

She narrowed her eyes. "No, we tell each other everything."

He groaned then started walking.

"Okay," she said, taking his arm and catching up with him. "What?"

He narrowed his eyes at her then shrugged. "Jules's dad is having some... health issues. Tutu asked me to take her out next weekend while they head to Pensacola to see a specialist. She didn't want Jules to worry too much. She's been... taking it hard."

"I wondered..." Zoey sighed. "She's been acting... quiet, lately."

He nodded. "Yeah, I noticed too."

"What can we do for her?" Zoey asked.

"Nothing. She hasn't told anyone because she doesn't want anyone to know. If her grandmother hadn't mentioned it to me during our lunch, we'd all still be in the dark. She'll tell us when she wants to." He touched Zoey's arm.

Zoey smiled. "Agreed. But at least I can convince chef Isaac to hook you up on your trip." She rubbed her hands together. "He knows all of Jules's favorite dishes and desserts." She clapped her hands. "It's decided. I'll arrange all the meals." She rushed down the pathway in the opposite direction of the parking lot.

He shrugged, knowing there was no use arguing or complaining. Besides, most of the time when he sailed down the coast, he ate sandwiches or grilled fish that he'd caught and had to cook himself. Having the entire trip catered by a top chef sounded very appealing. Almost as appealing has having Jules along for the ride.

# CHAPTER FOUR

That weekend the main hall was closed off for Hannah's and Elle's baby gender reveals. Most of the guests had come and gone for their early dinners while others who hadn't eaten yet were shown to the dining area by the main swimming pool.

The entire dining hall was decorated in soft yellows. Even though Hannah had less than two months before her due date, they had kept the gender of the baby a secret, waiting for Elle to get word.

Jules knew that the five friends did almost everything together.

"Wow, this looks amazing," Hannah said, stepping into the hall. She and Elle had been blocked from helping decorate for the evening.

"The benefits of owning the place," Elle said as she rubbed her belly. "We get to host as many parties as we want." She laughed as she and Hannah were shown to their seats by Aubrey.

"Get off your feet," Aubrey said, motioning to the two

chairs in the middle of a circle of other chairs. "I'll get you something to drink. We'll have food first, then presents, followed by games."

Both Elle and Hannah groaned. "Can't we just go to the big reveal first?"

"Nope, the men will arrive after the games, and we will do the reveals then." Aubrey shuffled off to get drinks.

Elle looked at Jules. "Help. Make them change the order."

Jules laughed and sat down beside Elle. "Just so we're clear, you want me to go against Aubrey, Zoey, and Scarlett?"

Elle slumped in her chair. "Yeah, okay, that was a stupid request."

"Who planned this party, anyway?" Hannah sighed and then took the drink that Aubrey handed her.

"I had better not hear a word of complaint from either of you," Aubrey said, narrowing her eyes. "Or the reveal portion of the night is off."

Hannah chuckled and then pretended to zip her lips closed.

Aubrey glanced over at Elle, who nodded and took the drink she was offered.

"Good, now, just relax while the rest of the guests arrive." Aubrey started to shuffle off, then turned around. "Keep them entertained?"

Jules nodded. "I got this." She waved Aubrey off so she could rush over and greet some of the guests.

For the next two hours, she enjoyed being surrounded by old friends and new ones. She ate some really great food, played silly games, laughed more than she had in months, and grew eager with the rest of the group for the reveal part of the evening.

When the men finally showed up, Jules felt her heart skip

when she noticed Damion among them. He, like the other guys, was wearing a button-up shirt and jeans, which was a lot dressier than the shorts and camp T-shirt that he normally wore.

She'd seen him in a tux several times and had instantly had images of him being a spy of some sort and coming in to sweep her off her feet and save her from the bad guys. She had a very wild imagination.

Tonight, he looked even sexier than he had in the tux. She watched his eyes scan the room and land on her. Then he smiled and her heart did more skipping.

"Can I have everyone's attention?" Aubrey said into the microphone. "We're going to head outside onto the back patio for the gender reveal. Please make your way out to the patio now."

She was standing up when Damion stopped beside her.

"Hey," he said casually.

"Hi." She smiled up at him.

"Want to head out with me?" he asked.

"Sure." She tried to dim her smile a little. It wouldn't do to have him see her beaming or blinding him with the largest of smiles.

"Lead the way," he said, and then he fell in step with her. "So, what did ya'll do before we got here?" he asked quietly.

"Ate, played games, that sort of things." She shrugged.

"Thought so." He nodded. "Some of the guys thought there were strippers involved."

She tripped when his words sank in. His hands came up and steadied her by taking her elbow.

"What?" she asked.

He chuckled. "Just kidding." He laughed. "Oh my god, you should see your face right now."

She took a couple deep breaths and silently wished that he

wouldn't let go of her arm. But he did as they stepped outside into the cooler night air.

"Thank you," Aubrey said into the outside microphone. "Everyone, please gather around. Since Hannah and Owen's bundle of joy is due first, we'll be revealing their gender first."

Hannah and Owen stepped up to the railing. Hannah was normally one of the fittest among the close friends.

Now, however, there was a massive bulge on Hannah's tiny frame, and it looked like she could topple over at any moment.

"Hannah, Owen," Aubrey started. She waved her other friends over and waited as the Wildflowers and their spouses all gathered around. "If you would direct your gaze to the skies," she said with a smile. Everyone glanced upward.

Within the next minute, a very large firework filled the sky with a massive blue explosion over the water beyond the grassy yard. The fireworks were a normal part of some parties at the campgrounds. They even had a barge out on the water holding all of the cannons for the ease of the light shows. New Year's, Fourth of July, any big parties they held—they took any excuse to set them off.

Everyone clapped as the happy couple hugged. Then her friends surrounded her and hugged the new family even more.

Hannah took the microphone this time. As she wiped tears from her eyes, she said, "We're having a boy." Everyone cheered again. "Thank you everyone for coming out tonight. Now, I'm going to hand this over to Elle, who, I'm told, doesn't know the gender of their child yet but has a special message first."

Elle took the microphone and hugged Hannah.

"We don't," Elle said, taking Liam's hand in hers. "But we do know something ya'll don't." She smiled and then nodded and turned to watch the fireworks.

This time, the sky filled with not one, but two massive

explosions. The one on the right side was blue, but the one of the left side, was pink.

Everyone gasped.

"What?" Jules asked.

"Twins," Damion whispered in her ear. "They're having twins."

"We're having twins," Elle confirmed happily into the microphone. "And apparently one of each sex," she said as Liam hugged her while everyone cheered loudly.

Jules glanced over at Damion. The look on his face instantly told her that he knew ahead of time.

"You knew. How?" she asked.

He chuckled. "I guessed." He shrugged. "She's the same size as Hannah but three months behind. That should have been a clue."

"You... seriously guessed?" She laughed.

"That they were having twins. Not the sex of them. A boy and a girl." He shook his head. "They're going to be busy."

"I think it's wonderful." She sighed as she watched the happy couple. Then the sky filled with even more fireworks, and she stood by Damion, a heartbeat away from him, watching the light show.

She could feel him inches from her. His body heat somehow penetrated her clothes differently than the warmth of the early summer evening did.

Maybe it was just her awareness of him that caused her body to warm. Maybe he was the reason she practically vibrated.

Damion laughed suddenly. "Two for the price of one."

"A very good bargain," Jules joked along.

"Champagne?" he asked, taking two glasses from the waiter that was handing them out.

She took the glass from him and sipped. "This was... an amazing night."

"Yeah, who else but the Wildflowers could throw a massive party like this?" Damion added.

"I know, right?" She turned around. Even here, outside, there were decorations. Everything had been just... perfect. Much like all of the parties they had thrown in the past. Birthdays, engagements, weddings, and Zoey's baby shower, where she had astoundingly gone into labor before the party had ended. Everything the friends did, they did completely.

Even when picking their husbands. Three of them had married brothers. Now, they were truly related with the last name of Costa.

Zoey, Elle, and Hannah. All of their children would be cousins.

Thinking of family had her remembering what her father was going through. How much her mother was even now struggling to keep him able to do basic things each day. The first time her dad couldn't remembered where he was had been scary. Then he'd forgotten her name during a dinner and when her mother had reminded him, he'd slammed his fist down on the table.

Her father had never shown an ounce of aggression her entire life. Hell, she doubted that he'd raised his voice even once. It had been so... strange.

Then, it had started happening regularly. The father that she'd known for her entire childhood was gone, replaced by a stranger who sometimes looked at her as if she wanted something from him.

Once, he'd even called Jules by her grandmother's name and had for almost a full hour acted as if he was a young child instead of his sixty-year-old self.

The first few doctor visits were helpful, or at least they

believed they were. An Alzheimer's diagnosis hadn't been shocking, not after the way her father had acted.

What had been shocking was seeing him deteriorate so quickly. By the fourth doctor's appointment, the diagnosis of Alzheimer's was in question.

Her mother was talking about taking him into Pensacola for more tests.

The fact that her father was having a difficult time walking and holding a fork scared her. Really scared her.

"Hey." Damion's voice broke into her thoughts. "Where'd you go just now?" he asked, leaning closer to her.

Taking a deep breath, she shook her head and tried to push the thoughts away.

"Sorry," she said. She leaned on the railing as music started playing through the speakers. Several couples filled the dancing floor while others sat or stood around chatting.

"How about a walk?" Damion suggested suddenly.

"Sure." She set her empty champagne glass down on a table as he did the same. Then she followed him down the pathway that led to the boathouse.

"I love that there are so many interesting places to walk here," she said as they headed down the lit pathway. "I can only imagine coming here each summer as a kid. It must have been truly amazing. As an adult, I totally pinch myself each day I get to work here." He laughed and glanced over at her. "What?" she asked.

"Do you know you get chatty?" he asked.

"Sometimes." She felt her face heat. He stopped under one of the lights and took her shoulders.

"No, don't be embarrassed. I like hearing you talk. I can tell a lot of times you hold back," he said, surprising her.

She was going to deny it, but his eyebrows rose, and she

sighed. "I get it from my dad's side of the family," she said, repeating what her parents always told her growing up.

He laughed at that. "Zoey has arranged for Isaac to supply our meals for the entire trip."

"Seriously? Wow. I dream about his strawberry salads when I'm not here for a day."

He laughed. "Salads? His burgers should be a sin."

Jules knew all too well just how amazing Isaac's burgers were. They alone were responsible for the almost ten extra pounds she'd put on that year alone. Pounds she was trying to rid herself of by eating his salads instead, along with walking during most of her breaks.

She'd never been, nor would she ever be, a skinny supermodel type. Nor did she really care to be. When she looked into the mirror, her heritage was the first thing she saw. The faces of her ancestors stared right back at her—her father's family along with a slight mix of her mother's Anglo-Saxon. Although that part she could only see in the straightness of her hair and her sky-blue eyes. Everything else was Hawaiian, or Kama'aina, through and through. She knew all about her heritage, since they visited her father's family often on the Big Island.

Her grandfather had abused her grandmother and her father and his two siblings when they were all younger. Her grandmother, or Tutu, as Jules called her, had divorced the man when her father was ten. When her dad moved to Florida, his mother had decided she needed a change and came along with him. His older sister and his younger one still lived on the island with their families and Jules's many cousins.

Jules had never met her grandfather, nor did she care to after hearing the stories her Tutu had told her.

"There you go, disappearing again," Damion said, stopping at the end of the dock to look at her.

"Sorry," she said, leaning on the railing and looking out over the dark waters. There was a supermoon out that night and, as if magic, she could see as clearly as if the sun was shining. "I was just thinking about family." She glanced over at him. The moonlight bounced off his darker skin, making him almost glow. "You used to live with your grandparents."

He chuckled. "Yes. One of the reasons I moved out shortly after getting this job was the lack of privacy." His smile slipped slightly.

"Do you miss it? The chaos? Being there for them when they need you?" she asked, thinking of what her mother and Tutu had to deal with on a daily basis with her father.

Damion reached over and took her hand in his.

"I think that... your family wants more than anything for you to be happy and, in order for that to happen, you need to live your own life. Let them handle themselves. If they need you, you're only a phone call away." He looked down at their joined hands. "My family is just down the street from me. I see them at least once a week."

He was right. She knew he was. Knew that she was worrying too much. Still, it was hard for her to let things go.

Even now, while she was standing at a very romantic spot, holding hands with the man of her dreams, she was worried about her family.

What in the hell was wrong with her?

———

# CHAPTER FIVE

D amion was pushing his luck. He knew exactly why she was talking about family. Since he'd promised her grandmother that he wouldn't let on that he knew about her dad, he was bound to keep his mouth shut on the subject.

But it was driving him crazy. Especially after seeing that lost and sad look in her eyes. He wanted to cheer her up anyway he could.

His first thought was to lean over and see what those sexy lips of hers tasted like. He'd been thinking about kissing her since the first moment he'd seen her over five years ago.

But he didn't want their first kiss to be just as a distraction. Glancing out over the water, he remembered the story his parents had told him of how they'd met. He turned until he was leaning against the railing and looking at her, and he started retelling the tale.

"Did you ever hear how my parents met?" he asked. When she shook her head from side to side, he started. "My dad and his parents used to live near the reservation just north of here. Since my grandfather wasn't Apalachee, once he married my grandmother, they moved into a small house on the outskirts of the reservation so my grandmother could be close to her family and roots. In the summer, my father used to work at a gift shop on the reservation, since his grandparents owned the little shop. My mother's family moved south to escape the Georgia heat." He chuckled. "Their words, not mine. They moved to Pelican Point back when my mother was just five years old. Anyway, sometime during my mother's junior year in school, her class took a field trip to the reservation."

"Did your parents meet there and fall in love?" she asked.

He shook his head no. "One would think, but no. They actually met because of the field trip, but my father wasn't working at the store that day. Instead, my mother was goofing off, like she tended to do back then, or so my grandparents have said on numerous occasions, and missed the bus back into town. When she found out she'd missed her ride, she came into the shop and, according to my great-grandmother, who was one hundred percent an Apalachee seer, a teller, knew by just looking at my mother that one day she would marry into her bloodline. So, she arranged for my father to drive her all the way back to Pelican Point himself. A two-hour round-trip drive."

Jules chuckled. "Your great-grandmother sounds like a meddler. Sort of like Tutu is."

Damion smiled. "I like Tutu."

Jules tilted her head and looked at him. He could see her wheels turning. Then her eyes grew large for a split second before they narrowed.

"She told you about my dad's health issues, didn't she?" she asked him, and before he could speak, she poked him in the chest. "Is that why you invited me on the trip?" she asked, poking him again.

He reached up and rubbed the spot, faking pain and shock.

"What?" Damion asked, knowing he couldn't keep the truth from her about what Tutu had told him. But her believing that he'd only invited her on the sail because of her family hurt. "No." He shook his head and became serious. "I asked you to come along because I want you to come and enjoy yourself. I thought we could have some fun together."

"But not..." she started, and he watched her face turn a slight pink.

He took her shoulders in his hands. "I invited you along on the trip because I thought we could have fun together. Yes, partially because you've looked stressed lately, but only partially. To be honest..." He took a deep breath. "I've wanted to ask you to go along with me for a long time."

He watched her eyes widen again but only for a split second. "Okay." She nodded. "So, Tutu didn't beg you to play with the poor lonely girl?"

He laughed and then pulled her in for a hug. "Naw, girl. She only mentioned that you were having a hard time. I'm the one who came up with the trip idea. Swear it."

She seemed to relax in his arms upon hearing that.

Then they heard a cough and turned to see a couple walking down the dock towards them.

"There you two are." Zoey and Dylan walked towards them. "We were just talking about going out tomorrow on the boat. The weather is supposed to be perfect, and Elle has assured me that you don't have any bookings." Zoey turned to him.

He had to think what day it was before nodding in agreement. "I have the day off." He had plans to sleep in and maybe go for a relaxing sail himself.

"We do too." Zoey motioned between her and Dylan. "My mom is going to watch Paige for us. We were thinking of heading to Crab Island."

"I can't," Jules said with a sigh. "I work."

"Elle already asked Beth to cover for you." Zoey waved her hand. "You're welcome," she added with a wink. "So?" She turned back to him. "Are you game for playing captain with a bunch of your friends?"

"How many is a bunch?" he asked.

"All of us... well, the dream team at least." She winked.

"Sure, I'm game," he agreed. "What time are we shipping out?"

Zoey glanced at Dylan, who shrugged. "Eight?"

"We'll take care of the drinks and food," Zoey added before jumping up and down and clapping. "A fun day in the sun. We haven't had one of those in..." She frowned. "Too long," she added with a laugh. "Let's go tell the others." She took Dylan's hand and pulled him back down the dock.

"You didn't have other plans for your day off, did you?" Jules asked.

"No, the only plans I had were possibly sleeping in and an afternoon sail," he answered. "Trust me, I'd rather spend my day captaining around my friends than spend a day alone." He glanced around and realized that the sound of the party had died down. Most likely, everyone had gone home, no doubt getting rest so they could meet first thing in the morning. "Why don't we head to our cars? Sounds like the party has wrapped up."

"Oh." She glanced towards the main building. "I didn't mean to keep you so long."

"You didn't." He smiled. "I'm the one who asked you to take a walk. Remember?"

"Right." She hid her eyes from him by dipping her head down. He knew that it was a move she did when she was embarrassed.

He took her hand in his, and they started walking down the pathway in silence.

"Can I ask you something?" Jules said when they made the turn towards the parking lot.

"Sure," he answered and glanced over at her, pausing under one of the lights.

"Why now?" she asked.

"Why what now?"

"Why ask me on a weekend sail and..." She held up their joined hands.

He looked at their intertwined fingers. His long dark, calloused fingers, and her small, much softer caramel-colored ones were mingled together. Then he looked up into her soft blue eyes.

"Because it's about damn time I did this," he said, leaning closer to her. Her body was like silk against his, almost as if they'd been made for one another. She was shorter than most women he'd dated, but this felt... right.

Using his free hand, he reached up and tipped her chin up by sliding a finger under it. Her eyes moved to his lips for just a split second before he covered her soft lips.

He'd been right all these years. The moment he kissed her, for him, there would be no going back.

It was as if her entire body melted against his while, at the same time, she came alive. Her hands moved to his shoulders, and her short nails dug into the button-up shirt that he'd worn that night.

He felt her body vibrate against his, or maybe that was him shivering with excitement? Her lips were by far the softest, the most luscious, he'd ever enjoyed.

Then she broke apart and chuckled as she looked over his shoulder.

"Someone's coming," she said, taking his hand and pulling him along the pathway.

Like a blind man, he followed her until they stood just outside one of the outbuildings. When he looked, he realized it was the woodshop where Liam worked. On the outside of the smaller building were hundreds of wood carvings either Liam or one of the guests had made and left behind.

Liam was a very talented carver, and his works were easily distinguishable from all of the novice carvings.

"We'll wait here until they leave," Jules said with a sigh. "Gosh, I always forget how talented Liam is," Jules said, reaching up and touching one of the man's carvings of a pelican.

"Yeah," Damion agreed. "He's talked me into trying my hand at carving a few times." He walked over to where one of his carvings of a turtle hung. "I'm not so good at it. Have you tried?"

She shrugged. "I made Liam burn all of my attempts." She laughed. "They were really bad."

"So, not an art major, I take it?" He leaned against the building.

She laughed again. "Singing and theater were more my pace."

"Girl, you kill it on karaoke nights."

She smiled at him. "I've heard your pipes as well. Not bad." She nodded her head.

"We should do a duet next time they break out the machine," he suggested.

She laughed. "What would we sing? 'Islands in the Stream'?"

He laughed. "Naw, how about..." He narrowed his eyes as he thought. "'Summer Nights'?"

"From *Grease*? I love that one." She started singing and he watched for a moment as her hips started moving as she danced around. "I played Rizzo in high school," she said between moves.

He laughed and easily joined in until they had sung the entire song. He was a little breathless and was sweating profusely thanks to the outfit he'd worn out to dinner with the guys before returning to the camp. But he couldn't remember the last time he'd had this much fun.

"Okay, girl, you got me all sweaty. Now it's time I went home and showered and got some sleep." He took her hand, and they started walking again towards the parking area.

When they stopped next to her car, she looked up at him.

"This isn't going to be all weird, is it?" she asked, motioning between them.

"No," he answered with a grin. "No." This time, he leaned in and brushed his lips across hers. "Friends first, coworkers second, and whatever comes next... we'll figure it out together."

"Promise?" she asked, her eyes narrowing slightly.

"Yeah," he said and kissed her again until he felt more centered.

"See you in the morning," she said, and he watched her climb in her car and leave.

"Dayammm," someone said from behind him, making him jump. Carter walked out of the shadows towards him, and he groaned.

"Dude, what'll it cost to keep your mouth shut?" he asked as he shook the man's hand. Carter was easily Damion's match physically. They both spent plenty of time in the gym together and could lift the same. Where Damion spent more time in the water, Carter spent time on the back of a horse or mucking out stalls.

Carter laughed. "It's about time you made your move on

Julie. You've been pushing the rest of us off from making our moves on her for years."

That was true. How many times over the years had he overheard Carter, Dean, or one of the other full-time employees talking about asking Jules out? Each time he had heard them, he'd warned them away with some excuse. In the end, the rumors had started amongst the guys that he had a thing for her.

"How much?" he asked again.

Carter slapped him playfully on the shoulder. "Cover for me on Tuesday and I'll let it slide." He nodded.

"Tuesday?" he asked with a groan.

"Just the morning ride. I've got this... thing in the morning," Carter said, glancing back down the pathway.

"Fine," he groaned. It wasn't the first time he'd taken over a morning ride for Carter. It wasn't that Carter was irresponsible in his work, but a lot of times his duties at the sanctuary got in the way of the scheduled morning horseback rides that guest booked.

Usually Scarlett took over, but with both Elle and Hannah being pregnant, Scarlett and the other Wildflowers were filling in for the pair a lot more.

"Cool, then your secret is safe with me... for a while," Carter joked. "The way the two of you were going at it, it won't be long before I'm not the only one getting a show." He wiggled his eyebrows, slapped him on the shoulder again, and then disappeared into the parking lot.

# CHAPTER SIX

Jules changed outfits at least six times. Normally, she wouldn't have cared so much about her attire. After last night, everything had changed.

She'd tried her standard one-piece swimsuit with a flowing cover-up covered in flowers. But that outfit covered too much. So she'd changed into her tiniest bikini and cut-off shorts and a white tank top.

When she looked in the mirror, she realized she looked a little too... desperate. She'd changed into several other swimsuit and cover-up combos before finally settling on a light purple bikini top with high-waisted pink and purple floral bottoms and her white and pink floral kimono-style cover-up.

Since she'd lightened her hair a few weeks earlier, the soft colors of the outfit made her skin practically glow. She threw her straw hat into her beach bag, pulled on her water sandals, and rushed out the door, hoping she wasn't too late.

When she arrived, almost everyone was already on the sailboat getting settled. She was slightly surprised to see Isaac and his wife Isabella carting containers into the lower deck of the sailboat. The pair were dressed for a day on the water.

"Wow, who let you off work today?" Jules joked with Isaac.

The man glanced at her and laughed. "Our boss," he answered with a wink. "I think she figured that if she gave me the day off, I'd arrange for the meals."

"We have been needing a day like this," Isabella said, touching her husband's arm. "My husband throws himself too much into his work and forgets that we moved to paradise to enjoy ourselves." She patted his arm.

"Well, I for one am very thankful you're here. And not just because of the wonderful food I know we're going to enjoy later."

"Thanks," Isabella said before Isaac could chime in.

Over the past five years, she'd come to know Isabella better than she knew Isaac. Mainly because the woman came in and used the facilities more than her husband, who was always stuck in the kitchens. She'd had more long chats with Isabella than she had with most of her friends.

"Here, let me grab that from you." Damion stepped up from the lower deck to grab the container from Isaac. For the first time since last night, she got a look at Damion. She felt her face heat as her eyes ran over his face and his bare chest.

He normally wore a camp shirt when he captained for guests, but since this was a group of friends, he'd removed his shirt. And she was very thankful he had.

She knew perfectly well where he'd gotten all those delicious muscles. Damion, Carter, and a few of the other full-time employees met at least three times a week and headed to the camp's gym together. On more than one occasion, she had rearranged her schedule and hit the gym while he was working out.

When his eyes met hers, his smile grew. God, he had such a

great smile. She felt her knees go weak and had to actually turn away from him before she fell down.

She set her bag down next to Zoey and sat down, trying not to feel awkward while everyone else rushed around to prepare everything for the day's journey.

By the time they headed out, it was half an hour past eight. Everyone was so excited, and no one seemed to mind that it was crowded on the sailboat. Normally, for guest sails they limited it to six couples and two staff. Now, there was double that. It didn't feel overly crowded, but she was thankful she'd picked a seat near the back where Damion stood at the wheel.

Some people sitting in the front ended up getting sprayed with water when they were heading out into the Gulf because the water was a little choppy. But the closer they got to Crab Island, the clearer and calmer the water got.

She'd been to the underwater sandbar area so many times in her life that she couldn't count. Most of the time it had been with her family on the Fourth of July. But since her father's health was failing, she had spent the last couple years celebrating at the camp instead.

It took almost a full hour for them to get from the camp to Crab Island. By then, it had heated up and a dip in the cool crystal-clear water sounded very appealing.

A few of the guys helped Damion make sure the two anchors were settled and the massive sailboat was clear from all the other smaller boats that surrounded them.

"I know better than to pick a spot in the middle," Damion said to her as a couple of people started to climb down the ladder into the water or jump off the sides of the boat. "My first year captaining, I got trapped in the middle of this mess." He motioned around them.

This early in the morning, there were only a couple dozen boats anchored off the sandbar. But any local knew that during the height of the day there could easily be hundreds of boats crowding in, blocking anyone's exit.

"This is perfect," she responded with a sigh. "My dad used to want to be in the heart of it all. Then when my mom would want to leave, we'd be stuck." She chuckled. "I think he did it on purpose because my mom would always want to leave after lunch and my dad likes hanging around until sunset."

Damion smiled. "Yeah, my parents are sort of the same way, but opposite. My mom likes to hang around and watch the sunset and wait for the crowds to leave while my dad usually complains about missing a game on the set." Then he nodded to the water. "Heading in?"

She glanced around and realized that everyone was now in the waist-deep water. Most of them had drinks, and Elle and Hannah had settled on a large floating mat that someone had brought along.

"Sure." She peeled off her cover-up and set it on her bag. When she turned around, she realized Damion was watching her. "What?" She instantly feared that something was wrong, but then that sexy slow smile he got made her realize he was checking her out.

"Girl," he said as he stuck his hand over his heart and banged his fist against his chest a couple times. "Had to restart my heart," he joked, and she smiled.

"Okay." She nodded. "I think you need..." She walked towards him slowly and finished her sentence as she pushed him overboard into the water. "To cool off."

He landed in the clear water and came up laughing and caught her as she jumped in next to him.

Feeling his hands on her skin had her body heating even more. It took almost half an hour before she finally felt cooled off. By then, she had a drink in her hands and was talking to

Lea about her and Brett's wedding plans, while Damion was tossing around a football with a few of the guys.

It had taken a few months for Lea to heal from the attack she'd suffered last year. Jules still couldn't believe how crazy people were, how full of hate they could be for someone they didn't know. Enough so that they would damage their own careers and lives just to punish someone they thought shouldn't exist.

Robbie Dixon Jr. was dead. Lea had shot the man who had terrorized and kidnapped her. Could Jules ever take someone else's life? She didn't know what she was capable of, having never been kidnapped and tortured like Lea had been last year.

To look at the woman now, you would never suspect that she'd gone through anything as crazy as that.

Jules knew that Rob Dixon Sr., a judge in the area, was now spending the rest of his life behind bars.

After the case went public, there had been a lot of changes in the local government. More than five county commissioners had been exposed for taking bribes and embezzling. They had been caught writing checks to friends or family members and then getting paybacks. The good ol' boys, as the five had been dubbed, were no longer in charge, and four of them were rotting in cells along with Rob Dixon Sr. The fifth had committed suicide after the story had broken, leaving behind his wife, three children, two mistresses, and a pile of debt for his family.

Shortly after all this went down, the town voted in a more diverse set of commissioners, both in gender and race.

"And you are no longer paying attention," Lea joked as she poked Jules's arm.

"Sorry." She laughed. "Okay, so, how many bridesmaids again?"

Lea shrugged. "Two. Only two. We don't want anything as extravagant as the last weddings."

"Right." Jules nodded, thinking back to Aiden and Aubrey's perfect wedding. "There have been some pretty amazing ones in the past few years. Are you going to have it at the camp?"

"No, Brett wants it on the beach."

"The beach at the camp is nice," Jules offered, making Lea laugh.

"That's what I said. But he's leaning more towards Destin so a lot of the on-duty officers can swing by. We're thinking of having the reception in the Grand. Owen says he can arrange for us to get a deal, since he owns the building." She rolled her eyes.

"Right, they just purchased that a few months ago." Jules glanced over to where the three Costa brothers were wrestling for the football. Two of them were holding the other down. At this distance, with all of their dark hair wet, it was hard to distinguish who was who. Especially since they were all very tall, tan, and quite muscular, more so than most of the men around them. With the exception of Damion, of course.

Jules's eyes moved to Damion, and she watched him laughing and catching the football that one of the Costas had thrown.

Just the way he moved had her mouth watering. Remembering what the kiss last night had done to her, what it had awakened in her, had her knees going weak again.

"Oh!" Lea said suddenly, getting Jules's attention.

"What?" Jules instantly looked around the water for a shark.

"You got it bad." Lea poked her again. "I see you looking at Damion." Lea's eyes narrowed. "Has he finally made his move on you?"

"What?" Jules's face heated, and she wished she wasn't wearing makeup so she could dunk her entire head under the water. "No," she lied.

Lea's eyes narrowed slightly, and she tilted her head. "I'm a doctor. I know the signs of someone lying to me." She moved closer. "Tell me everything." Then her chin rose. "There is such a thing as patient-doctor confidentiality."

Jules smiled. "You're not my doctor."

"But I am your friend. So, spill," Lea retorted.

Jules glanced over to where Damion was now wrestling Brett for the ball. She remembered how she had begged for details when Brett had made his move on Lea, how she'd been there for Lea when she needed help after the attack, and softened.

"He kissed me last night," she said quietly. "Just a kiss but..." She took a deep breath.

"Need me to restart your heart with some paddles?" Lea joked.

"If you had been there, yes. It took me two hours to fall asleep last night."

Lea laughed. "You know he's been crushing on you for years, right?"

"No." Jules shook her head. "No, he hasn't." She shook her head again. "He has?"

Lea just laughed and then the conversation changed when Zoey asked them to play volleyball with the rest of the gang.

They took a break for lunch and ate a variety of wonderful sandwiches and snacks that Isaac had made in the full kitchen below deck. She and Damion, along with Dylan and Zoey, sat off the back of the sailboat and ate while dangling their feet into the water.

After lunch, she went with Elle, Hannah, Lea, and Scarlett as they weaved around the floating boats, making a point to not trip over any anchors. They crossed the shallow waters and waded through the crowd of people to use the porta potties on a floating barge.

When they returned, Levi, Brett, Owen, Dylan, and Aiden were pushing and shoving a group of overweight, exceedingly intoxicated men while Liam and the rest of the men were either standing in front of Damion or holding him upright.

Jules rushed over to Damion's side and that's when she noticed his fat bloody lip and swollen eye.

"Are you okay?" she asked him, but his eyes were focused on the other group of people.

The presence of two pregnant women seemed to bring people somewhat to their senses and the fighting miraculously stopped.

"You just crossed the wrong people," Brett said. "I'm a cop." That only seemed to piss the other men off even more. Even though Brett had officially retired last year, she knew that he still thought of himself as the law and always would.

Slurs and curses filled with racial hate were being shouted at them, aimed at Damion, Lea, and even Jules herself, along with hate aimed at law enforcement, but no more fists flew. Even the women in the other group seemed to get into it, and they pointed at Damion, her, and Lea. More racial slurs were thrown their direction than she'd ever heard.

Brett turned and said something to Owen before he made his way back to the sailboat and climbed aboard, no doubt to call it in.

The Costa men, Aiden, and Levi made a blockade to protect Damion and the women. It seemed they had made a decision that no one was going to cross them.

Then she heard one of the women with the other group say something about her ugly swimsuit and how she was obviously a nigger lover.

Jules couldn't help it, she laughed at the woman, a brunette that easily outweighed her by fifty pounds. The woman rushed through the men like a lineman in football and headed directly towards her.

When the woman started rushing towards her, Damion put himself between them, but Jules touched his arm.

"I've got this," she said softly.

Damion looked down at her and nodded. "I'm here for backup," he said softly.

Jules knew better than to throw the first punch. Letting the woman grab her hair and yank hard took courage. What didn't was easily slamming her palm into the woman's chin, a move she'd learned in one of Aubrey's self-defense classes. The heavier woman fell backwards, landing in the waist-deep water as blood gushed from her obviously broken nose.

"Damn girl," she heard Damion say behind her. "Where were you when this all started?" He chuckled.

"You bitch," the woman came up screaming. "I'm going to sue you. You did it now. You and your kind deserve to rot in prison." The woman screamed at Jules as she held her broken nose.

"You assaulted her first," someone new said, getting their attention. A woman was rushing towards them through the water, holding up a phone. "I have the entire thing on video." She was a blond woman in one of the smallest bikinis Jules had ever seen. To say this woman was beautiful was an understatement. She was... gorgeous.

She rushed closer, waving her phone, and added, "I'm still recording. When the cops get here, you and your friends are the ones who are going to go to jail," she said to the bloodied woman.

The woman turned to Damion and asked, "Are you okay?" and a wave of jealousy washed over Jules.

# CHAPTER SEVEN

Damion held the ice pack to his eye and watched Jules. The move she'd used to take down that racist bitch had been damn impressive.

He couldn't get the image of her taking the woman down out of his head while he sat and listened to everyone give the coast guard details of what had happened.

It appeared that the woman who had caught it all on video was a semi-famous swimsuit model. She'd been doing a social media post on a boat nearby and had been doing a live stream when she caught the entire thing on camera. Needless to say, the video had gone instantly viral.

While the woman showed one officer the video and gave her account, Brett filled another officer in on what had happened.

Everyone gave their statements and photos were taken of Damion's cuts and bruises.

When that was all done, Jules sat next to Damion on the sailboat and held an ice pack to his lips.

"What happened?" she asked after he was done answering

some basic questions. She needed the entire story and had only heard snippets of it so far.

By now, his sailboat was surrounded by coast guard and police boats, as was the other group's boat.

"Shortly after your group left to go the bathroom, these guys showed up. Apparently, they'd been partying further in the crowd. They were trying to make their way out and decided to anchor here to continue partying. The big one there"—he motioned to a heavyset man who was now being cuffed and hauled out of the water onto a police boat— "chucked the anchor right at me." He motioned to his leg where a long red mark had formed and it was starting to bruise. Thankfully, it wasn't bleeding. "I said something like, hey, watch it, and he came back with..." He closed his eyes and shook his head. How many times in his life had he been called a nigger? Too many to count. "Words," he finished, not wanting to upset Jules any further. As it was, she looked slightly pale and a little green. Her eyes were filled with worry for him and her friends. "Then, before I could respond, he jumped in the water, landing directly on top of me. I thought for a moment I was going to drown under a three-hundred-pound racist," he said, meaning it as a joke. "Thank God for Brett and the others. They pulled him off me, but not before the man got in a few good punches." He touched his lip with his tongue and winced. "You guys showed up right after that."

"What is wrong with people?" she asked softly.

"I guess they were mad that I had a bigger boat than them," he joked, taking her hand in his.

She sighed and then glanced over. "They're all getting arrested," she said, nodding.

He glanced over and, sure enough, all six of the people, including the woman who had attacked Jules, were being hauled onto the police boat.

"They'll impound their boat too," he said with a smile.

"I've never had anything like that happen before," Jules admitted.

"We have," Lea said, sitting next to her. Then she took Jules's hand in hers. "Don't worry, we are not going to let this spoil our fun today. Are we?" Lea turned to him.

"Hell, no, we aren't." He smiled and then winced.

"Scoot over and let the doctor take a look at your man," Lea said, nudging Jules aside.

He couldn't help but smile at Lea's words or the fact that Jules didn't correct her friend. Then Lea touched his lip, and he had to focus on not crying like a baby in front of his friends.

Lea examined him from his bruised shin to a small bump on the back of his head that he didn't even know he had.

"We need to take pictures of all these before I bandage you up. Sorry, but you shouldn't get back in the water today," Lea added, snapping a few photos on her phone.

"It's okay." He was done with it at any rate. They only had about another two hours before sunset. After what had happened, he was thinking of heading below deck and taking a nap to recover.

"After that..." Jules glanced around at the other boats that had moved aside to allow the police in. She could feel everyone staring at them. "Why don't we just go?"

"No," Lea said before he could answer. "If we tuck our tails and leave, they win."

"Besides, I'm pretty sure everyone else around us is on our side," Damion said, taking Jules's hand in his. "Did you hear the cheers when you knocked that woman on her ass?"

"Kick-ass move by the way," Aubrey said as she climbed aboard and sat down. "You did pay attention to my class."

Jules smiled. "Yes, I did."

"You should hand out business cards for your classes," Lea

joked. "I'll bet all the women who saw Jules kick ass would sign up."

"That's not a bad idea," Aubrey joked.

"This is a good time to bring out dessert," Isaac said, holding out a tray of cookies and brownies.

Damion grabbed a brownie. Jules shook her head, but he grabbed a cookie and handed it to her.

"Thanks," he said as Isaac moved around the boat. By then, the police had pretty much disappeared. There was still one police boat next to the other boat, no doubt waiting for the tow.

Everyone from their group was onboard, enjoying the treats.

"You shouldn't turn down one of Isaac's treats. Betty probably made them, and you know how amazing of a pastry chef she is," he said, finishing off the brownie.

He glanced over at her cookie, which she was eyeing. He reached for it, but she laughed and held it away from him.

"I think you're right." She took a huge bite of it while he laughed.

After everyone was hopped up on sugar, they jumped back in the water and started another volleyball game while he and Jules watched for a while.

When Jules leaned against his shoulder, he wrapped his arm around her and leaned against the side of the cabin. There was a row of cushions that the camp guests normally sat on. Now, his legs were stretched out, cushions propping him up, and Jules was practically lying in his lap.

With the sunshine warming them, the sway of the boat, and the sound of happy people cheering, and Jules held tight against him, he drifted off to sleep.

They both woke sometime later when the group came back onboard.

"Did you get some rest?" Lea asked the both of them.

"Yes," Jules said, stretching her arms over her head. "How are you feeling?" She turned and looked at him.

"Much better," he answered truthfully.

Jules's eyes narrowed. "You don't look any better." She reached up and touched his eye and then his lip.

"Is it bad?" he asked.

"It's not good." She tilted her head.

"But you're still handsome as ever," Brett joked as he climbed aboard. "Now how about you point this colossus towards home?"

"You don't want to say for the sunset?" he asked.

"We can watch it from closer to home and somewhere less crowded," Liam answered as he wrapped a towel around himself.

The guys helped him pull up the two anchors, and he carefully maneuvered the massive sailboat through the few other boats that had anchored behind them. When they hit open water, he decided the winds were too rough to let the sails out and he'd just use the motor to get them home instead, which would take a little longer.

No one complained. Several of the women had gone downstairs and changed into drier clothes, while the guys pulled on shirts or hoodies. The wind had kicked up and even he reached for the hoodie he had.

Jules made her way back to him and handed him another brownie.

"A little pick-me-up." She leaned against him. He nudged her to sit on his knee and steer while he enjoyed the brownie.

"I've never driven a sailboat before." She laughed as he placed her hands on the wheel.

"A sailboat isn't a lot different than a regular boat when you're using the motor. Steer into the waves and aim for where we're heading," he said between bites.

"How is it you know where we're going?" she asked, glancing around. "Everything looks so small out here. Right now, I couldn't tell you where I am, and I've lived here my entire life."

He pointed. "Do you see that house there." He pointed to a massive mansion. The pristine green yard was lined with palm trees. "We'll go past it and then take a left."

"You can't always navigate by sight though." She glanced back at him.

"Nope, that's what this baby is for." He patted his GPS computer screen. "Right now, it's off, but if I'm going on longer trips, it's on, navigating for me the entire way. When you've been out on the water as much as I have around here, you remember a few landmarks."

She was quiet for a moment then asked, "Has anything like today ever happened to you before?"

"It's not the first time someone has gotten violent," he answered. "It is the first time I was almost drowned by a three-hundred-pound drunk guy."

"I'm really glad you're okay." She leaned back into his chest.

He'd finished the brownie and wrapped his arms around her.

"Want to take over?" she asked.

"Naw, you got this." He was enjoying letting her steer them home.

He killed the motor just outside the small inlet to their beach area so everyone could watch the sunset and sip champagne. He wanted more than anything to kiss Jules as the sun disappeared, but not with all of their coworkers and friends around them. He wasn't sure just how public she wanted what was between them to be.

He was determined to ask her before the night ended.

Navigating back to the camp in the dark wasn't hard. He could probably do it with one eye shut. Once they docked, the gang quickly gathered their items while he closed up the sailboat and made sure everything was secure.

When Jules tried to head off down the path with the rest, he took her hand and stopped her.

"Hang back for a minute, if you will?" he asked her.

She glanced back at the group of their friends, who were too busy chatting amongst themselves to notice his request.

"Sure," she said, setting her bag down. "Did you need some help cleaning up?" She looked around.

Instead of answering her question, he pulled her into his arms and kissed her, remembering the split lip too late. Wincing slightly, he shifted until most of the pressure was on the good side of his mouth.

"That has to be killing you," she said, pulling back slightly.

"It is, but the pain is worth it." He rested his forehead against hers. "What is this we got going on?" he asked her.

"You tell me?" She looked into his eyes.

"I've liked you for years," he admitted, and her smile grew.

"I've liked you for years too," she said easily.

"Okay, so..." He sighed as he ran his hands up and down her arms, noticing the chill.

Once the early summer sun went down, the temperature dropped quickly. He knew she was probably uncomfortable. It was late and she had to work the next day. He did too. He had an early morning of cleaning out the pools before guests would want to swim.

"Let's see where this goes," Jules finished for him. "For now"—she touched his split lip gently with her fingertip—"heal. I'll see you tomorrow." She leaned up on her toes and placed a kiss on the good side of his lips.

He stood there like a statue watching her go. Only after did he decide not to drive back to his place. Instead, he went down into the cabin and crashed on the king-size bed down there.

The next morning, he was adding salt to the largest pool when Elle found him.

"Do you have a moment?" Elle asked him. She winced when she saw the black eye and puffy lip.

"For you?" He smiled and felt his lip cut open again. "Sure thing." He dumped the rest of the salt into the water where it quickly disappeared. Then he tossed the bag into the trash can and followed her into her office.

He was surprised when they walked in, and a few people shouted "surprise" at him.

"What's this? It's not my birthday." He tilted his head. "Is it?" That got a couple laughs.

"It's your five-year anniversary," Elle cheered.

"Wouldn't that make it everyone's five-year anniversary?" he joked as he blew out the small candle on a cupcake Zoey held up.

"We officially opened the camp a few weeks from now five years ago, but we brought you on board five years ago today." She handed him the cupcake. "So, yay!" Zoey rolled her eyes. "I think this is just Elle's way of justifying the cupcakes," she whispered.

"I heard that," Elle said. "And I don't need an excuse to eat cupcakes. I have two right here." She rubbed her belly.

Jules stepped up beside him, holding her own cupcake with a blown-out candle on it.

"They got you too?" he asked her.

"Yes." She smiled. "I was hired half an hour before you were... apparently." She chuckled then held up her cupcake. "To five years."

He lifted his cupcake and tapped hers. "To five years." He took a bite.

The rest of the day he thought about the last five years. How he had pretty much danced around asking Jules out that entire time. He remembered seeing her for the first time standing in the sunlight just out front of the main building. Zoey was showing her around as Elle started showing him around. Then, somehow, the four of them continued walking around the campgrounds together.

He thought he'd said maybe two words to her that entire time. He'd never felt shy around a woman before, and so hadn't been sure how to behave, feeling that way around her.

When in doubt, keep your mouth shut. His mother used to say that all the time, so that's what he did. For five long years.

He even tried to convince himself that it was just a crush. That worked at first. Then it didn't.

Now, he couldn't wait for the trip the following weekend. He made sure his place down the coast was cleaned and that the fridge and pantry were stocked. Even though Isaac was sending along complete meals for them to heat up, he didn't want Jules to feel like she was missing a thing.

He was halfway through his day when he got the call from the local police department. Brett had told him they might end up calling him.

Still, having to excuse himself from helping a couple with a rowboat and take the call was disturbing enough. Then he got word that all six of the people that had been arrested had been released with minor charges and fines.

The guy could have killed him. They should have at least been charged with assault. Instead, all six had been charged with public intoxication, a minor offense compared to what had happened.

He tried not to think about what he would have been charged with if the roles had been reversed. Or even if there hadn't been video evidence of what had happened.

That news put him in a sour mood for the rest of the day. Thankfully, he didn't have a sunset tour scheduled for that evening and, after he locked the boathouse up, he headed home for the night.

After showering and falling into bed, he heard his phone chime and was just about to ignore it when he thought of the possibility that it might be Jules. He reached over and smiled when he saw her message.

# CHAPTER EIGHT

Jules waited for Damion's response to her meme. She'd heard from Lea, who had heard it from Brett, that the other group from the day before had been released from jail with minor charges.

The biggest expense was probably getting their boat back, if it was even their boat. The group was from out of town, so it was most likely a rental.

"You just made my night better," Damion responded. "Thanks."

"Any time. I hated to hear that they aren't rotting in jail right now for what they did to you," she responded.

"Me? What about what that woman did to you?"

"I think I did more to her than she did to me. A few strands of my hair versus a new nose job." She laughed as she sent a funny emoji along with the text.

"Girl, you got me laughing so hard it hurts." His response had her thinking about his laughter. It was warm and rich, and she loved the sound of it.

"I like hearing your laughter," she responded. Then she quickly added. "Have a good night. See you tomorrow?"

"It's my day off. But I might stop by if you promise me that you'll eat lunch down at the beach with me."

She smiled and hugged her phone to her chest for a moment before responding. "I can do that."

"Eleven. Okay?"

"See you then," she answered, and then she lay in bed and reread every single message twice before falling asleep.

The next day, Jules watched the clock continuously. She counted down the minutes until Damion would show up. Every time the front doors opened, she grew happy and then disappointed when it wasn't him.

He was ten minutes late but walked in with a bundle of flowers in his hands.

"My truck had a flat tire," he said with a frown.

"Oh no." She took the flowers from him. "But you had time to pick these up?"

He chuckled. "I picked them from the flower beds along the pathway."

She laughed. "Don't let Tommy hear you say that."

"Tommy?" he asked with a frown.

"The guy who plants these and takes care of them," she answered with a shake of her head.

"Why have I never met him?" Damion asked with a frown.

"Because he's shy and works in the evenings when you're normally out on a sunset cruise."

"Since I had to deal with the flat tire, I didn't have time to stop and grab a lunch. Mind if we stop off in the dining room and grab a sack lunch?"

"Sounds good. I didn't pack one either. I was hoping we'd grab something as well." She didn't want to tell him that she'd been so eager for today that she'd forgotten to pack one.

He held out his hand for hers. She set the flowers in the vase along with the bundle that normally sat on the front counter.

"Have a good lunch," Beth called after her.

"Thanks," she said.

They walked through the short line of other employees getting lunches and each grabbed one of the sack lunches they made for employees who wanted to enjoy their food outside. The meals were pretty much the same as the ones you could get in the dining room but packaged in recyclable containers. The fact that everyone called them sack lunches was kind of an employee joke.

It had actually been Jules's idea to switch to the reusable containers for the meals. She'd watched a documentary with her father on plastics in the oceans. After doing a little research, she'd come to Elle with the idea and proof that, over the long haul, the campgrounds would save money as well as help save marine life and the planet if they switched over.

Elle had loved the idea instantly. Over the past five years, Jules had come to her with several more ideas, all of which Elle had implemented.

They took their lunches and started down the pathway to the beach area. Normally, there would be a bunch of guests or employees enjoying the white sand and the sun, but today was a little cloudy and most people seemed to have other ideas.

"Looks like we have the beach to ourselves." He motioned to a table under a large palm tree.

She walked over and sat down and tried to hide a smile when he sat next to her instead of across from her.

"What did you get?" he asked as she opened her lunch.

"Chicken salad. You?"

"Burger, fries, and a brownie for dessert," he answered. "Want?" he asked, holding up a fry.

Yes, she did want, but she started to tell him no. But the moment she opened her mouth, he stuck the fry in it.

"I knew you were going to deny it, but seeing that look in your eyes, I can tell you really wanted it," he explained. "My mother taught me never to question what a woman eats, but you can't tell me you seriously want to eat those twigs over this." He motioned to her food.

"What I want and what my body can handle are two different things," she admitted, reaching over and taking another fry. "But two fries won't hurt too much."

"Trust me when I say nothing would hurt that kickin' body you have." He nodded and then picked up his burger and took a bite. "Bite?"

She shook her head. "There I do draw the line. I'll stick with my twigs and chicken. So, what do you do on your days off?" she asked, suddenly feeling conscious that they were basically on their first date.

"Sail, but I also do other things. Usually, errands for my folks or helping them with a project around their house. My mom has been remodeling the house since before I was born," he joked.

"I like your parents' house," she admitted. His parents owned a couple of local home furnishings stores. His mother was a complete genius when it came to decorating homes. Their home had always been magazine worthy. "I wish I had as much style as your mother does. She has a knack for decorating." She thought about her little apartment and the hodgepodge of things she'd collected over the years to put in it.

"My dad likes it except when it comes to paying for the renovations." He laughed.

"Your dad retired a few years back, right?" She tried to remember the full story of how his dad used his retirement to help in his wife's business. It wasn't a conversation she'd had with his family often, but she remembered hearing something about it.

"Yeah, he was a general in the navy. He never pressured me to go into the military but had hoped." He shrugged. "After he retired, he helped mom get the second store opened and that took off quickly."

"Every time I walk into your parents' store, I walk away with something. Of course, I don't have the style your mother does, so none of it matches what I've purchased in the past." She laughed.

"I like your place. It's you," he said. "I let my mother decorate my place. It's nice..."

"It is freaking gorgeous."

He nodded. "It could easily be a rental. I keep adding some of my own style. I feel like I have to sneak it in behind her back."

Jules laughed. "Parents can be a little much sometimes." She thought of her own mother's constant advice on what styles Jules should wear. "With your mother it's furniture, with mine it's clothing. Every time I have lunch with her, she points out something wrong with what I'm wearing or gracefully mentions that I shouldn't be eating so much."

Damion frowned. "Okay, now I don't feel so bad when my mom complains about a neon lamp I bought."

"It's not as bad as I'm making it out to be." She felt her face heat. "It's just... She's extremely petite and I... take after my father."

"You're petite," he said. "And perfectly curvy in all the fun places." He smiled.

"Thanks." She focused on finishing her lunch, suddenly feeling very self-conscious. She wasn't used to compliments. From him, they made her feel heated. Actually, every time she was around him, she felt heated.

"I embarrassed you," he said, breaking into her thoughts.

She glanced up at him as he reached over and took her hand in his. "Although it's true—I and a lot of people find you perfect—I didn't mean to make you feel awkward around me."

She relaxed. "It's not you. I think that it's compliments in general that I'm uncomfortable with. I didn't get a lot of them growing up. Not about my looks, at any rate." She shrugged and looked at their joined hands. The way his fingers easily interlocked with hers had her relaxing even more. It felt right, natural, to be touched by him.

"You should have. If you'd gone to my school, you would have. I would have made sure of it." He winked at her, and she couldn't help but laugh.

"If I had gone to your school, I would have been wise to your games a lot earlier." She nudged his shoulder with hers.

"Games can be fun. If you play them with the right people." He wiggled his eyebrows and had her laughing even harder.

A few moments later, a crowd of people showed up and started a beach volleyball game. They watched the guests as they finished their lunch, then she suggested they take a stroll around the grounds until her lunch break was up.

"What are your big plans for the rest of your day off?" she asked him as they headed down the pathway towards the zip line area. There were dozens of secluded cabins along the pathways that jutted off the main path. For the ease of the guests, there were also golf cart pathways to each of the cabins to deliver luggage and for guests with special needs. The cleaning crew and food delivery folks also used them. Each cabin had two beach bikes sitting out front for guests to use at their leisure. There were more bikes at the main building and pool areas.

They had talked about getting a handful of scooters but

decided they didn't like the idea of people zipping that fast down the pathways.

When she wanted to make some extra cash during the holiday season, she picked up a few shifts delivering meals to the cabins. The tips were good, and it was easy work she enjoyed. Either that or she'd work behind the bar at dinners or parties.

Last Christmas, she'd earned enough during one holiday party to buy her mother a new iPhone.

"I was thinking of heading out on the water. Maybe paddle-boarding for a while," he said.

"Working here does have a lot of perks," she said with a sigh. "I mean, if you need extra cash, there's always something to do around here. Or if you want to relax..." She motioned to the zip line area that they were passing. "You can always just join an activity during your off hours."

"It is pretty much the perfect place to work," he said. "Though the camp has had its fair share of problems." He glanced over at her.

"Remember Ryan?" she asked, rolling her eyes. "That woman wasn't right from the moment she stepped foot on the grounds."

"Yeah," he agreed. "She tried to hook up with me the first day I met her."

"She did?" She instantly wondered just how many employees Damion has hooked up with over the years. She knew her score. Zero. She'd tried dating a few times, but nothing had ever led to the bedroom. The last time something *had* led there, she'd been eighteen and stupid enough to believe that Brian Gruber was the real deal. He'd spent one night with her and then stopped answering her texts and calls.

"I can spot crazy from across the room," Damion added. "And that woman was oozing it."

"She was. It was pure luck that Dylan and Zoey weren't hurt. Still, she did stab Hannah."

"Then Hannah was kidnapped by Owen's cousin," he added with a shake of his head.

"Yeah, I guess when I think about it, crazy stuff has happened here. Just last year with Lea and Brett. Of course, that had nothing to do with the camp directly." She took a deep breath, remembering how scared she and the rest of the group had been when Lea had been kidnapped. Then she thought back to yesterday and shivered and wrapped her arms around herself.

He stopped and pulled her into his arms. "Thinking about yesterday?"

"Yes." She sighed and rested her head against his chest. "I'm sorry you have to deal with stuff like that.

He shifted slightly. "It's not typically to the extent it was yesterday. In recent years it's gotten worse, though. I did grow up in the south and my family is one of the only mixed families in a small southern town." He leaned back and looked into her eyes. "I doubt there's a black person or American Indian in the south that hasn't experienced some form of hate at least once in their life."

"Your mom?" she asked. For some reason, she couldn't imagine anyone being mean or hateful towards the woman. She'd oozed class and friendliness every single time Jules had seen her.

"Oh, especially her. I learned my fight from her." He smiled. "As a business owner and a woman, she has a few doozy tales to tell. One Karen even recently called the cops on her in her own store. The woman had the audacity to claim that my mother was trying to steal something. From her own store." He shook his head.

"That's terrible," Jules said with a frown.

"Girl, she knows how to handle herself. She's been dealing with it a lot longer than I have. Being married to a white man, she gets all the hate when they go out together. My dad has had some thrown at him too. When I was young, he had stories of how people, both white and black, would question why he had a black baby or kid with him. I can't remember it, but one of the first days of school, he came to pick me up instead of my mother. I apparently ran to him all excited, but the teacher was upset and claimed that my dad was trying to steal me. The police were called. Before they got down there, my mother showed up. They almost pulled me out of the school. Needless to say, that teacher was reassigned." He sighed. He ran his hands over her shoulders. "I'm making it sound worse than it is. It's not like I walk out my door each day afraid of being called a nigger."

She winced. "I hate that word."

"So do most people, but there are plenty that don't know it's wrong. Not as many as you'd think though. They just have louder voices and recently they've gotten caught on camera a hell of a lot more, so they're highlighted."

"Good, they should be shamed in society. Everyone should know what kind of heart they have."

He smiled. "I'd like to tell you that yesterday is most likely going to be the last day I experience something like that."

"But it wouldn't be true." She nodded. "I get it. It just sucks. You were minding your own business. You hadn't even said anything to the guy until he hit you with the anchor. And from the video, it appears as if he was aiming for you."

"He was. I could see it in his eyes. It's the only reason he didn't kill me with it. I was paying attention."

"It burns me that they're free," she admitted.

"No doubt already headed home," he said with a shrug.

"Enough about all that." He took a deep breath and then smiled. "Let's talk about our trip this weekend."

Her smile doubled as he took her hand and started walking again. "Okay, what about our trip this weekend?"

He laughed, then went on to tell her all the fun things he had planned. For the rest of the day, she dreamed about being with him. And not just because of all the fun things he had planned.

## CHAPTER NINE

Why was it that when you wanted time to slow down, it seemed to rush past you? But the moment you wanted a day to get there, time seemed to stop altogether.

Damion watched Jules head back inside the main building, then he headed off to the boathouse to grab a paddleboard and enjoy the rest of the afternoon.

His mind was consumed with the kiss she'd given him before she'd darted inside. It had been quick, he understood, so that no one they knew or worked with would see it. Still, the kiss had been more potent than any he'd had before.

He grabbed a paddleboard, life vest, and a paddle and stripped off his shirt and flip-flops. He left his clothes and his phone and keys in his locker in the boathouse.

He launched from the docks and headed out across the dark fresh waters of the inlet. Most guests liked to launch the paddleboards from the beach area, since the waters of the Gulf were a lot clearer than that of the inlet. He, however, liked the quiet of the inlet, the nature of the smaller streams that weaved through the swampy areas. There were sporadically placed homes along the banks, most with their own boat docks. Some were mansions with swimming pools, but there were also a few run-down trailers.

One property in particular he'd watched for years. Not for the run-down trailer, but for the land. It was perfect. There was an old dock, one that could be rebuilt to hold his own sailboat and also had enough room for two more boats.

The long grassy yard was fully overgrown now, but with some minor work, it could be just as beautiful as the yard of the mansion that sat next to it.

The dilapidated trailer would be hauled away. He'd dreamed of having Aiden design and build his dream home on the land.

But every time he'd looked into the lot, the owner refused to sell it. He didn't know if it was because he was the one asking or if he was really not interested in selling.

However, today, he almost fell off his paddleboard when he noticed the For Sale By Owner sign amongst the tall grass. Damn. He hated that he'd left his phone back in the boathouse.

Deciding the paddleboard trip was over, he turned and headed back as he chanted the phone number over and over in his head, trying to remember it so he could call the moment he got back.

The moment the man answered, he asked the asking price. Moments later, he was making an offer. Of course, the man refused to agree to anything until he met him in person.

Damion's heart sank. Then it jumped when he thought of an idea. He agreed to meet the man in an hour, then hung up and quickly called in reinforcements.

Exactly one hour later, he parked his truck in the overgrown driveway. The owner, a man he'd already met on several occasions in town, stood by his beat-up truck, watching him.

Before Damion could get out, two other vehicles parked beside his.

He jumped out and quickly smiled at Owen Costa, then glanced over at his dad as he climbed out of his parents' car.

"Nice," Owen said under his breath. "This the guy?"

Damion nodded. "Johnny Rowlings." He walked over and held out his hand to the man, who quickly glanced between the other men before shaking it. That was a first. Normally, the man refused to shake his hand or to talk to him. "This is my father, General Wells, retired."

He watched with pleasure at the surprise on Johnny's face as he took in the presence of a famous American hero. Anyone who'd followed the news in the past ten years knew who his father was. Knew what he'd done for their country.

"Sir." Johnny shook his father's hand eagerly.

"This is my good friend and financier, Owen Costas," Damion added, motioning to Owen.

Johnny turned to Owen and, once again, Damion watched with pleasure as the man's eyes widened. "I know your old man."

"Yes, so I hear," Owen said easily.

"He lived next door. I remember the three of you boys running around that yard." He motioned to the yard a ways down from the land. "Back when I lived here with my family."

"Yes, I remember your daughter Kaley," Owen said easily. "How is she?"

"Married with five kids of her own," the man said as his chest puffed out.

"Good," Owen said and then turned his eyes to the land. "The old place has seen better days."

"She has. After Mary passed, I moved into a smaller place in town. Doctors told me I wasn't supposed to do too much yard work." He patted his leg. "Not after the last surgery."

"My son has mentioned what you're asking for it. Mind if we have a look around?" his father asked.

Johnny motioned with his hand. When Owen and his father started walking the land, Johnny turned to him. "You never mentioned you were a Wells."

"You never let me get that far in the conversation before." He held out his hand again. "If you're agreeable, I'd like to offer you what you're asking. A deal between you and me before those two sharks come back and try to talk you into a lower price."

Johnny looked down at his stretched-out hand for a split second, then easily put his hand in his and shook it vigorously.

Four hours later, he strolled through the camp's doors with a bottle of champagne and a proper bouquet of flowers in his hands.

Jules looked up from her computer screen and her eyes widened.

"Hey," she said as he set both in front of her. "What's all this?"

"We're celebrating," he said with a smile.

"What?" she asked, burying her face in the flowers.

"I am now an official land owner. Well, I will be in about a week," he added with a shrug. "But the legal paperwork is all signed to put things in motion."

"You are?" She looked up at him. "You... bought a house?"

"Land. There is a house of sorts sitting there, but it's going to be hauled off and a proper home built in its place." He leaned on the counter. "So, I figured as celebration, I'd take you out to dinner. By taking you out," he added quickly when her eyes narrowed slightly, "I mean grab a couple Isaac-packed dinners and go watch the sunset on my new property," he finished quickly."

Her eyebrows arched up. "Now that's a date I can get

excited about." She nodded. "Let me finish up here. Five minutes?"

He nodded. "I'll go get us some cups and some dinners to take with us." He started towards the dining hall but stopped and said over his shoulder, "And I will not be getting you a salad."

He enjoyed her laughter as he walked away. Since it was past normal business hours, most workplaces would be quiet, but the camp was still full of employees. Most of them were just coming on shift or taking their lunch breaks, which happened to be during dinner time.

The fact that there were employees pretty much around the clock was another reason he liked working here. His hours were pretty close to normal workday hours, except twice a week when he had sunset sails booked. But if he was being honest, he lived for those evenings.

He was standing in line for food when Andrea came and stood next to him in line.

"Hey, I didn't know you were working today?" she asked him.

He liked Andrea. Had even taken her out on a date. But they just hadn't clicked. Instead, they'd fallen into a very comfortable friendship, almost like brother and sister.

"I'm not. Just here to grab some food." He moved forward in the line and picked up two premade meals.

"Eating for two?" Andrea nudged his shoulder playfully.

"Jules and I are going to head out and have these on my new property," he said proudly.

"What?" she asked, excited. "The land you've been wanting?"

He nodded. "Just made the deal today. It's not final but..." He didn't get any further because she practically jumped in his arms. He was still holding the dinners and had to make sure he didn't drop them but laughed at her excitement.

"Congratulations," Andrea said cheerfully.

That was when he happened to glance over and see Jules standing in the doorway to the dining hall, frowning as she took in the scene he and Andrea were making.

"Thanks," he said, stepping back. "Talk to you later." He quickly rushed after Jules, who had disappeared through the doors.

He caught her outside the front doors, looking up into the night sky, just... standing there.

"Hey," he said softly. "Andrea was just congratulating me on—"

"I know," Jules interrupted him. "You don't have to explain anything to—"

She stopped when he set the meals down on the stone wall and took her shoulders in his hands and pulled her closer.

"I've kissed you. I owe you an explanation for why another woman had her arms wrapped around me," he said softly. "Andrea is like a sister to me."

"You two went out," she said, her entire body stiff.

"Once. And we determined we pretty much thought of each other as brother and sister," he explained. "She was excited when I told her I'd made the deal for the land. Back when we went out, apparently it was all I could talk about." He smiled.

He felt Jules relax slightly. "She's just so..." She glanced at the doors. "Pretty."

"Yes, she is, but I only have eyes for you. Besides, you're more than just pretty. You're knock-out gorgeous. Sexy as hell and the only woman I currently want to kiss and be with."

"Currently?" she teased.

He would have pulled her into his arms, but at that

moment, a couple of employees were heading towards them. Instead, he grabbed their meals. "Did you get the champagne?" he asked her.

"I put it in my bag." She showed him the huge bag that she carried with her every day. "What did you get us for dinner?" she asked as they headed down the main stairs towards the parking lot.

"Roast beef sandwiches, homemade chips, and brownies."

"I think you are a brownie-aholic," she joked.

"Take that back." He stopped and looked at her. "There's no such thing. I can eat a dozen brownies a week and quit anytime I want."

"Oh yeah?" She started reaching for the containers, but he held them away and added.

"I'll quit tomorrow." He started walking again as she laughed and caught up with him.

As he drove the short distance to the land, he filled her in on the property and how long he'd been in love with the place. How he'd convinced Owen and his dad to go along today, after his unsuccessful attempts to talk to the owner.

"I don't think my color had anything to do with it. I've heard the guy is all about the good old boys club. He likes making deals with men in power," he added as he pulled into the dirt driveway.

"Wow." Jules's attention was on the scene in front of them. They had about an hour before sunset, but already the sky beyond the run-down trailer was filled with soft colors.

"The trailer will be the first thing to go," he said. He turned off his truck and jumped out. He made it around to her side just as she stepped out into the tall grass. "Of course, I'll get the yard under control." He frowned down at her low-heeled shoes. "I should have let you change after work first." He groaned.

"Oh." She laughed and then jumped back up into his truck.

She scrounged around in her big bag, pausing for a moment to hand him the bottle of champagne, then pulled out a pair of sneakers and replaced the heels. "There, problem solved." She jumped back out of the truck.

"Let's go for a walk before we eat." He took her hand in his.

As he moved around the land, he told her all his plans. He had dreams of a massive three-car garage near the front of the lot, closer to the road. Big enough that he could work on a boat if he had to. Then there'd be the house.

"Four bedrooms and an office. Maybe a library combo type thing?" He shrugged. "A kitchen big enough that when I have people over, the entire group can stand around in it, if needed." He chuckled. "My mother always jokes that whenever she has guests over, most of the time they stand around in the kitchen."

Jules laughed. "It's the same at my parents' house."

"Then back here." He took her hand again and they walked towards the old dock. "I'll fix this one up. Maybe add a lift for a smaller boat on this dock area." He motioned to the smaller space. "The *Wind Chaser* can go here," he added, moving over to the last slip, "instead of being docked at the camp all the time. Security has caught a couple of people in the last year trying to sneak on her and take her out. I've had to add locks on the chains."

"It's amazing what drunk people think they have the right to do," Jules said. "Nice view." She motioned to the water. "That's Reed and Kimberly's place, right?"

"Yes," he answered. Reed Cooper was retired military of some sort. He was very secretive, but the man had helped find Hannah back when Owen's cousin had kidnapped her. Reed was dating Zoey and Scarlett's mother, Kimberly. The woman had moved into one of the cabins when the friends had opened the camp. About two years after that, she'd moved in with Reed.

The pair spent almost as much time traveling as they did at home. Although, after Zoey gave birth to Paige, they were home more often.

"Wow, that place looks bigger from this close," she exclaimed.

"Of course, what I build won't be half that size, but it's going to be all mine." He turned and looked back at the land, his back to the water now.

She turned too and looked along with him.

"It's a nice spot. Those huge oak trees are beautiful." She motioned to two huge trees that sat off to the side.

"I plan on keeping them. I'll maybe even hang a swing from one of them. You know, so my kids can swing under them."

"Kids, huh?" She turned to him. "I can picture you with a handful of them running around."

He laughed. "Two. At the least. Three if I'm lucky."

"Lucky?" she asked.

"To be with someone who wants three kids," he answered easily.

# CHAPTER TEN

Jules thought about her own dreams for children. She'd always thought that three was a perfect number. Two boys and a girl. At least in her mind, she'd always imagined so.

Then her mind turned to images of what her and Damion's children would look like. They'd be beautiful, she surmised quickly. They'd have his smile and his dark rich eyes, which laughed and sparkled when he talked.

"Come on, let's get the food and champagne. This is a good spot to watch the sunset." He took her hand, and they walked back to his truck and gathered the things, including an old beach blanket that he kept in the truck.

While they ate, they talked about each other's plans for their dream futures. After he filled her in on his dreams for the home that he was going to have Aiden build, she told him about the online classes she was taking and how she had hoped that they would allow her to take a bigger role in the business side of the camp.

"Not that I don't love working at the front desk, because, hello, best job in the world." She paused as he agreed. "But I want to make more of a difference around here. I want to do what I can to make the place successful. Maybe expand it a little more..." She dropped off and took the last bite of her food. She pushed the empty container aside when she realized she had finished the entire meal while they had talked.

She normally didn't eat more than a salad with some turkey or chicken in it for dinner. She'd shoved the entire roast beef sandwich down her throat as they dreamed together.

"I'm sure with both Hannah and Elle heading into maternity leave, they'll be begging you for help," he said.

"I've already talked to Elle about it," she said with a strained smile. "If all goes well while they're out, they think I can take a bigger role permanently."

"You sound as if that's a problem."

Sighing, she leaned back on her elbows as her feet dangled off the docks. The sunset was in full force, and the sky was flooded with bright hues of some of her favorite colors.

"What if I screw something up?" she asked suddenly, turning towards him.

"You won't," he said easily, leaning next to her.

"But what if I do?" she stressed. "This place is... well, everything. I can't imagine going back to work in an office or waiting tables somewhere else. Having a dead-end job." She sighed.

"The camp does spoil you for any other jobs," he joked.

"I just don't know if I have the strength to lose it," she admitted.

"Then don't screw up." He took her hand in his and pulled her against his chest. "You'll do great." He kissed her forehead.

She relaxed back against him, and they watched in silence as the sun slipped completely beneath the horizon.

"Jules?" he asked when they were shrouded in darkness.

"Hm?" She closed her eyes and tried to hold onto the feeling of being held by him.

She felt him take a deep breath, as if he was going to say something. But then he shook his head and sat up. "I'd better get you back."

She stopped him by leaning over and kissing him. She'd wanted to feel his lips against hers again. Wanted to hold onto his sexy scent. Carry his sexy taste with her to bed. Wanted to dream of him.

Taking what she wanted, she closed her mind to the fear of this not meaning to him what it meant to her. Even if this was one sided, the way she felt, she was going to enjoy every moment with him.

"My god," he moaned against her lips when she pulled back for a breath.

Her heart felt like it was going to leap out of her chest. Her breathing was erratic, causing her head to swim.

"Jules, I'm not going to tell you that I don't want you," he said, running his hands over her bare arms. "But it's cooled off and there are a gazillion mosquitos out here." He chuckled. "Let me take you back. We can finish this..." He rested his forehead against hers. "This weekend." He kissed her again.

He dropped her off at her car in the camp's parking lot, and she headed home. Alone. She thought about spending more time with Damion, dreaming of what it was going to be like with him.

She was supposed to have the following day off work, but since she was trying to save up for a new sofa, she'd scheduled to work in the dining room for both lunch and dinner, which gave her a few extra hours in the morning all to herself.

Normally, she'd grab a bowl of oatmeal or some fruit and eat it at work. But today, she had arranged to meet her parents at a local café instead.

She arrived a few minutes early and grabbed them a table. She wasn't surprised when her parents showed up a few minutes late. Her mother had taught her to be early or on-time for everything in life, but her father was always late for personal functions.

Her mother always joked that he was too busy in life to care what others thought. She knew that deep down it bothered her conscientious mother, as was evidenced by the look of irritation on her face when they walked in.

In the past few years, her father, a man she'd always deemed strong as an ox, someone who could easily surf big waves in his family's home on the Big Island while clutching a delicate flower between his fingers, had grown more frail looking. He had a difficult time holding things, talking, and even sometimes walking.

The man was everything to her. Had always been. She had more in common with her dad than she had ever had with her mother.

Jules used to believe it was because of her mother's ridiculously high standards. Nothing, according to her mother, was ever good enough. Even her own daughter.

But the older Jules got, the more she understood that she had played a role in their separation. Jules had given up trying to have anything in common with her mother years ago, and she'd never really done anything to change that.

Until recently.

"Mom." Jules got up and hugged her and whispered. "Dad making you late again?"

Her mother chuckled. "It's what he lives for." Her mother hugged her back.

"Daddy." Jules turned to her father and hugged him. His body seemed so small when she held onto him.

"Bean." Her father hugged her, using the nickname he'd

given her on the day she'd been born. He'd called her that not because of her small size, but, according to him, because she came out the color of a Kona coffee bean, a subtle light cream color.

They all sat and after they'd ordered their drinks and meals, she turned to her mother and said, "I've decided to take a sailing trip with Damion this weekend."

Her mother's smile grew. "That's good. Tutu told me that she'd talked to Damion. She told me that the boy asked her if it would be something you'd be interested in."

She didn't know what was funnier. The fact that her mother called Damion a boy or that he'd actually asked her grandmother if she'd be interested in going sailing with him.

"Yes, he mentioned it to me. He just bought the land right next to Reed Cooper," she informed them.

They chatted about that for a few moments until their food arrived. It was strange to hear how her parents basically thought of Damion as part of their family. They'd always liked him, she knew that, but hearing them talk about him, she realized that it was more than just liking him. They actually adored him.

Her mother talked about him as if she were a proud mother. She couldn't remember ever hearing her mother talk about her in that way. Her father, yes, her mother... no.

Before their food arrived, a friend of her parents stopped by and briefly talked to them. Her parents knew almost everyone in the small town, even though they had only moved to Pelican Point six years ago, shortly after she'd graduated from high school. She'd grown up in the Panama City Beach area.

After her father's retirement, they'd bought the house they were in now and, as they put it, settled down away from the hustle and bustle of tourists on the other side of the bay area.

It was halfway through that conversation when her father suddenly went still. His eyes grew large and then he gasped.

At first, Jules thought he was having a heart attack. But then he turned to her mother and shouted, "Why did you do that? I told you we weren't going to come today."

Everyone looked very confused for a second. But then Jules's mother quickly apologized and told the other couple that they'd chat with them some other time and that he wasn't feeling himself.

From there, things got worse. Her father's voice got louder, and nothing seemed to settle him down. Not even after the food arrived.

"Mom," Jules said softly.

"I think we're going to head home," her mother said suddenly.

"I'll get this." Jules motioned to the table. "Daddy, I'm sorry, I need to go to work," she said standing up.

"Oh." Her father seemed to come back to himself for a moment. "Okay, bean. Will we see you tonight?"

She didn't know what he was talking about but nodded just in case it set him off.

After her parents left, she bumped into the other couple at the cashier's station.

"Is everything alright with your parents?" the woman asked.

"Yes." She held her head up. "My father is showing early signs of Alzheimer's."

The woman nodded and looked at her husband. "We went through that a few years back with George's father. I'll give your mother a call later this week. Maybe we can help her out. She shouldn't have to go through this alone."

Jules wanted to tell the couple that she was not alone, but she smiled and nodded in reply instead.

By the time she arrived at work, she had a slight headache from worrying about her father. She sent her mother a text asking how he was. Her mother replied quickly that he was resting and enjoying watching a game on television.

Just knowing her father wasn't affected as much as she and her mother were should have relaxed her. But it didn't. Instead, she worked through the entire evening stressed.

Working the dinner hour should have been fun. After all, tonight's dinner theme was a luau. She'd changed into the traditional attire that she'd grown up wearing around her father's family whenever they returned to the Big Island.

When they were with family, she and her cousins would usually make actual grass skirts, but tonight she was wearing ones made of synthetic material instead.

Still, she felt very comfortable walking around the dining hall and the patio area serving food in basically a swimsuit with a skirt.

But then one of the guests cornered her outside. She hadn't talked to the man before but had noticed that he was there with a younger woman who was easily half his age of around sixty.

"Well, well, aren't you a luscious little exotic flower?" the man said, blocking her from entering the building. She had a pitcher of ice water in her hands. The moment he cornered her, she used it to block his body from pushing up against her own. If she had to, she could either pour the ice water over the man's head or knock him out with the heavy metal material instead. At any rate, she didn't feel too threatened by him, since there were a dozen people within shouting distance that she knew would come to her aid.

"Did you need something?" she asked him, lacing her voice with a non-friendly tone. It normally did the job to let men know she wasn't interested. However, the guy continued to lean into her.

"You know, I'll be here for an entire month. Why don't we set a time to..."—his hand moved up to her arm as she jerked away— "play." He wrapped his fingers around her upper arm.

Dumping the ice water on him felt so good. He screamed and jerked away from her, giving her the opening to dart past him. The moment she did, she saw Damion rushing towards her from the pathway that led from the boathouse.

"Are you okay?" he asked her, his eyes running over her entire body.

"Never better," she said and stepped inside.

"That man..." He trailed off when the guy started shouting about getting her fired.

"Is a dick," she finished. "And I'll make sure to tell Elle and the others exactly what happened. But there's no need. He did all of that directly under a security camera." She smiled and set the empty water pitcher down. "God, it feels good to work for friends who are smart women who stick up for each other." She sighed. "What are you doing here?"

He seemed to relax for the first time since she'd seen him. "I heard you were working the night shift and thought I'd come say hi." He leaned against the counter. "What time do you get off?"

She glanced at her watch. "An hour. Have you eaten?" He shook his head. "Grab an empty table outside. I'll order us something and we can eat together once I'm off."

"Sounds like a plan." He turned to go but stopped and twisted back and gave her a kiss. "You're super sexy when you kick ass."

"Thankfully I didn't have to kick anything this time." She laughed. "Just pour."

When she went back to the kitchen, Elle was sitting down on a tall barstool, holding her stomach.

"Are you alright?" she asked, rushing to her friend's side.

"Yes, just…" She took Jules's hand and held it to her side. Jules felt a bump against her hand. "They're playing soccer in there, I swear it," Elle said with a laugh.

Jules relaxed and enjoyed feeling the new life kicking against her hands.

"Oh, I should warn you, I had to dump a pitcher of ice water on a guest," she said with a smile.

"Had to?" Elle frowned. "Are you okay?"

"I love that that is the first thing you ask me. Not if the guest was mad. Which he was, by the way. He promised to get me fired."

Elle shrugged. "He probably deserved it. I can cut his stay short if you want?"

Jules thought about it for a moment and shook her head. "No, I think he got the point."

Elle smiled. "Mighty, mighty Jules. Okay, on that note, I'm going to head to bed. These two have had enough for one night."

"Goodnight," she said, and went back to work.

Sure enough, when she stepped outside, the man was talking with Zoey, who was patiently listening to the man scream while his wife sipped her drink as if the entire thing was a show.

The moment the man saw her, he pointed and raised his voice. "That's her. She ruined my Versace. This is an eighteen-hundred-dollar shirt. Not to mention my shorts." The man was on a roll now. Jules didn't know if he enjoyed all the attention he was getting or was really that upset she'd cooled him off.

Zoey reached up and rubbed the sides of her forehead as she quietly got the man to stop yelling.

There were only a handful of guests still out on the patio at this time of night. Most had eaten their dinners and retired or headed back to the pool area where they could relax and take a dip to cool off.

Even thought it was early summer, tonight was one of the first really hot nights. There would be more, lots more, but this was the first of the year. Which is why the luau was perfect for tonight.

Knowing that Zoey would handle things, she made her way over to Damion.

"Know what you want?" she asked him as she set down a glass of water in front of him, then took a sip of her own and sat it down where she would be sitting in about an hour.

"Do you really think he's that upset that you ruined his shirt or is it more that you denied him?" Damion asked, watching the show.

"The latter. I would guess he has plenty of money to buy another shirt. Men like that have fragile egos and when they see someone they want and can't have, they turn into two-year-olds who can't have the toy they want," she said with a slight sigh.

"Does this happen often around here?" he asked, looking up at her.

"Enough that Zoey knows exactly what went down without having to ask me my side of the story." She waved to Zoey who rolled her eyes while her back was turned to the man.

Damion was quiet as she turned back to him.

"Does it happen to all the women working here?" he asked.

"Most, which is why we all attend Aubrey's self-defense classes."

"But you feel safe here, right?"

"Of course. There are cameras everywhere." She motioned to the few covering the patio area. Seeing Damion's worry had her sitting down next to him. "Hey, stuff like this doesn't happen every day. I'm normally standing behind the front desk. Far away from drunk men who want to hit on me. Besides, have you seen my outfit?" She waved her hands up and down her body. "I'd want to hit on me. I should have worn a warning label. Look but don't touch."

Damion smiled and she saw him relax. "Jerks like that should be taught a lesson." He sighed. "And yes, how could I not notice your outfit. I'll be lucky if you don't douse me with ice water before the night is over."

Jules felt her knees go weak and was thankful she'd sat down moments before. Damn, Damion had a way about him that no other man had. With a simple look he caused her heartrate to spike and her breathing to double. Her body wanted him. Needed him. Her heart jumped at the chance to be near him. Every fiber of her being wanted to be near him.

She was in deep trouble.

CHAPTER ELEVEN

Damion was thankful Mr. Versace had left the patio area finally. He'd yelled at Zoey until Dean Wallis finally walked over there and told the man and his wife to go back to their cabin and sleep it off or he'd call the police.

He knew Zoey would have done it herself, but she was trying to be diplomatic for some reason.

After they left, Dean walked over to his table.

"Thanks for that. I was just about to head over there and help out," he admitted.

"Zoey hates it when we step in, but I'd had enough of that asshat's bullshit," Dean said with a sigh.

Zoey walked over and sat down. "Are we having a party?" She groaned. "Cuz I could use a drink."

"I'll get you one, darling," Dean said. "What's your poison?"

"Mai tai," she said, putting her feet up on an empty chair. "Is Jules joining you?"

"She's getting our dinners," he told her as Dean disappeared.

"What took so long getting Mr. Versace to leave?" he asked her.

Zoey rolled her eyes. "That guy, Joe Tribberton, owns one of the largest local online travel magazines and used to be a friend of my father's."

"Your dad died a few years back, right?" he asked.

Zoey nodded. "Mr. Tribberton and my father were close. I had hoped..." She shook her head. "He's loaded. I mean... really loaded. If he enjoyed himself here he could not only do a piece in his magazine but..."

"Money talks to money," he said, and Zoey nodded.

"Now, knowing what kind of creep he is, I should send him packing. I mean, he took a page out of my father's book and married someone half his age." Zoey rolled her shoulders.

"Yeah and look at all the problems Bridgette caused you and Scarlett." He remembered how the woman had kidnapped Aubrey after she and her mother had sunk their claws into Aubrey's wealthy father.

"I doubt Lisa, Joe's new wife, would lift a finger to do anything except order another drink," Zoey added as Dean set a drink down in front of her.

"I'm just finishing up." He motioned to the last guests on the patio. The yelling had scared all the others away. "Then I'll join you. Want food?" he asked Zoey.

"Sure, whatever they have left in the kitchen," she said with a sigh. "I'm exhausted."

Just then Jules came out with their food. She set it down and sat down next to him.

"I guess the drama was good for something. Everyone has gone, making it possible for me to sit down half an hour early," Jules said as she picked up a French fry and ate it.

He noticed that she hadn't ordered a salad for herself and instead got a cheeseburger and fries like he had.

Another thing he appreciated about this job was the instant friendships he'd gained. There were a handful of people that worked at the camp whom he considered close friends. He'd spent the last few years growing even closer to them and, for the most part, his friendships outside had fallen to the sidelines. Not that he'd had a bunch of friends before, but the few casual friends he'd had dropped away after he'd started working here.

The friendships that he'd gained at the camp were some of the best that he'd ever had.

For the next two hours, he laughed and joked with the employees that came and gathered around the table. By the end of the evening, there were almost a dozen sitting around.

At one point, he reached under the table and held onto Jules's hand. He'd forgotten to have that talk with her about showing affection in front of everyone. He wanted their friends to know he had finally made his move.

Hell, a few of his friends had been joking for almost a year about it. But he wasn't going to pressure her into anything, not when this was more important to him than any relationship he'd ever had before.

Shortly after midnight, after everyone had left, they walked to the parking lot, hand in hand.

"What are your thoughts on this?" He held up their hands.

"Hand-holding?" She smiled. "I like it."

"I mean, in front of others," he clarified.

She stopped and turned to him, then lifted her arms and rested them on his shoulders. "Are you asking me what I think of PDA?"

He nodded as his hands moved to her hips.

"Yeah, something like that."

"I'm okay with it if you are," she said easily.

"Even in front of the gang?" He motioned behind them.

"Especially in front of them. It's going to be such a relief to stop answering everyone's questions about when we're going to hook up," she joked.

"Is that what this is?" he asked. "Just a hookup?"

"No." She shook her head. "I think we both know it's already gone beyond that. Even before we've officially done the hooking part." She smiled.

"One day left." He sighed. "Then we head out for four days, three wonderful nights." His hands started moving slowly over her hips. "Nights during which I know exactly what I plan on doing with you. To you."

He felt her shiver. "We could..." She motioned to her car.

He leaned down and kissed her. In his heart, he knew he wanted to wait. He'd never wanted anything to be as special as his first time with her. That didn't mean he couldn't enjoy the moment with her.

After all, just feeling her lips under his had him growing harder than he'd ever been—physically and mentally—for someone.

They were both a little breathless when the first raindrop fell on their heads. He leaned back and looked up into the dark night sky. He could see the lighter grey clouds rushing past them.

"We'd better..." He didn't finish getting the words out before the sky literally dumped on them.

He took her hand and pulled her the rest of the way to the parking lot.

The torrential rains in Florida were nothing to be ignored, but most of them were quick to pass. He opened his passenger door and helped her inside, then rushed around and climbed in behind the wheel as the rain continued to fall hard over them.

"We'll wait it out." He shook the rain from his hair, then he looked over at her.

The raindrops had caused her hair to almost glow, much like her skin was doing.

Without a word, he slid across the seat, pulled her back into his arms and covered her mouth with his. "I want you so bad," he groaned. "But I'll be damned if the first time is in my truck when I have to be at work in a few hours." He sighed. "The trip…"

She nodded in agreement. "I wonder what else we can do to pass the time until the rain stops?" she asked, and then bit her bottom lip.

"Oh, you're in trouble now." He shifted his hands on her. Her eyes closed as her head leaned back against the seat. Her breasts felt like silk even through her wet clothes. He cupped her as he trailed his mouth down her neck.

Her hands bunched in his wet shirt, then he felt her nails scrape his shoulders as she tugged his wet shirt over his head. He pulled back and tossed it aside, then slowly unbuttoned the shirt she'd put on over the floral swimsuit top that was part of her outfit for the evening.

"God, you should wear a bikini every day to work," he said, looking at her. She gave a nervous little giggle and then gasped when he dipped his head down and trailed his tongue across the skin between her breasts.

She tasted like fresh rain and sex. Hooking her top with a finger, he nudged it aside and lapped at her erect nipple. He took it deep into his mouth, sucking until he felt her buck under him.

"Damion, I need…" She groaned as he pushed his hand through the fake grass skirt that she was wearing to cup her through the bikini bottoms she wore underneath.

She jerked against his palm, then moaned when he shifted the material until he felt her soft warm skin against his fingertips.

"Please," she cried out, jerking her hips towards his fingers. When he dipped them inside her, she exploded and came more alive than anything he'd ever witnessed before. God. She was even more amazing than he'd expected.

His body ached to fill her, to be surrounded by her wet pussy. He wanted it more than he'd wanted anything in his life.

But he suddenly realized the rain had stopped and the parking lot wasn't as empty and quiet as they'd expected.

Had she screamed? Hell, yeah, she had. Had anyone heard? Probably. He shifted her swimsuit back into place to cover her before leaning up and kissing her lips to keep her from begging him for more.

"I think we have an audience," he said softly into her ear. "I'm hoping they missed the main show." He motioned to a dark figure standing across the parking lot.

"Oh god." She groaned. "When did it stop raining?"

He chuckled. "I thought the same thing. I was too busy watching the fireworks to notice," he joked as he pulled his shirt back on. "I'll walk you to your car," he said, but she stopped him. "It's right there." She motioned. "It's still raining, but not as bad. Stay, you can watch me from here." She leaned over and kissed him again. Then she took her bag and dashed through the rain to her own car.

When he looked, the dark figure was gone, so he turned back to watch Jules's taillights disappear down the road.

Then he drove home and had one of the worst night's sleep in his life. He tried not to be grouchy when he showed up to work shortly after six the next morning.

The heavy rains had dumped a bunch of leaves and debris in all three pools, so it took him longer to clean them out than it usually did. When he was done, there was a bead of sweat dripping down his back, so he did what he normally did—he jumped in the pool to cool off.

"Are you supposed to be doing that?" someone called to him when he surfaced.

He glanced over and saw an older man sitting on a chair watching him.

"Yes," he responded. "I have to test the salt levels," he lied, somehow not rolling his eyes. It wasn't the first time he'd been asked that. Nor, he doubted, would it be the last.

The truth was that no one that worked at the camp cared what he did. Just as long as his job got done. It was the same with all the employees.

Employees were allowed to use any of the facilities as long as they were off duty and didn't make a scene. They were even allowed to invite a guest or two, just as long as they scheduled it ahead of time.

The perks of the job were almost as good as the job and the pay itself.

"I have a pool of my own. I know for a fact that's not how you check the salt levels," the man persisted.

Deciding he didn't want to argue, he climbed out of the pool just as Zoey was coming around the corner.

"Oh, there you are Damion." She smiled when she saw him. "Cooling off?"

"The young man was taking advantage of the pool," the old man jumped in.

Zoey turned to him and in a cheerful tone replied, "He's allowed. Thank you."

Instead of it ending there, the old man looked taken aback, shocked that he would have permission to jump in an empty pool he'd just spent half an hour cleaning.

"Ignore him," Zoey said softly. "His wife says he's got dementia." She took his hand and they walked towards the pathway. "The reason I came looking for you is to ask you to take over my shift at the volleyball net on the beach at noon."

He started to mentally run through his day. "You're free. I checked," she added with a smile.

"Sure," he answered. "Anything wrong?"

"No. No." She shook her head, and he watched a frown form on her lips. "No," she said again.

"Are... you sure?"

"No, it's just... I'm late," she blurted out.

"Well, then you'd better..." The sentence was halfway out before her meaning sank in. "Oh!" He froze. "Oh!" he said again.

"I know!" Zoey shook her head. "I mean, Paige isn't even a year old," she said, pacing in front of him as her hand resting over her stomach. "We were trying, but I just didn't think it would happen this soon."

He took her shoulders and stopped her movement. "You want two kids?"

She smiled. "Yes, we both do. Actually, we've talked about a houseful of them."

"Then relax. Go, do whatever you gotta do. I'll take the volleyball game. I got your back." He leaned in and hugged her, only then realizing he was still a little wet. "Sorry." He pulled back.

"Thanks, Damion. You're the best," she called out as she headed towards the parking lot. "Don't tell anyone... just yet."

"I won't," he promised. But when he turned to go, Jules was standing there smiling at him.

"Tell me," she said, crossing her arms over her chest.

"Nope." He shook his head. "I just promised..."

"You didn't promise. You just said, I won't. That's not a promise. So..." She waved her hand towards him. "Spill."

He sighed. Just seeing the look in her eyes, he understood there was no way he was going to get out of telling Zoey's secret to her.

"Fine, but we have to walk as we gossip. I've got a volleyball game to oversee." He took her hand in his and headed towards the beach area.

After dishing out the scoop on Zoey's possible family expansion, Jules informed him that she was on her lunch break and agreed to head up and grab them both sandwiches that they could eat while he oversaw the volleyball game.

They were missing a few people, but the game was more exciting than the last few ones he'd refereed. The group of guests were younger, and they all seemed to know each other.

Between games, he wolfed down the sandwich while Jules sat and watched the game from the shade of a palm tree. When he looked again, she'd gone, most likely back inside to work.

After he was done with the game, he walked into the water and cooled off again before heading to the gym to spot a few customers and enjoy a workout himself. After hitting the showers in the locker rooms he changed into his outfit for the evening sail.

Before making it to the boathouse, he stopped off and figured he'd flirt with Jules for a while.

She was busy on the phone when he leaned against the counter. There was a slight frown on her lips and a little line between her eyebrows she always got when she was upset.

He only heard the last part of the phone call, but it didn't sound like it was anything that should have upset her.

"What's wrong?" he asked the moment she hung up.

"You know that guy from last night?" she said as she leaned on the counter.

"Is he bothering you?" he asked, motioning to the phone.

"No, that was...another guest. But he did corner me as I was leaving the beach."

Damion stood up straight. "I'll—"

Jules reached across and took his hand.

"Do nothing about it. I've already told Elle and Brett. He's going to have his new guy, Aaron, check in on me and maybe walk me to my car each night until the guy is gone."

"I'll walk you to your car each night," he jumped in.

"You'll be out on your cruise when I get off work," she reminded him. "Aaron can do it, or Brett said he would himself. But you can spend my lunches with me and meet me in the morning if you want." She leaned on her elbows. "If you think you're up to the task?"

He moved behind the counter and wrapped his arms around her. "I am," he said into her hair. "I should have punched the guy out first thing."

"No, you shouldn't have. We'll deal with it. Besides, they aren't going to give him another warning. Next time he bugs me, they're cancelling the rest of his and his wife's time here." She leaned up and kissed him. "Don't you have a sail you're supposed to go on soon?"

"Yeah." He sighed and thought about getting someone else to cover for him.

"Go, I'll be okay." She nudged his shoulder. "I still have an hour before I head home. Besides, I want to go and pack for our trip tomorrow. Are we still leaving at eight in the morning?"

"Sharp." He smiled. "I'll have breakfast all ready for you. Just... get here," he said and kissed her again. "See you then."

"Okay." She smiled as he turned and walked away. "Damion?" she called after him. "I can't wait until tomorrow."

"Me either." He smiled all the way down to the docks.

## CHAPTER TWELVE

Jules must have packed, unpacked, and repacked more than a dozen times. She wished she'd had enough time to run into town and buy a couple new swimsuits and maybe a sexy dress or two as well.

In the end, she settled on packing five of her nicest bikinis, two sundresses, a sexy evening dress, some cotton shorts, a couple of T-shirts, two sweatshirts, and shoes to go with each outfit. She threw in her makeup kit after getting ready the next morning and hauled the two suitcases down to her car from her apartment.

She doubted Damion would have two suitcases and thought of repacking everything to make it fit into one, but then figured she had to stop second-guessing herself and shoved it all in her trunk.

When she arrived at the camp, Damion was sitting in a golf cart in the parking lot, waiting for her.

"Morning." He smiled at her and when she got out of her car, he walked over and hugged and kissed her.

"Morning." She smiled up at him.

"I figured you'd want a ride to the docks." He motioned to the golf cart.

There were more than twenty golf carts on the campgrounds. When the camp had opened, there had only been five or so. But as the camp grew, more golf carts were needed. The employees used them to haul guests and their luggage to each of the cabins or just to race each other around the grounds.

Scarlett held the record for winning the most races. Everyone was pretty sure she was cheating. Somehow.

Damion loaded her luggage up on the back of the cart and, to his credit, he didn't complain or even say anything about her two suitcases.

After everything was stored below deck, she sat next to him while he navigated out to the bay area.

"We'll be heading back to Destin first, then out to the Gulf and down the coast. Isaac's team loaded us up this morning. My little kitchen below has never been fuller." He patted the spot next to him. "Wanna drive?"

She shook her head. "Maybe later. Right now, I want to sit back and enjoy being on my very own private sail with a sexy man at the helm." She wiggled her eyebrows.

"We'll stop off at Crab Island for breakfast," he said. "We won't anchor close. It'll still be too early for most of the tourists."

"Sounds good." She leaned her head back to enjoy the warmth of the sun. Since it was early, it wasn't roasting them just yet. She had brought a couple different sun hats for when it got too hot.

It was a short trip to Crab Island and when they were a few yards from the clear shallow water, Damion cut the engine and tossed one of the anchors overboard.

"Won't we need both of them?" she asked, motioning to the bigger anchor that sat at the front of the sailboat.

"No, this'll hold us in place long enough for us to enjoy our breakfast. Besides, no other boats will dock near us out here. They're all closer in at this time of day." He was right. There were more than a dozen boats already crowding around one another in the center of the shallow sandbar.

"Now sit back. I'll get our breakfast." Damion disappeared down the narrow steps.

Since the sun had warmed up, she removed her shirt and shorts and sat back in the bikini she'd worn underneath.

When Damion came back up carrying a large tray filled with food, he whistled.

"And to think all I had to do was feed you to get you to undress," he joked as he set the tray down on the bench. He reached over and flipped a lock holding a flat surface that he used as a table.

She moved over and sat on the bench after he moved the food to the table. "Wow, this looks amazing," she said, taking a slice of watermelon.

"Isaac's best." He headed back down the stairs. When he came back this time, he had a bottle of champagne and two glasses. "He thought of everything." He sat next to her.

They ate fresh fruit, small muffins of every flavor, and her favorite—little quiches with bacon, ham, egg, and cheese.

"I'm so stuffed. If we eat like this for the entire trip, I'm going to have to go on a diet when we get back," she joked.

"Me too." He rubbed his flat stomach.

"You're joking." She shook her head. "You have a six-pack. Trust me, I've seen and felt it." She motioned to his stomach area. Even though she couldn't see it now, since he was wearing a shirt, she remembered how wonderful it was. How sexy it felt under her fingertips. "You're perfect," she added.

He turned to her and pulled her into his arms. "So are you." He kissed her. For a split second, she felt perfect. But then her mind recovered from the kiss and all of her insecurities returned.

They raised anchor and, once the sailboat was out into the Gulf of Mexico and heading south, he showed her how to open the two large sails. The biggest one was white and the smaller one was blue-and-white striped. He took his time and showed her how everything worked, telling her all the names of things. Not that she would remember, but she enjoyed hearing him talk.

The moment the wind caught the sail, the boat started moving at a steady pace. At one point, they were traveling faster than they had using the motor at top speed.

She'd been in a few speed boats that were faster, but there was something magical about the large sails above them filling with wind. The silence of traveling without a motor was inspiring.

"This is... amazing." She laughed and turned to see Damion watching her. "I can see why you love it."

He smiled. "It's the one place I feel that I truly belong."

She thought about those words. Let them sink in. As much as she had felt like an outsider her entire life, she understood that he had felt the same. Maybe even more so.

The more she thought about it, the more her eyes burned and her heart ached. So, she did what she always had. She began to talk nonstop.

She asked him question after question. How did he get into sailing? Was it hard to learn? When and where did he go on his first solo trip?

He let her steer for a while when he went downstairs to get them drinks and a bag of chips to snack on. They were halfway through the trip, and it felt like they had just left Crab Island.

Damion tied off the wheel with a rope that hung close by

and then moved over to sit on the cushioned bench with his arm wrapped around her.

"Don't you worry you'll run aground like that?" she asked, trying not to let her own worries show.

"No, I'm right here." He smiled at her. "I never leave her like this for too long," he added as he took another chip.

"This is nice," she admitted after a while. She'd relaxed and pushed the images out of her mind of them hitting the shoreline, which happened to be about a mile from them on the left.

There wasn't another boat in sight. The only sounds were that of the gulls overhead and the water lapping at the front of the boat. There wasn't even a cloud in the sky. She couldn't imagine being out there in a storm.

Lifting her face to the sun, she took a deep breath and felt more at ease than she had in years.

"Tell me about this place we're staying at. Your family owns it?" she asked him. He'd rested his head back and had his eyes closed. His arm was still around her, and she could tell he was just enjoying the moment like she had was.

"Yeah, they rent it out from time to time. But for the most part, it sits empty. I go down every few weekends to check on things. Do some minor fixes or repairs. My folks pay a cleaning crew to come in after each rental, but I like to check up on things myself every now and then." He shrugged.

"How long has your family owned it?" she asked.

"Since I was a kid. My uncle and my dad went in on it together. After my uncle Gary died, my dad gave me his share in the property." He glanced up as a helicopter flew over them. It was one of the tourist services, and they waved at the people waving back down at them.

"We're off Mexico Beach," he said as he watched the helicopter disappear. "They're finally rebuilding after Hurricane Michael wiped the entire town out."

"I noticed. My parents and I drove down here last month. So much of it is still gone, but they finally have some of the basics back. The store, a hotel, and gas stations. It was terrible how everything was just gone. The camp was lucky to survive the last hurricane," she added, remembering all the devastation the storm had caused.

"We hightail it to my aunt Gene's place in South Carolina when it gets bad down here," he admitted. "Where do you go?"

"Hotels. Wherever we can." She shrugged. "My mother was an only child. Her parents died shortly after I was born. Both of them were taken by cancer. My dad's family still lives on the Big Island in Hawaii."

"Yeah, I remember him talking about it. You have a ton of cousins there, right? I've seen some pictures hanging up at your parents' place."

She laughed. "Six cousins and more than a hundred aunts, uncles, grandparents, distant cousins... I think I'm related to everyone on the island."

He smiled. "It must be nice, going back there."

"It is, but still, this is home." She sighed and looked off to the land in the distance. There were homes all along the shoreline, most of them clustered together. To the right, there was a massive void, empty of buildings.

"St. Joseph Peninsula and Cape San Blas," he said as he got up and unhooked the rope and started to steer them a little further away from the land that was getting closer. "We're going around this and then we're only an hour away." He turned the wheel.

"What's the farthest you've traveled?" she asked, lying down on the cushion and stretching out in the sunlight.

"The Keys," he answered quickly.

"Oh, right. I knew that." She yawned and closed her eyes to the brightness.

She hadn't planned on falling sleep, but the sunlight and the full stomach helped. The quiet sounds of the water lapping at the boat and the birds overhead soothed her and the gentle rocking of the boat all must have lulled her to sleep.

She woke to Damion's kisses. His hands were on her shoulders and arms, rubbing slowly in circles.

"Did you have a good nap?" he asked. She realized he was sitting next to her and that the sails were down. More importantly, the boat was no longer moving.

Wiping her hands over her face, she sat up and stretched before looking around.

They were docked.

"We're here?" She blinked a few times.

"Yup." He smiled and helped her stand up. "Welcome to the Hideaway." He motioned to a blue metal-roof home nestled amongst trees.

An extremely long raised walkway led from the dock over the shallow Gulf waters to a private white-sand beach area. There was a plush green yard between them and the three-story home that held a fairly large swimming pool.

"This place is massive," she said, taking it all in.

"It has seven bedrooms for larger family gatherings or guests who rent the place with friends. But we'll just be using one." He pulled her into his arms.

She couldn't help teasing him. "Oh? Will you be sleeping outside then?"

"You wound me," he said before kissing her. "Come on, I'll give you the tour before we drag our stuff inside." He took her hand in his and helped her out of the boat and onto the dock.

"My dad and I rebuilt this dock a few years back. Every now and then a couple of boards need to be replaced," he said as they walked side by side down the narrow wood planks.

"How shallow is the water out here?" she asked, knowing

most docks in this area that could accommodate boats as large as his sailboat had to be extremely long to reach out to the deeper waters. It was the reason the docks at the camp were along a narrow waterway instead of on the bay or Gulf sides.

"At the dock? About fifteen feet. Right here, about two feet."

"How many parties have you had here? I bet you used to come down here all the time in high school." She stepped onto the green grass.

"Only one. You'd think I'd be more popular than I was." He laughed. "I was pretty much ignored, which was better than being bullied all the time," he said as they walked past the pool.

"Any neighbors?" she asked, looking to the surrounding trees.

"Someone owns the lots on either side, but they haven't built on them yet. My dad has been trying to buy them for years. Even though he's officially retired, he'd like to build two more of these places and retire in *style*," he said as they stepped up to a door.

The entire bottom floor was nothing but exposed stilts. A hammock hung between two of them. There were parking spots along with kayaks and a canoe. There was a large deck off the back of the house with stairs leading up, but they headed towards a doorway that opened to a narrower set of stairs. In the front of the home, towards the roadside, there were wider exposed stairs that she expected went to the front doors.

"We'll go in the back way," he said, using a code to unlock the door. He quickly stepped inside and disarmed a security system, then turned to her and motioned for her to go on up the stairs.

At the top of the stairs was another door. This one was unlocked, and she stepped into a large laundry slash mud room.

"Nice." She looked around. There were hooks with beach

towels hanging off them. Weaved baskets sat on a shelf above the washer and dryer along with laundry detergent and other soaps. Everything someone would need while away on vacation.

"You think the laundry room is nice, wait until you see the rest of the joint," he joked as he opened another door.

She stepped out into a massive two-story living and kitchen space. There were huge windows on the wall facing the water. Somehow the view from up here was even more spectacular, as if seeing it behind glass made it more desirable. The high ceilings in the great room were done with wood planks in a light wood coloring. There was matching wood on the floors with huge area rugs in a soft grey in several places, giving it a cozy feeling.

A dark grey sofa and chairs sat in front of the windows. A massive flat-screen television was on one wall and a twelve-person dining table in grey and white sat along the other wall. The kitchen was near the back of house relative to where they had arrived, but she realized it was actually the front of the home if you had arrived from the road.

The kitchen was modern and done in the same light colors. Honestly, everything was so amazing. She just knew that his mother had decorated everything. The class and comfort screamed of his mother's influence.

There was a hallway leading off to one side and a wide staircase led up to the top floor.

"There are two bedrooms and bathrooms down here and five bedrooms and four bathrooms upstairs. There is a small bathroom downstairs for pool guests, so you don't have to run up the stairs," he said as they walked around the room.

She turned to him and watched his face closely for his response as she asked, "Which bedroom are we going to take?"

# CHAPTER THIRTEEN

Damion's body instantly responded to Jules's question. However, he had a few things he wanted to do first. Like eat and shower.

"Whichever one you want. I would, however, suggest one of the main bedrooms on this floor. Taking those stairs for a midnight snack can be a bitch."

She laughed. "Only you would think of stairs as an inconvenience to get to food." She shook her head. "Let's go look at them, and I'll decide."

"You go. I'll start bringing in the food and our things," he suggested, needing some time. "Then we can eat out by the pool and take a dip."

He saw her eyes run over his face before she nodded. "Sounds perfect."

He left her and went back outside to gather their things. There was a massive cart that helped him carry most of the things up the dock. Still, he had to take three trips to get it all. Isaac and his crew had packed more food than the two of them would need for a month.

Her bags were easy enough and after she'd picked the guest room facing the water, the one he always stayed in himself, he set their things in the large walk-in closet. She helped him cart up the rest of the items and they put the food in the fridge and cupboards together. The menial task seemed a whole lot more fun with her by his side.

Then they mixed Jules a drink, grabbed him a beer, and headed back down the stairs. The dip in the pool was well needed and hard earned.

It felt good to wash the salt spray and sweat from his body while rubbing his body up against Jules as they played in the water together. He left her in the water and went back upstairs to make them sandwiches and grab them a couple more drinks.

When he came back out, she was lying in the sunlight on a lounge chair, and he felt his heart practically stop. She was a goddess in the sun. Her soft skin practically glowed. Her hair shone and looked silky soft.

He wanted to drop everything and run to her. Hold her. Consume her.

Instead, he set the tray with their food and drinks down on the table, which sat on the side of the pool area in the shade of the trees along with a massive hammock.

They joked and flirted with one another while they ate.

"God, do you know how long it's been since I've taken any sort of vacation?" she said between bites.

"You went to Hawaii last Christmas," he pointed out.

"Being around my ohana does not count as vacation. Even if I get to stay in paradise, eat amazing food, and go surfing every day."

"It doesn't?" he asked with a laugh. "Sounds pretty amazing to me."

"That's because you don't know the rest of my family. We spend most of our time running around, arguing, or fighting for attention. My cousins are always causing some sort of fight, which then lasts the entire trip." She rolled her eyes.

"You love them," he said, seeing it clearly in her eyes.

"Of course. That doesn't mean they don't drive me nuts at times." She smiled. Her eyes moved out to the water. "God, this is so amazing."

He glanced out over the water and saw the amazing view. There were big puffy clouds floating across the bright blue sky. The emerald-green water was so clear, you could see the fish swimming in the shallow water.

"Yeah," he agreed, "it is."

"Don't get me wrong. Hawaii is pretty amazing, but the long flight, the feeling of not being able to hop in a car and take a long road trip..." She glanced over at him.

"You could always get a sailboat," he joked.

She rolled her eyes. "What is it? A four-week journey to the mainland?"

He shrugged. "Depends on how good the winds are."

"Yeah, not like a weekend road trip up north." She relaxed back. "I'm thinking of crawling in that hammock and taking another nap."

"I'll join you," he said, feeling a little exhausted himself. Normally when he made the trip down here alone, he would get right to work fixing whatever needed repairing. But this trip, he was on vacation.

He wanted to enjoy every moment with Jules. They tossed their empty paper plates into the big, covered bin under the stairs. Then he climbed into the hammock and pulled her down beside him.

She laughed when they almost spilled over, but he steadied them quickly enough. He'd spent so many hours in the hammock, it was like riding a bike to him.

"There." He held onto her. "Is this what you wanted?"

"Yes." She sighed, and he felt her completely relax. "I think it's more than that. I think I needed this. Things were getting too... big."

"Life is big. But taking time like this helps you realize some of the things you thought were too big, weren't."

"Exactly." She rested her chin on his chest and looked up at him. "Why did we wait five years to do this?"

He thought about it for a moment before asking. "Have you ever danced the tango?"

She half sat up and looked at him in shock. "Hold the phone... You can dance?"

He shrugged. There was one point in his life he would have been embarrassed about the admission. He no longer was.

"An old girlfriend made me take a class with her that she'd won in a raffle," he explained. "In the tango, just before you make the first move, there's this sort of... flirtation that happens between partners. A couple beats filled with eye contact, elevated heartbeats from the closeness of one another, the anticipation of the first beats of the music." He shifted to look down at her. "That's what the last five years have been. We've been building up to the dance."

She shifted slightly until her body covered him, then her lips brushed across his.

"I don't think I want to wait any longer," she said against his mouth. "Why don't we head inside?"

He moved so quickly; they ended up sprawled on the soft white sand below the hammock. Thankfully, he was quick enough to twist their bodies so that she landed on his chest instead of under him. Still, whatever breath her request hadn't knocked from him, the fall took out of him.

"Are you all right?" she asked with a chuckle.

"Yeah," he said with a wheeze, causing her to laugh some

more. "Okay, dip in the pool to wash the sand off first, then we head inside."

She nodded in agreement, and he rolled until they were both clear of the hammock above them. Then he playfully picked her up in his arms and rushed to jump into the deep end of the pool, still holding her tight.

She gave a brief squeal before they hit the water with a splash. As their limbs tangled, his desire for her grew to an almost unbearable level.

They came up for air kissing, her arms wrapped around his shoulders, her mouth fused to his.

"We're clean. Let's go," she said breathlessly.

He nodded in agreement, unsure if he could trust his voice. Then he gathered her in his arms again and swam towards the stairs.

He climbed out, still holding her.

"You can put me down," she said as he started towards the back door.

"I'm good." He smiled down at her. "Grab us a towel?" he asked as they passed the towel hooks that sat right outside the door.

He kicked the outside door shut as he started up the stairs. She used the towel to dry her hair, shifting slightly in his arms as he headed back to the bedroom she'd picked out.

When he got there, he slid her down until her feet touched the ground. She tossed the towel down and reached to pull her wet swimsuit off, but he stopped her.

"I like to unwrap my own gifts," he said as he kissed her again. Their bodies heated as their hands ran over bare skin.

He untied the swimsuit top that she was wearing and it dropped to the ground with a wet plop. He cupped her bare breasts in his hands, enjoying the way her nipples puckered for him.

He enjoyed the taste of her skin on the tip of his tongue as he trailed it over her, lapping up the drips of water still on her. Her fingers dug into his shoulders as he reached to untie the bottoms on her swimsuit. Each side had little ties on them that rested just above her hips. He'd dreamed of undoing them from the moment she'd taken off her shorts earlier in the day.

When they joined the top of her suit on the floor, he cupped her and returned to kiss her lips as she moaned his name over and over.

Hiking her leg up, he dove his fingers deep in her and she came on his fingers, juicing them until he swore that he could no longer hold back. He had to feel that sweet wetness on his dick.

Then he realized what he was thinking. For the first time in his life, he cursed at having to wear a rubber. Walking over to the nightstand, he pulled out one of the packages he'd placed there earlier.

When he came back to her, she was sitting on the edge of the bed, looking satisfied and eager at the same time.

"Here, let me." She took the condom from him and smiled as she slid his wet swim trunks off his hips. Her fingers cupped then circled his length. Instead of sliding the condom on, she stroked him a few times and he mentally counted to keep himself from coming in her hands. He wanted, needed, to be inside her.

"Jules," he growled as he closed his eyes. "Don't torment me."

He heard her chuckle and then felt her slide the condom on. "Later," she said, "I'm going to enjoy taking you in my mouth."

"Fuck," he cursed as he pinned her to the bed. "You make me lose control." He spread her legs and settled between her.

"Good," she sighed as she wrapped her ankles tightly

around his legs. "Now you know how you make me..." She gasped as he plunged into her. "God!" She arched back and he felt her nails scrape his skin.

Good. He wanted her to leave marks on him. He needed the pinch of pain to help him realize that this was really happening. That she felt as wonderful wrapped around him as he'd imagined.

"There's no going back now," he said next to her ear.

"No," she said as she shook her head. "Please." It was nothing more than a whisper, but the simple word had him moving inside her. His hips arched back until his cock was almost dislodged, then he jerked forward again, and once more she cried out his name.

He felt her convulse around him, wished more than anything he could feel her slickness against his own skin.

He covered her mouth with his as she continued to beg and moan with pleasure. He wanted everything she offered him. Wanted to taste it, feel it, swallow it whole.

When he felt his own release building, he leaned back.

"Look at me, Jules," he begged.

When her blue eyes opened and focused on him, he let himself go. Let everything he'd been holding in for her over the past five years explode.

No. There was no going back now. Damion Wells was in love.

# CHAPTER FOURTEEN

**W**hat in the hell was that? Jules had never experienced anything like it before.

Sure, she'd had sex. More than a dozen times by her count. With two different partners and spread over the course of eight years.

But nothing, and she did mean absolutely nothing, had come close to what had just gone on between her and Damion.

Damn, the man could move. He seemed to know every place to touch her—to lick, suck, and kiss her—that would cause her body to explode.

It was as if he'd found and read the entire manual to her body. Hell, more than that, he'd memorized it.

She had never come twice so quickly before in her life. Not even when she was using her vibrator on herself.

Even now, as his body pinned her to the mattress, she ached for him. And he was still inside her.

It felt damn good to have his weight pinning her down. He was lean and toned, and his warm skin felt so nice and slick next to her own.

She tightened her pussy muscles around his length and felt him flinch.

"You're trying to kill me," he groaned next to her ear.

"Just... testing something," she replied with a smile as she did it again. She felt him grow harder inside her, so she did it a few more times.

"Damn," he said, shifting until he looked down at her. "Is this what you want?" he asked, shifting his hips and filling her completely again.

"Yes," she said with a gasp.

"Don't blame me," he said between pumps, "when you can't walk tomorrow."

She laughed. Then she held onto his hips and groaned his name when he continued to move inside her.

He bent his head down and sucked her nipple into his mouth, mimicking the motion his hips were making.

"You taste like summer," he said against her skin. Then he ran his tongue up her neck before kissing her so deeply, her soul ached.

What power did he hold over her to make her react so intensely?

"Look at me, Jules," he said again. When her eyes focused, she expected him to come again, only he didn't. This time it was her who let go. Her body wracked under his, convulsing as if by his command.

"That's it, baby, come for me again. You've got one more for me." He leaned down and trailed his lips across hers. "You can do it for me, baby." His hips continued to pump, his dick filling her, retreating, then filling her again. She felt him push harder, farther, faster, and knew that he was right. She had one more in her. One more build and fall into the blinding light. One more sweet release. Only for him.

When she locked with his eyes this time, she felt him tense with his release and mirrored it with her own.

No. Whatever this was, she'd never had it before. Nor, she doubted, would she with anyone else.

This was for him alone.

She woke sometime later when Damion stirred and left the bed. It was dark and, for a moment, she forgot where they were. Then the light in the bathroom flickered on.

"Sorry," he said softly.

"No, it's okay." She rolled over and watched him walk back towards her, gloriously naked. A slow smile crept onto her lips. "Am I allowed to say wow? Or is that too cliche?"

He sat next to her, his hand going to her bare hips. "You can say it just as long as I can say... damn." He dragged out the word and she laughed and hugged the pillow. "Hungry?" he asked.

"I could eat," she admitted. "After I use that." She motioned to the bathroom.

"We can shower, then eat."

"I'm fine with that." She rolled over. "But you'll have to wait... I need the room first." She started to get up, but he stopped her and kissed her. "I'll go use the one across the hall, then meet you in the shower." He kissed her again. "But you don't have to be shy around me. The toilet is in its own private room."

"I don't think I could go knowing you were just outside the door," she admitted, feeling stupid.

"Someday you'll be so comfortable around me, you'll burp and fart in front of me," he joked.

"No." She laughed. "I won't."

He smiled and laughed as she disappeared into the bathroom. She made sure to shut both doors, the outer one and the one to the smaller room that held just the toilet.

When she was done, she gathered her shampoo and conditioner, unlocked the outer door for him, and stepped into the shower.

Moments later, he joined her. She'd showered with a man before, but with him, it felt more right. She was more relaxed. Maybe because he was running his hands all over her again?

He even started helping her shampoo her hair. He ran his fingers along her scalp, through her long hair, and her body reacted again.

She figured that two could play at that game, and she started running her soapy hands all over him. He was perfection.

"I can't believe I get to play with these," she said, running her fingers over his muscles. "I mean, look at you. You're built. Built, built." Her eyes locked on his chest and six-pack.

"And I can't believe I get to play with these. You're stacked," he said, cupping her breasts in his hands. "Stacked, stacked."

She laughed. Then her laughter died and turned to moans when he dipped his head down and started sucking on her breasts.

"I don't know why I'm enjoying this so much," he said. "I'm a leg man."

She laughed again. "I'm really into asses," she admitted, reaching around and grabbing his butt. "Really, really." She sighed feeling his firm cheeks in his hands. "But that doesn't mean I don't appreciate a six-pack now and then." She reached back around the front of him with one hand and ran her fingers over the toned muscles that lay over his stomach.

"This is going to be one long shower," he teased as he pinned her against the tile wall. Then he was kissing her again and slipping on a condom before sliding slowly into her.

She was thankful for a few things. One, that he was strong

enough to hold her up, and two, that there was a large tile seat in the shower that she could collapse on after he'd turned her legs to jelly.

"Food," she groaned. "If we're going to do that again anytime soon, I need sustenance." She leaned back against the shower wall.

"Agreed." He shut of the water. "I think we're as clean as we're going to get." He reached over and helped her to her feet. "Let's go see what Isaac packed for us."

They ate smoked chicken sandwiches on wheat buns and pita bread with hummus, then finished the meal off with some of Isaac's key lime pie. Since it was already dark out, they ate in the dining room instead of taking the meal out to the large deck that overlooked the water.

She was more relaxed after talking and joking with Damion over the food. She'd always felt relaxed around him, comfortable, even with the sexual tension they'd had before. Now that they had made that move, the tension had shifted. It was still strong, but the last barrier of the unknown had been finally removed. In its place was a new hunger. One she doubted would be filled in just the one weekend they had together.

"There are some board games." He motioned to a bookcase full of family games. "I've never been beaten at Monopoly," he challenged.

She laughed. "Oh, challenge accepted." She reached over and grabbed the game and set it up while he cleared the dishes and grabbed a bottle of wine.

"You get the race car. I'm the dog," she said, waiting for him to challenge her. Instead, he smiled. "I've always wondered why they didn't have other animals. I mean, dogs, cats, horses, cows, you know? Wouldn't that be more fun than a thimble?"

He held the small piece up. "Why a thimble?" He shook his head.

"And one shoe? What's up with that?" She held up the small piece.

"It should have been high heels. Those are sexy." He straightened the money she'd set in front of him.

"You aren't a cheater, are you?" she asked suddenly.

He gave her an I'm-wounded-you-asked look, then took her hand in his.

"I'm not a cheater in any sense. That extends to all parts of my life," he said in a calm tone that had her heart skipping.

"Me either."

He smiled. "Good, then let's play." He rubbed his hands together. "I've got to add one more notch on my belt of Monopoly winnings."

Two and a half hours and another bottle of wine later, Damion frowned over at her.

"How'd you do that?" he asked, waving his hands. "How?"

"Easy, buying land is—" she started but stopped when he held up his hands.

"I know the tricks to Monopoly. But..." He motioned to the board. "You kicked my ass. I mean, wiped the board with it and everything." He held up his single dollar. "I'm broke."

She laughed. "So, you can't pay your rent?" She waved to his piece, which was currently sitting on her land.

"Hell no, I can't." He narrowed his eyes. "Do you take credit?"

She laughed. "Maybe. What do you have as collateral?"

As an answer, he moved closer to her. "How about other forms of payment?" he asked. His eyes moved to her lips and, suddenly, the game was completely forgotten.

In one quick move, he swooped her up and carried her over to the sofa a few feet away. There, he kissed her senseless while his body covered hers.

She didn't know when he'd removed her cotton shorts and

tank top or his own shorts and T-shirt. She lost track of time when his mouth dipped lower to cover her pussy.

As he ran his tongue over her, he slid a finger into her and had her convulsing and crying his name. When he built her back up, this time, he slid over her and into her.

Wrapping her legs around his hips was by far the most surreal feeling in her life. He fit perfectly against her. He fit perfectly inside her.

She could no more stop herself from releasing, from doing what he demanded of her body, than she could stop the sun from rising the next morning.

They fell asleep on the sofa, wrapped around one another. He tossed a throw blanket over them both sometime during the night.

She wanted to stay right there, in his arms, wrapped around him for the rest of the weekend. But this was real life, and her bladder was yelling at her from the three glasses of wine she'd drank the night before. With the added weight of Damion pushed tightly against her, she was trying to figure out if it would be unclassy of her to push him to the floor and make a run to the bathroom.

"What's wrong?" he asked, rubbing his hands over his face.

"I need the bathroom. I'm about to knock your ass on the floor and make a run for it," she admitted.

He laughed and, to his credit, quickly rolled away.

What happened next was like every scene in any old horror movie, where the victim is frozen in place and can't run from the killer.

She tried to get up from the sofa, but her body wouldn't work. She actually had to wiggle and rock her entire body. There might have been several choice curses that flew loose when nothing seemed to work to dislodge her from the deep cushions.

Finally, Damion reached over and pulled her easily to her feet.

"Thanks," she said, rushing out of the room.

When she came back out to the living room, having washed her face, combed her crazy tangled hair, and put on a new swimsuit under a pair of shorts and a tank top, Damion was standing at the stove making bacon and eggs. He was wearing a new pair of swim trunks and swaying his hips to music playing out of a speaker somewhere in the room.

"Hungry?" he asked over his shoulder.

"It was one of the reasons I woke up. That and the wine. What can I do to help?" She moved to his side.

"Drinks. There are fixings for mimosas if you want."

They moved around the kitchen like her parents used to, easily avoiding bumping into one another as if it was a dance.

When the food was ready, they stepped out onto the deck and ate out there. There was a large table and chairs as well as a sofa and chairs that sat around a firepit.

"Maybe we can watch the sunset from here tonight," she suggested.

"That sounds like a plan. I saw the makings for s'mores."

"I love it when we do s'mores at the camp. I always help out on those nights." She remembered the last time she'd sat out in the cold around one of the campfires. Her parents had decided to take a night at the camp for their anniversary. She'd gotten them the honeymoon cabin. They'd spent a full day at the swimming pool, then had a black-tie dinner, before meeting her at the campfire for s'mores and champagne.

That had been one of the last nights her father had been normal. Shortly after then, something had... clicked on. Or off, rather.

They had noticed a few hints that his memory wasn't what

it used to be. The first time he'd lashed out, both her mother and she had been confused. From there, it had grown worse.

"What's the plan for today?" she asked, pushing the thoughts of her father's problems away.

"This, maybe some of that." He motioned to the pool. "What do you want to do?"

"This and that sounds good." She sighed and leaned back. "Maybe a dip in the Gulf?"

"Whatever you want." He leaned back himself. "We've got two whole days to do whatever we want." His hand moved to her thigh. "Whenever we want." He wiggled his eyebrows.

# CHAPTER FIFTEEN

The last thing he expected to be doing shortly after breakfast was sweating his balls off. But when Jules suggested they take the paddleboards out on the water, he followed along, hoping to maybe spend a little energy and then come back and get lucky again.

How was he supposed to know that she'd want to explore as much of St. George Island as she could. They made it almost to the state park before she suggested they turn around.

Thankfully, the water was calm enough that it was easy going. But with the sun beating down on them, he had to jump in the water several times to cool off.

She'd grabbed a large straw hat and a sun shirt before they'd left so she wouldn't burn her skin. He'd packed a water-safe bag with their phones and had put a couple bottles of water in there, along with a bag of chips and a few granola bars, just in case he wanted a snack, which he always did when he was out on the water.

By the time they returned to the house, he'd eaten all the snacks and was so ready for lunch. Jules had only drunk a bottle of water the entire trip. Even though he tried to convince her to eat a granola bar, she said she was happy with the water.

He did notice that she grabbed an apple while he grilled the fish that he'd caught on the paddleboard trip and put in the small live-well bag that he always hung off his board. Paddleboard fishing was something he and his father always enjoyed when they came down here as a family. He hadn't caught anything big, but the four small groupers would be good in sandwiches.

They ate their lunch by the pool then jumped in and cooled off further. He couldn't stop himself from touching her while they played around in the water.

He'd never felt so free with anyone he'd been with before. He was pretty sure it was because they had been friends before they'd started dating.

Most of the women he'd been with, he'd had a few awkward dates before getting together with them. He'd learned their quirks after sleeping with them, which is why most of his relationships hadn't lasted long.

Jules was different. He knew almost everything there was to know about her.

He knew how she liked her coffee. Which wines she liked. Which foods she liked and, more important, which ones she loved but avoided because she was always trying to lose weight. He didn't think she had to do. As it was, he could see her hip bones. When he'd first seen her five years ago, she'd probably been ten to fifteen pounds heavier than she was now, and she'd looked happier.

Still, feeling her legs wrapped around his hips, he had to admit, no matter what she weighed, she felt perfect.

"How about we head upstairs for a nap?" he asked as his hands cupped her butt.

"We could," she said a little breathlessly. "Or we could..."

She reached down, her fingers going underneath his swim shorts, and cupped him.

"Damn, girl." He groaned. "Here?" He glanced around and realized there no way anyone would see them. The nearest house was almost five lots away and on the other side of the road.

As far as perfect places to have sex outside, this was it. Funny, he'd never thought of that before.

"All right," he said, taking her lips with is. "Let's play." He hoisted her up and made his way to shallower water, then set her on the side of the pool deck and undid her bottoms, tossing them on the side of the pool as the sun beat down on her exposed skin. "Spread those legs for me."

She smiled and did as he asked.

"Don't let me get sunburned," she warned. She took his shoulders and pulled him towards her.

"Never," he said and covered her pussy with his mouth.

He hadn't planned on having sex in the pool, so he knew he'd have to take her back upstairs to grab a condom. But that didn't stop him from enjoying her or making her come a couple times outside.

When she was totally relaxed after multiple orgasms, they headed inside where they spent time exploring every inch of each other until they fell asleep holding onto one another.

The nap was short enough that they woke in time to heat up one of Isaac's premade meals and eat out on the deck to watch the sunset.

This time, he brought a condom with him and was thankful, since she pulled his shorts off and took him into her mouth right there on the back porch. He was never going to be able to be anywhere in the house or outside the house again without remembering what she had done to him.

When he was on the brink of coming, he flipped her onto

the sofa and took her, enjoying the way her soft moans of pleasure disappeared into the night air.

When they were lying there, naked and breathing heavy, she sat up suddenly.

"Let's go skinny dipping in the pool. I've always wanted to but have never had a place I felt safe enough to do it." She glanced around. "There isn't anyone for miles." She took his hand.

He didn't want to tell her he went all the time while he was here. Instead, he followed her down the stairs and into the water.

She was kissing him and wrapping her body around his again, but he knew he'd forgotten his condoms upstairs again.

"What's wrong?" she asked when she reached for him, and he slid back slightly.

"I left the condoms upstairs."

"It's okay. I've been on birth control since I was thirteen. It's helped regulate…" She shook her head. "Things. Anyway, and I'm clean." She tilted her head. "You?"

"I'm clean," he about burst out. "I've never… I've always worn…" He sighed and noticed her smile grow.

"Damion. I trust you. I would really like to feel you against me. In me." She pulled him back to her.

He didn't need any further encouragement. It was as if after getting the go-ahead, his dick took complete control of his mind and body. He'd never felt anything more powerful or more intimate in his life.

"Are you okay?" he asked after he felt her tighten around him with her release, which had caused his own release to follow.

"I'm better than okay," she said with a chuckle. "We're going to have to do that again tomorrow, when I have more energy." She took his hand and started floating in the water in front of him. "Float with me for a while. Gosh, look at all the stars."

He leaned back and happily floated next to her and looked up at the stars, while they were both completely naked.

They skipped on the s'mores that night, and headed back up the stairs and inside, where they fell into bed and went straight to sleep. They had stayed out in the pool almost half of the night, talking about their future. About his plans for his house. About her family.

He wanted to take her mind off her dad, but he knew that most of the worry was from not talking about it. So he listened to her. Listened to all her fears and worries about what would happen to her mother if her dad couldn't be there for her.

Which made him think of his own parents. Both he and Jules were only children. Which meant when their parents grew older and became unable to care for themselves, that responsibility fell on them.

He knew he was years away from that happening to his parents, but still, accidents or diseases happened. He supposed he'd never thought about it before.

The following day they went on a short bike ride. Since the main road didn't have sidewalks, they had to ride on the side of the road. The traffic to the state park was light for a while, but shortly before noon, it picked up and they headed back to the house for another swim.

"I can't believe we leave tomorrow," she said, adjusting her big straw hat. "It's been a dream being here."

"You'll just have to come back with me next time," he said easily.

"I'd like that." She looked at him from under the brim of her hat. "I think your nose is getting sun burned." She reached over and touched the tip of his nose.

"Yeah, I should've put something on it." He leaned back. "I

have a couple places on me that my dad says come from his side of the family. My nose is one of them." He smiled.

"What are the other parts?"

His mischievous smile grew, and she slugged his arm playfully. "I like your dad. He's funny. I've always been wary of military types. You know, the grouchy general types. Your dad is nothing like that."

"No, he isn't. At least not to people he likes. I've seen him pull off the grouchy general type to some. It's not a pretty picture."

"Why didn't you go into the military?" she asked. "Don't most military brats follow in their parents' footsteps?"

"For as long as I could remember, I knew I wanted to sail." He glanced off to the water. There were dark clouds in the distance, and he knew that tonight they were due for some rain. But by the morning, they'd have clear sailing back home. "The military would have just prevented me from my dreams."

"You really lucked out working at the camp, didn't you?" she asked.

"Yeah, if this hadn't come along, I'd be doing charters in Destin." He shrugged. "I did that most of my summers through high school."

"You did?" She sounded excited.

"Yeah. Not on my own boats, but still, I was on the water. I earned enough money the three summers I did that to buy the *Wind Chaser*." He motioned to his sailboat.

"I wondered how you could afford such a big boat," she said. "I'm still making car payments on my secondhand car." She rolled her eyes.

"Tips help," he explained. "You probably don't get a lot of those sitting behind the counter every day."

"My pay rate is higher to compensate for it, but still, it's why I work dinners or other events every now and then, when I really want to save money for something."

"I could teach you to work the sunset sails with me. I only go out twice a week," he suggested, wanting to have her along so he could spend more time with her. "It's basically doing what you do for dinner. Serving drinks." He shrugged.

"I'm not sure how good my sea legs are. I'd probably spill drinks over everyone. But I'll give it a try. How much do you usually make on tips?"

"A couple hundred each trip."

"What? Seriously? A couple?" She gasped. "I'll freaking grow sea legs for that much."

He laughed. "You can practice tomorrow on our trip back by serving me drinks the entire way."

"It's a plan." She stood up and did an amazing cannonball into the pool.

After dinner and the sunset, they decided to watch a movie together. She picked a scary movie that he'd watched a couple times before. Even though she'd admitted she'd seen it before herself, she still jumped and held onto him each time something scary happened.

Later, when she was fast asleep in his arms, he thought about missing the feeling of her next to him in bed when they returned. She'd go back to her apartment, he'd go to his.

Already, he ached for that to change. Would it be too soon to ask her to move in together? They had known each other for over five years. That was longer than he'd known anyone else he'd dated before. Not that he'd lived with anyone before, but still. It had to count for something. Right?

With his mind on that, he fell asleep and had dreams of their future, living in a dreamhouse on the land he would be closing on next week. In his dream, they had three beautiful kids and two dogs, ugly-looking mutts that were loyal and goofy and ran around and went sailing with them.

When they woke, they made breakfast together after showering.

"What are your thoughts on dogs?" he asked her, remembering his dream.

"I love them. Are you thinking of getting one?" she asked.

"Two. I want two of them," he said, suddenly knowing he was going to go to the pound when he got home. "Rescue dogs," he added. "My folks rescued Cooper and he's the best dog they've had."

"My parents used to have a dog, Bailey. She died when I was thirteen. It broke my father's heart when she went, and they've never gotten another one since."

"It's not fair that they don't live longer," he said. "But that just means we get to get more and give them their best lives while we have them."

"I agree." She smiled. "My place won't let me have pets."

He frowned. "Mine either."

She laughed. "Isn't that going to hinder you from getting two dogs?"

"Yeah." He sighed. "I could find us a place to live, together. One that allows dogs?" he said, holding his breath.

She stilled and turned to him. "Did you really just ask me to move in with you?"

"That depends." He moved over to take her hips in his hands and pull her closer. The eggs were probably going to burn on the stove, but he didn't care.

"It does? On what?" she asked, putting her arms around his shoulders.

"On your answer," he said, holding his breath.

"Let me think about it," she finally said. "I want to say yes, but…" She bit her bottom lip, then shook her head. "Find a place first. It'll have to be close to the camp."

"Yes," he agreed eagerly. "It'll probably only be temporary anyway. Aiden's going to start building the house on the land after I close on it next week. When that's done, we can move in there." He watched her face for any signs of fear.

Instead, he saw she was thinking hard about it.

"I'd have a few stipulations," she said slowly.

He reached over and turned off the stove. "I'd be happy to go over whatever rules or stipulations you have." He leaned in and kissed her. "I want to spend my nights with you in my arms."

She melted against him. "I'd like that too. I just want to make sure my parents are okay first."

"And you living with me might change that? If anything, I'd think it would help out. Rent would be cheaper. We could carpool to work." He pulled her closer. "You wouldn't be going through this alone. I'd always be there to listen to your fears and help you through the rough patches."

"You make it sound magical," she said with a sigh. "Find a place. I'll get you an answer after I talk to my parents. I promise."

"That's good enough for now." He kissed her. "Now that the eggs are overcooked, let's eat." He pulled the pan off the stove.

In the end, he made them more eggs. After they ate, they cleaned up, carted their luggage back to the sailboat, and locked up.

"I'm going to miss this. Not working. Lazy days." They pulled away from shore and she sighed as the house disappeared from view.

"I am too. It sucks knowing I'll be sleeping in my own bed

alone tonight." He pulled her close to him. "If I didn't have to be at work at five..." He dropped off.

"I know." She sighed. Then shifted. "Now, I guess I'd better practice walking around and serving drinks." She laughed. "If I'm going to pay off my car in this lifetime."

# CHAPTER SIXTEEN

It took them an hour longer to get back home than it had to get down to St. George. Damion said the winds were not strong enough to fill the sails and they ended up having to use the motor for more than half the trip back.

She didn't mind, but when they hit a little weather when they were coming back into the bay, she felt her stomach lurch. Of course, an hour earlier she had just eaten a full lunch complete with a slice of chocolate cake.

Damion had her sit down and help him steer, which helped steady her stomach. By the time they pulled back into the docks at the camp, she was feeling back to her old self.

"It just takes some getting used to," he said to her as he tied off the boat. "I remember the first time I hit choppy waters. I hung over the side of the boat until we returned to shore." He walked over to her and ran his eyes over her face. "You're not green anymore."

She laughed. "I wasn't really green, was I?"

He shook his head and kissed her. "No, but you did look pale."

"Thanks for talking me through it." She laid her head on his shoulder and wondered what happened now? Would they go back to just being work buddies?

He'd asked her to move in with him. That was a pretty big move. Right?

She'd been so shocked she hadn't known what to say. Her first instinct was to say yes. But then she'd thought of the logistics of it all.

Living with a guy was a lot different than spending a weekend with him. Were they really compatible? Again, her gut said yes. But she wanted some time to think about it.

Besides, the lease on her apartment wasn't up for another three months.

"Let's get your stuff to your car," he said and stepped back.

"Three months," she said suddenly. "My lease is up in three months. Find a place and you'll have your answer before then."

He smiled at her. "I'm a very patient man." He ran his hands over her arms. "After all, I waited five years to finally work up the nerve to ask you out."

She smiled. "Was it worth it?"

He leaned down and kissed her. "Totally."

Most of the clothes she'd packed she hadn't even taken out of the suitcase. Putting them away, she looked around her one-bedroom apartment.

She loved the place, even with its mishmash of furniture and styles.

If she moved in with Damion, she knew that their items would be combined. Yes, she loved the style his mother had decorated his place with, but how would it feel having her things mixed with the nicer, more expensive items?

She remembered him telling her that he'd given his mother full rein to decorate his place and that he'd wished he could have more freedom to decorate it himself. Did he like her style? He'd said so, but was he just being polite?

She hated that she doubted herself. Doubted them together. They'd been good together all weekend. It had been… well, magical. Then again, they had been away from all responsibilities.

She wanted, no needed, some time being with him around work and their friends.

She flopped down on her bed and stared up at her ceiling and cursed. She should have just said yes. She missed being around him already.

Would it be strange to call him now? Strange to ask him to come over? Rolling over, she glanced at the clock. It was only three o'clock.

Getting up, she changed into an outfit her mother would approve of and drove over to her parents' place.

Her mother was sitting on the back deck reading and her father was taking a nap on the sofa. She didn't know where Tutu was. Probably in her room, reading or watching television.

Without disturbing her father, she stepped outside after grabbing a bottled water from the fridge.

"How did it go?" she asked, sitting down next to her.

"Hey, sweetie." Her mother's eyes ran over her, like they always did. "How was your weekend?"

"Good," she said quickly. "How was Daddy's appointment? What did the doctor say?"

Her mother sighed and put her e-reader down. "Nothing much. Not anything new. She said that it does appear to be Alzheimer's, but they're testing him for any sort of brain disease. We won't know until the results get back next week. She suggested that when and if things got worse down the road, that he might be more comfortable in a home. Someplace more prepared to help him through what he is going through."

"You're not going to do that? Are you?" she asked, suddenly afraid.

"Not without talking with you first." Her mother shifted and then surprised her by taking her hands. "Jules, something has shifted in your father. Something that..."—her mother shook her head— "I'm not sure I'm prepared to handle on my own."

Jules's heart sank. "Do you need me to move back..."

"No," her mother interrupted, dropping her hands and looking slightly shocked. "I'm thinking of having your aunt Rita move in here." Jules instantly relaxed. "Her divorce is final, and she's spending a fortune on renting her place on the island. Besides, I think it will help your dad having his favorite sister around."

She felt her heart skip at the thought of having her favorite aunt nearby instead of thousands of miles away. "That's a wonderful idea. What does Aunt Rita think of it?"

"She's on board with it. She's been thinking of getting off the island anyway, now that her kids have moved to New York and Chicago. Besides, she's tired of running into your uncle Rob everywhere. It is an island, after all. She's decided that she's going to sell most of the things that she got in the divorce settlement and figures that she can be here by the end of the month." Her mother reached over and took her hands in her own. "Now, tell me about your weekend."

"Mom, Damion wants to move in together," she blurted out.

Her mother's face stilled and then a slow smile crept onto her lips. "And? Did you say yes?"

"What?" she asked in shock. "What in the... what?" She stood up and started pacing, then turned to her quickly. "You think I should?" she asked, shaking her head.

"Honey, the two of you have been dancing around each

other longer than your father and I were married before we had you." Her mother laughed. "He's good for you. We like his family. He's a good, hard-working, honest man, and judging by the way he's looked at you for all this time, he's totally over the moon for you."

Jules rolled her eyes. "Who says 'over the moon' anymore?"

"Old people. People who know what they're talking about because we're so wise." Her mother stood up and took her shoulders in her hands and then pulled her close into a hug.

It wasn't as if her mother hadn't hugged her before. But she'd just never done it out of the blue like this. Normally, it was on birthdays or special occasions.

Still, it felt pretty damn good. Whatever was changing her mother's outlook on their relationship, Jules couldn't fault it. Her mother hadn't said a single harsh word towards her that day.

"You really think it would be a good idea to move in with him?" she asked her.

"You're going to do what you think is best." Her mother leaned back and looked down into her eyes. Her mother was almost a half-foot taller than Jules. At one point in her teen years, Jules had hoped that she'd keep growing to be as tall as her mother. Just one more thing she'd been disappointed about in life. "No one can tell you what path to take in love or in life. All I can do is try to encourage you to follow your heart. Don't let what's going on with your father be a barricade to your future. He has made himself perfectly clear that he doesn't want to stop you from living a happy life. It was his idea, actually, for Tutu to talk with Damion about taking you on the trip."

"What?" Jules jerked back. "It was?" She shook her head in disbelief.

Her mother smiled and walked back over to sit down. "Your father hasn't completely lost it. He's seen the way you look and act around Damion. Everyone has," she added. "Now, are you staying for dinner?"

Jules thought to say no, but then glanced in and saw her father waking up from his nap. She needed to spend as much time with him as possible. There were no guarantees that she would have many more days like this.

"Yes," she said.

"Good. I'm making your favorite and you can help me in the kitchen." Her mother stood up again, then she walked over and hugged her again. "You can tell me all about your weekend while we work on dinner."

That evening, when she finally crawled into bed, she was more sure about moving in with Damion. Not that she was going to give him an answer right away. After all, Tutu had suggested she let the man sweat it out a little first.

She typed Damion a text message, then after a few deep breaths, hit send and waited.

"Thanks for the amazing weekend. I really enjoyed spending time with you."

She watched her screen, as if willing him to respond.

Within minutes, his response came back.

"So did I. I can't wait to see you again tomorrow. I already miss you. Have lunch with me?"

She smiled at the message and then typed. "Of course." Then she sent another one. "I miss you too."

"Did you see your folks?" he texted.

"Yes. My aunt Rita is moving in with my parents."

"Is that good?"

She knew that he'd never met her aunt Rita before. "Yes, she's my dad's older sister. Recently divorced her husband of thirty years after he decided he liked twenty-one-year-old models instead."

"Ouch. Stupid man. When you find someone who can put up with your shit for thirty years, you've found gold."

"Good answer," she typed and then added an emoji of a gold star.

"Hey, my parents are proof that you stick with love and not mess around," he texted.

She felt her stomach flutter a little as she relaxed back in bed.

"Aren't you supposed to be asleep?" she asked after seeing it was past ten.

"Morning does come early. I've got to clean the pools before guests start jumping in."

"I'll see you tomorrow. Goodnight." She smiled at the emoji he sent of a sleeping bear.

"Night."

The next morning, she had to fill Beth and then Zoey in on their weekend. She knew that she would probably have to answer questions about her and Damion's weekend more than a dozen times before lunch.

When he strolled in to get her for lunch, she was so excited to see him again. She tried to convince herself that the weekend hadn't been that breathtaking.

Then she saw him walk through the front doors wearing a pair of grey board shorts and a white camp shirt, and her heart literally jumped in her chest.

Damn it. She was in love.

"Hey." He walked over behind the counter and hugged and kissed her. "Missed you," he said into her ear.

"Ugh," Beth groaned as she flipped her long dark hair out of her face. "You two are already acting like the rest of the love-struck couples around here. Go have lunch before you make me puke," she joked.

Beth was basically Jules's height. They both wore heels behind the counter most of the time just to see over the computer screens. But where Jules was wider, Beth was petite. Very petite. So much so that Jules would have bet that she could place her hands around Beth's waist and have her finger touch.

Jules laughed at Beth's joke as she grabbed her purse and took Damion's hand and headed towards the employee dining room.

Normally, she would take a walk or eat her lunch outside if it wasn't too cold or too hot. Today, she enjoyed sitting at a table with him near the windows.

The employee's dining room was about a quarter of the size of the main dining hall. Instead of facing the water, this room faced the woods. To Jules, the view was even better since there was normally not a soul in sight out the windows.

She loved the woods that surrounded the campgrounds. There were cabins scattered throughout the trees, some facing the beach, others on the Gulf side.

"How does it feel being back?" he asked her after she took a bite of her salad.

"Boring. It's strange. When we were away, time seemed to go by so quickly. The weekend was like..." She snapped her fingers. "Now, it's not even halfway through my workday and I feel like I've been here for days."

Damion laughed. "I feel the same way. It took me forever to clean the pools this morning. I was counting down the minutes until we could have lunch."

"You have a sunset sail tonight?" she asked.

He nodded. "It's a small group. Private party. That group of friends that are here for a week."

"Right, someone's birthday or..." She tried to remember.

"Anniversary," he corrected. "Ten years."

"Right." She nodded.

"Zoey's working tonight. Otherwise, I'd invite you to come along." He took her hand in his.

"I'd have to pass it up. I had made plans to work in the pool bar. Britt is out sick," she explained. "Zoey asked me this morning."

"Then you'll be around after I'm back from the sail?" he asked.

She smiled. "Yes, I will."

"I'll come find you." He squeezed her hand lightly.

"I'll look for you."

Somehow, the time after lunch flew by more quickly. Maybe because she was extremely busy. The phones continued to ring while guests checked out and others checked in.

A couple years back, they had opened a little gift shop in the lobby area, where guests could purchase camp logo items such as shirts, beach towels, cups, mugs, souvenirs, and other trinkets. Guests brought their items to her desk to either add the cost to their bills or pay cash for. After lunch, there was an influx of guests wanting to purchase items. The entire gang that Damion would be taking out on the sunset sail all came through and purchased several hundred dollars of items each.

She was almost half an hour late shutting down the gift shop and the front desk, which meant she had to rush to change into her shorts and camp tank top in order to work behind the bar at the pool.

She slipped her swimsuit on underneath just in case she had time to jump in and cool off at some point during the evening.

By the time she arrived at the outdoor pool bar, there was a line of people waiting for drinks. It was a couple of hours before dinner, which meant there would be a huge rush, then a long lull while guests changed and ate dinner, followed by another huge rush of people returning to the pool area for the evening.

She loved working behind the bar. They had a standard menu of drinks that Britt, the head bartender for the camp, had come up with. The drinks were all named either nautical or tropical names, much like each cabin had its own unique name.

Just another thing about the camp that she and everyone else found utterly charming.

She knew how to make all the standard camp drinks. Usually, when a customer ordered something special, Britt was there to fill the order. Tonight, however, it was just Jules and McKenna, a new hire, working behind the bar. She doubted that McKenna knew much about special drinks, since she was obviously barely twenty-one herself.

However, after the first hour, she realized that McKenna was as good of a bartender as Britt.

"How'd you learn all this stuff?" she asked when the guests started to thin out. Most everyone had left the pool area and headed to dinner at this point.

McKenna, a tall blonde who had the body of a supermodel, shrugged. Her long blond hair was braided in twists and piled on top of her head to make it look like she had a mohawk. Her clothes were extremely fashionable and, from what Jules could tell, far more expensive than anything she owned. They were also tight enough that there was no doubt that she would be making far more tips than Jules would that night.

"Growing up, my mother was a serious alcoholic. She made me mix all her drinks," McKenna said, leaning against the bar.

"I'm sorry." Jules felt instantly terrible for bringing it up.

McKenna just shrugged. "She's clean and sober now, going on five years. But after I graduated, I knew what I wanted to do."

"Serve drinks to other alcoholics?" she said, wishing she'd

just shut her mouth.

McKenna chuckled. "No, I'm saving up to go to med school. This is just something that helps pay the bills."

"Wow, that's... amazing," Jules said, handing a couple their drink orders. That looked like it would be the last one for a while. "I'm going to jump in. Did you wear your suit?" Jules asked.

"We can do that?" McKenna stood up straight and looked at her.

"Sure, if there aren't any orders. Everyone's gone to dinner at this point. They'll be trickling back in about an hour." She pulled off her shorts and shirt. "Until then, I'm cooling off."

"I... didn't. This is only my second day. Last night Britt wasn't feeling well and barely talked to me. She threw up like ten times." McKenna glanced over at the pool. I can stick my legs in though." She toed off her shoes.

"You'll want to get some comfortable flip-flops. Your feet are going to sweat too much in those. At least for the summer months," she suggested as she stepped into the pool, then dove in. The water was refreshing. There had been sweat beading down her arms and back the entire time she worked.

The pool bar was in a tiki style building with three sides exposed, which meant no air conditioning. There were fans, but they were so loud, most of the time you couldn't hear orders, so they were shut off a lot.

McKenna leaned back with her feet dangling in the pool.

"So, you and Damion are a thing?" McKenna asked her.

Jules swam over and leaned against the edge of the pool. "Yes," she answered with a smile.

"How long has that been going on?" McKenna asked.

"Technically, five years." She laughed. "But we just made it official this past weekend."

"He seems nice. I met him earlier before you arrived when

he had to come fish someone's sandwich out of the pool." She motioned to the water.

"Yeah, he's constantly complaining about people dropping food in the water. Where are you going to school?"

"Right now, I'm taking online classes. Until I get my associate's degree. Then I'm planning on going to Florida State."

"How wonderful. I'm taking online classes too. For business. I'm wanting to help out around here as much as I can."

"You like it here?" McKenna asked.

"It's the best. Where else can you work and have all this to play with?" She motioned around. "Just as long as it doesn't hinder your work." Just then someone stepped up to the bar.

"I'll get it." McKenna jumped up to take the order. Jules stepped out of the pool and sat on a chair, knowing she had to dry off soon.

She had at least another half an hour before guests would flood back to the pool area, so she leaned back in the chair and allowed the sun to dry her skin, her hair, and her swimsuit.

When McKenna came back and sat next to her, she glanced over at the pretty blonde. There was a new frown on her lips.

"What?" Jules sat up, prepared to fix whatever had gone wrong with the order.

"I...It's just... It's going to be difficult leaving this job." McKenna leaned back in her chair and Jules relaxed. "I mean, have you seen the guys that work here?" She nodded as Dean delivered some food to some customers.

"That's Dean. He's a huge flirt," Jules said. "I'm surprised he hasn't asked you out yet."

As if her words had willed it, Dean headed their way. Without asking, he scooted Jules's legs aside and sat down on the foot of her lounge chair.

"Is it break time already?" he asked, playfully.

"It is for us." She nudged him with her feet. "Don't you have food to deliver?"

He nudged her back. "Don't you have drinks to mix?"

"Not at the moment."

"You get a break, so do I." He turned to McKenna. "I'm Dean Wallis."

"McKenna."

"Are you working the bar with our Jules?" Dean asked.

"I'm not a possession," Jules said, but Dean ignored her.

"She's the one working with me," McKenna said quickly. "She has to tolerate training me since Britt is out sick."

"Right," Dean said with a smile. "If you want, I can show you the ropes," he offered, leaning his elbows on his knees, trying to get closer to McKenna.

"Thanks, but Jules is doing a great job," McKenna said easily.

"Well, then, maybe after hours, I can give you a full tour of the place?" Dean said smoothly as he shifted his entire body as if to say to McKenna, *I'll only focus on you.*

"Thanks." McKenna chuckled. "I'm good. I got the tour yesterday."

"Oh, but you haven't seen the well. You simply have to see the well."

Jules rolled her eyes and, thankfully, McKenna saw and sighed. "Thanks, but no. I'm good. Sorry, I've got another customer. Nice to meet you, Dan." McKenna got up and quickly left.

Jules laughed at McKenna getting Dean's name wrong. She was almost hundred percent sure she'd done it on purpose.

"And he strikes out," Jules said, making a swing with her arm and then cupping her mouth and making crowd noises.

"Bite me," Dean said playfully, nudging her feet again. He

didn't make a move to get up and leave. Instead, he asked, "So, it sounds like you and Damion had a good weekend. You know, I was slated to go with him instead of you. When he asked you, he dropped me like a rotten lunch. I guess hoes do come before bros." He nudged her leg again. "In this case, I'll allow it, seeing as you're my adopted sis."

"Gee, thanks, bro." She nudged him back, then pushed him off the chair completely. "Go flirt with guests. Maybe you won't strike out and finally have that threesome you've always dreamed about."

Dean laughed. "Who says I haven't already had one. Your mom seemed to enjoy it."

Jules laughed and stuck out her tongue at Dean as he shifted to sit were McKenna had just been.

Shortly after she'd gotten the job here, Dean had taken her under his wing. He had protected her like a sister and, after that day, she hadn't gotten offended that he'd never asked to show her the well.

The well was a hot spring of clear water bubbling up in a swampy area on the campgrounds. They didn't allow guests to wander there, since it was fairly dangerous, plus, there had been rumors a rather large alligator had been spotted not far from the area.

Still, some adventurous employees snuck out there and enjoyed the warm fresh water.

"But you did enjoy your weekend?" he asked, growing more serious.

"Yeah, we had a great weekend. Thanks for giving your spot up. How's are things going with your sister?"

Dean's younger sister by almost ten years, Sophia, was battling breast cancer. Thankfully, it had been caught early on. Even though she was only in her teens, their mother had demanded early screening, since it ran in the family. If she hadn't, it could have been too late for the eighteen-year-old.

Jules knew that Dean, for all his outward appearance of being a player, was deep down an extremely nice guy. He'd been raised by a single mother, and he'd helped raise his younger sister when she came along. It ate at him, what Sophia was going through. She knew that he spent most of his free time driving back and forth to the hospital to be with his sister in Tallahassee.

"She's hanging in there." Dean's entire persona changed at the mention of his sister. He looked happy, but underneath, Jules could see fear and sadness in his eyes.

"Tell her I said hi," Jules said, laying a hand on his. "McKenna's not your type." She squeezed his hand. "She's far too smart for you," she teased.

He smiled. "Thanks for that." He held his fist over his heart. "The arrow dove in deep. With that, I'd better get back at it. The dinner rush is almost over."

"Yeah, now that I'm dried off, I'd better go help McKenna." She motioned to the bar where several guests had bellied up to sit down.

Dean got up but stopped and looked down at her. "You and Damion. You're good together. But if you break my man's heart..."

She laughed. "I won't. If anything, it'll be the other way round."

Dean shook his head. "If you think that, then you don't know Damion that well." He nodded to her and then disappeared down the pathway that led to the main building.

She thought about Dean's words for the rest of the evening.

Shortly before sunset, she watched a very drunk Joe Tribberton stroll towards her, and she cursed under her breath. In the afterglow of the weekend, she'd forgotten all about the man.

# CHAPTER SEVENTEEN

Damion removed the drunk woman's hand from his butt for the tenth time as the *Wind Chaser* bumped against the dock. Then he had to reach up and steady her to stop her from falling overboard.

Why wasn't her husband with her? He remembered the busty plastic-looking blonde being with Joe Tribberton, the man who had harassed Jules.

The moment he'd noticed that she was on board, he'd sent a text message to Brett and Aaron asking for an update on the guy and asking them to check in on Jules. He hadn't heard back from either of them until halfway through the sunset trip.

Aaron promised Damion that he'd check in on Jules at the bar several times, but he had his hands full with a couple other issues that night.

He'd also sent a text to Jules but knew that she had probably locked her phone in the cabinet behind the bar after a string of thefts had targeted employees' belongings last summer.

Damion counted the minutes until he could rush to watch over Jules and make sure that she was okay.

"Why don't you and I go make some fun?" the woman, whose name he hadn't even gotten, purred in his ear.

"Sorry, I'm seeing someone and I'm still working." He cupped her wrists to remove her hands from his butt once more.

"Oh, boo. I'm married and that doesn't stop us from having fun with others. While my husband runs around and chases skirts, I'm here..." Her voice dropped. "Chasing you. Is it true what they say about black men?" She started to reach around to the front of his shorts, but he stopped her by gripping her wrist tightly. "You know what they say, once you go black..."

"That's enough," he interrupted her firmly, tightening his grip on her wrists and pushing them away from his groin. "This game is over."

"Boo." She giggled.

Damion glanced around and realized that everyone had exited the boat without his help. Not only had the woman pissed him off and accosted him, making remarks that were racist, but she was blocking him from doing his job and getting the tips that most gave as they exited the docks.

He called out to the guests leaving the dock. "Thanks, I hope you enjoyed the trip."

Several of them waved back at him but continued on and left him fending off the drunk woman.

Thankfully, Zoey stepped up from the cabin at that moment.

"Do you need help locking things up?" Zoey asked him, her eyes zoned in on the drunk woman.

"Yes," he answered a little too enthusiastically.

"Mrs. Tribberton, Lisa, why don't I walk you back to your

cabin..." Zoey started, but the woman jerked her gaze towards Zoey.

"You can go," Lisa said sharply. "Your help is no longer needed." She waved her fingers at Zoey as if she could magically make her disappear.

Zoey visibly took a deep breath. "We're here to do a job. Not to be accosted by guests. I think Damion has made it clear that he's not interested."

The woman dropped her hands to her side and turned towards Zoey.

He knew that Zoey could fend for herself. After all, she was the one who had fought off Ryan when the woman had come after Dylan with a gun five years ago. Still, after Zoey had confirmed to him earlier that she was indeed pregnant again, Damion felt the need to step between the women and fend off any attacks from Lisa.

"I think it's best if you call it a night," Damion said in a calm tone.

The woman's eyes narrowed past him to Zoey. "I could have you fired for this," she started, but Zoey laughed, causing the woman to jerk forward and swipe out at her. Her hands somehow managed to ball up in Zoey's shirt.

Damion's hands moved to the woman's arms. He jerked them off Zoey and held the woman away from her.

"She's pregnant," he said in a harsh tone. "You won't be laying a finger on her or anyone else in this camp," he warned.

Lisa laughed. "Of course. After all, women like you are only good for breeding." She rolled her eyes. "You'll never be anything more."

"I'm the owner of this camp," Zoey said in a sharp tone. "When I say you're done, you're done. If you don't return to your cabin now, I'll be forced to ask you and your husband to leave River Camps."

Lisa made another jerking motion towards Zoey, but he was there, holding her back.

"This isn't over. I'll see that you're ruined," Lisa growled.

"You can try." Zoey laughed. "My friends and I built this place from the ground up, ourselves. I'm sick of people like you and your husband thinking you can strip away what someone has worked hard to build by raising your money-backed voices and screaming foul, when you're the one accosting us, the hard-working people. You cry foul because you can't have something you want and then cry that someone has damaged your frail ego. Enough is enough. It's time you were taught a lesson. You can't have everything you want. Now leave."

Damn, Damion thought. Zoey was on a roll.

This time, Damion had to hold Lisa's entire body back. He'd never witnessed Zoey's verbal wrath firsthand, but he had to admit, it was very impressive.

Somehow, Lisa managed to wiggle around him and got a strong grip on Zoey's shirt and hair, but Zoey fought back and managed to shove Lisa a few steps away from them, though not before receiving a nasty scratch on her arm from the woman's long nails.

Lisa's swimsuit cover-up skewed to the side, sliding off her shoulder as she jerked back a few steps. Just as she steadied herself by the edge of the boat, a large smile crept onto her face. Seconds before Lisa made the move, Damion knew what the woman's plan was. Sure enough, he watched in horror as she tipped backwards over the edge of the sailboat, her arms reaching out as if she'd changed her mind seconds too late or maybe it was just for show.

Lisa landed in the water with a loud splat. Both Zoey and he ran to the edge of the boat and watched her surface, her blond hair covering most of her face in a heap of tangled mess just before the screams started.

"Shit," Damion and Zoey said under their breaths at the same time.

"Damion, we have to call the police," Zoey said before they raced to help her out of the water. She was still flailing around, as if for show, even though the ladder on the dock was less than five feet away from her.

"Is she expecting me to jump in and save her?" he asked Zoey.

"I don't know, but you'd better while I call Brett." Zoey nudged him.

"Well shit." He handed Zoey his phone and keys. Then he toed off his shoes. The water near the docks was only ten feet deep so he had to be careful as he jumped in.

When he wrapped his arms around Lisa, she shoved at him and fought him for a moment. Then she realized it was him and melted against his body. Her nails dug into his soaked shirt.

"Oh," she said softly. "I thought it was that woman come to drown me."

Damion didn't say anything, just hauled her to the stairs and helped her out of the water. Aaron was now standing on the dock, and he helped Lisa out of the water.

"Oh, thank you," Lisa sniffled.

Zoey handed Aaron a towel, who then handed it to Lisa.

"I came as fast as I could," Aaron said to Damion as he climbed the ladder. "Brett's on his way too."

"I want this woman arrested," Lisa said, pushing her wet tangled hair away from her face.

"If anything, you should be locked up. I'm bleeding and have the marks on my body to prove you attacked me." Zoey held up her arm. A trickle of blood from the cut dripped down her forearm.

"Lies. She's jealous of my wealth. She said so herself," Lisa screeched.

Zoey chuckled and then sighed. "I said no such thing. I'm too tired for this bullshit." She walked over to sit down on a bench a couple feet away. It was then that Damion noticed Zoey was looking very pale and sick. Instantly, he worried.

"Are you okay?" Damion asked her.

"No, I'm not okay," Lisa started.

"I was asking Zoey," he clarified, moving to kneel by Zoey. "Are you okay?" he asked again.

"Yes." Zoey smiled at him. "Just..." She rolled her eyes. "Tired." Her voice lowered. "I shouldn't have baited her. Chalk it up to hormones."

He smiled. "It was impressive, seeing you in action," he said in a low enough voice that only Zoey could hear.

"Well?" Lisa said loudly. "Are you going to call the police and have her arrested or do I need to call my lawyer?"

"Enough. I think it's time you and your husband left River Camps," Zoey said, standing up suddenly.

When Damion saw her sway, he gripped her elbow, knowing Zoey wouldn't want to show any weakness to the woman.

"As of this moment, you and your husband are no longer welcome on my property." Zoey leaned a little more on Damion.

He didn't like her coloring. She was paler than normal, and he could see that she was sweating more than she should have been.

"Zoey?" he said as she slumped against him and passed out cold. "Call Lea," he yelled at Aaron as he lifted Zoey's limp body into his arms. It was then that he noticed the blood trickling down Zoey's legs. "Fuck that, tell Brett to meet us in the parking lot, we'll drive here there ourselves." he said to Aaron as he ran with her in his arms towards the parking lot.

He had never been more afraid in his life. His heart

pounded so loudly that he could barely hear Zoey talking to him. She was telling him to call Dylan and to tell him that she was sorry she got so worked up.

"You just hang on," he told her over and over.

When he arrived at the parking lot, Lea was there with Brett. He slid into the back seat of Brett's car, still holding Zoey in his arms.

Seconds later, Dylan rushed up from the main pathway, looking scared and worried.

Lea climbed in the back seat with Zoey and tore off Zoey's shorts in one quick movement as Dylan slid into the passenger seat. Brett gunned the car and spun out for a moment before the wheels caught on the gravel and they headed towards the hospital at high speed.

Dylan held onto Zoey's hand and talked to her while Lea examined Zoey. He avoided looking down, but there was so much blood coming from between Zoey's legs, he couldn't help but stare.

He'd never seen so much blood. When Lea slapped his arm, he focused.

"Your shirt, now," Lea said again.

He lifted Zoey slightly until he could pull off his still-wet camp shirt and handed it to Lea.

He lost track of time. Lost track of everything. At some point, Zoey passed out. He held her head, stopping it from rocking back and forth with the movement of the car.

He focused on her face, listened while Dylan kept promising the world, promising anything just for her to be okay. To wake up.

Through it all, Brett and Lea were the only two calm ones in the car. Brett was talking on a phone as he zipped through the traffic quickly.

They were three quarters of the way to the hospital when flashing lights started following them.

"They're going to escort us the rest of the way." Brett explained quickly.

Sure enough, the cop car sped past and pulled in front of them, paving the way through the rows of cars for them.

When they stopped in front of the ER, he helped slide Zoey's limp body out of the back seat and onto the stretcher. Lea and Dylan rushed through the double doors with the gurney while he stood there, still covered in some of Zoey's blood, holding his hands out as if unsure of what had just happened.

Brett moved to his side. "Come on, we'll head inside and get you cleaned up. Maybe find you another shirt." He took Damion's arm and led him inside.

"What just happened?" he asked.

"My guess?" Brett said, looking over at him and then taking a deep breath. "Miscarriage. Lea had told Zoey that the pregnancy had complications."

"Will she be okay?" Damion asked.

"Lea will take good care of her," he assured Damion. "Come on, we'll head in and wait with the rest when they get here."

"Lisa... Aaron." He shook his head. "The woman..."

"Aaron will handle it," Brett assured him. "Let's get you cleaned up before the others arrive."

Within the hour, the waiting room was flooded with camp employees. Zoey was loved by everyone.

When Jules walked in, he relaxed finally. He'd been worried about her all this time, just knowing what Lisa had said about her husband chasing skirts. Brett had informed him that Aaron had escorted the couple off the campgrounds. But that didn't stop him from worrying until he saw Jules for himself.

"Any news?" Jules asked him after she hugged him.

"She's resting. They'll keep her overnight," he explained. "Dylan should be coming out soon."

Zoey's family was back with her now. Each time someone brought flowers, they were handed off and taken to Zoey.

"I shouldn't have let..." he started and heard his voice hitch.

"Hey." Jules took his hands until he looked at her. "Aaron filled us in on what happened. These things happen. They've been happening to women since the dawn of time," she said easily. "Zoey's strong. She'll get through this." She nodded and smiled.

"Yeah," he sighed. "You should have seen her." He shook his head. "Standing up to that woman. She was a freaking warrior."

Jules smiled. "I've witnessed her and her sister verbally take down many unruly guests. I'd like to think they helped me find my inner warrior when handling situations like that."

He nodded. "I could have done something to not make her so upset," he said.

"Damion. She didn't miscarry because she was upset. That isn't..." Jules shook her head. "In most cases, it doesn't work that way. I'm positive this is one of those cases. Whatever set this off had nothing to do with you or what happened on the dock."

"She's right," Lea said, coming to stop in front of them. She'd come out a few moments earlier to talk to everyone. "The pregnancy was nonviable. It was an intrauterine pregnancy." Lea knelt down to his level. "The baby never had a heartbeat. Zoey knew this. But she couldn't get the medical help she needed because... of new laws. We were trying to come up with a plan for her care. Tonight was her body correcting the wrong all by itself. She was extremely lucky it did. Dylan and Zoey had prepared for this." Lea smiled at him. "I'm sorry you got mixed up in this. This in no way—" Lea shook her head and took his hand in hers. "This had nothing to do with you. You couldn't have prevented this. Unless you suddenly became a deity," she added with a smile. "Zoey is fine. She and Dylan will still be able to have more kids."

He took a deep breath and closed his eyes. "Okay." He nodded. "Thanks, doc."

"Any time," Lea said, looking between them both.

"Hey, why don't we get out of here? Grab some food?" Jules suggested.

He turned to her as Lea moved around the room to answer any more questions and fill everyone else in on Zoey's status. "That sounds... wonderful."

Since he'd ridden with Brett to the hospital, he climbed into Jules's car and let her drive him wherever she wanted to go.

"I like your shirt," Jules said as she drove.

He glanced down at the T-shirt Brett had gotten him from the hospital's gift shop. "At least I survived" was written on the front in bold letters.

"Yeah, my camp shirt got ruined." He looked out at all the traffic. "What is everyone doing out at this time of night?" he asked.

"It's only eight."

"It is?" He frowned. "It's only been an hour?" He shook his head. It seemed like a lifetime ago he was picking up Zoey on the dock.

"Is Grimaldi's Pizzeria okay?" she asked, pulling into the parking lot.

"Sounds perfect." He wasn't really feeling hungry, but when he stepped inside the restaurant and the smell hit him, his stomach growled loudly.

"Miss Julie," the host greeted them. "Your parents and Tutu were just in here yesterday," the older man said with a smile.

"Jerry, when are you going to ask Tutu out on a date? You know she expects it of you," Jules said easily.

The older man laughed. "A date? No, I'm waiting until she'll agree to marry me." He winked.

Jules laughed. "Do you have two seats for us?"

"Is this Damion?" The man turned to him. "I've heard so much about you. Not from this one." He pointed to Jules. "Tutu can't seem to stop talking about you." He leaned closer to Damion. "I think she has a crush on you and not me."

Damion smiled. "You'll have to get in line for her. This whole ploy of mine"—he motioned between him and Jules— "is just so I can win over Tutu."

Jerry laughed. "I like him," he said, "Come, I have my favorite table waiting for you, along with a bottle of wine."

After they sat down, Damion asked, "Friend of the family?"

Jules smiled. "My parents like Italian." She shrugged. "A lot. Over the years, we sort of became part of the family here."

He nodded. "I think I've only eaten here a handful of times."

"It's one of my favorites," she told him, then her smile slipped. "How are you doing?"

He took a deep breath and cleared his mind. "Better."

"It must have been so traumatizing." She took his hand.

"I don't know how women do it." He shook his head. "Just dealing with the ups and downs of monthly cycles, then childbirth, and the possibilities of stuff like that happening. I guess I never thought about miscarriages before. I mean, I knew they happened. I'd just... never known anyone who'd had one."

"You'd be surprised," she said tilting her head. "Around ten to fifteen percent of pregnancies end in miscarriages. My mother had three of them herself before finally having me."

"Really?" He frowned and thought of his own mother. Maybe that was why he was an only child. Had she had problems too? Suddenly, he realized he'd never talked to his mother about it. About why they had never had more kids.

"Hey," she said, getting his attention. "Women are a lot stronger than men believe they are."

"I don't doubt that." He thought about what Lea had said as they ate their pizza and drank the wine Jerry had delivered to them himself.

There was so much he didn't know about things. So much he'd never thought about. What would have happened if Zoey hadn't had a miscarriage? You'd have to be dead or have your head buried in the sand to not know what was going on in the country, the heavy debate over choice.

Zoey didn't choose for her pregnancy to not take. She'd seemed so excited—scared, but excited—about the prospects of a new little one. Paige had been born healthy enough last year.

He'd ignorantly figured that any woman who chose to end her pregnancy had done so for non-medical reasons. Not because the baby—or whatever it was or wasn't at that point—had no heartbeat. Did the lack of a heartbeat make it less loved?

"You're very deep in thought." Jules's voice shook him from his own internal debate. "How about a walk on the beach to clear your head?"

"It's dark."

Jules smiled. "Has that ever stopped the relaxing sound of the waves or the wonderful feeling of soft sand between your toes?"

He smiled and shook his head. "No, I suppose it hasn't."

## CHAPTER EIGHTEEN

Jules held onto Damion's hand as they strolled along the soft sand. She was thankful the moon was full and lighting their way down the white sandy beach.

"Did you know that only one in about ten thousand sea turtles will survive to adulthood?" She asked as they went along.

"Seriously?" He frowned. "I'm beginning to think I know nothing."

She laughed. "Isn't that what life is all about? Learning as we go?"

He stopped and pulled her into his arms. "Yes." He sighed. "You're amazing. You make me want to be better."

"Better than what? Because from where I'm standing, you're looking pretty amazing," she told him. He continued frowning down at her, so she added, "Just because you don't know all the ups and downs of the female reproductive experience, or odd facts about sea turtles, which I learned one summer when I volunteered to find nests, doesn't mean you're ignorant. What makes a person ignorant is knowing these facts and still pushing agendas that fall in line with their own views or so they can get more money." She watched his shoulders rise and fall. "I would say you came away from today enlightened." She smiled. "So, what is Damion going to change in his life because of his newfound knowledge?"

He was silent for a while. "Well, for one, I'm going to stop thinking that women complaining about their periods is a ploy to get attention."

"You thought that?" she asked, her eyes narrowing.

"Not really, but my father has always mentioned it when my mother cries for no reason."

Jules smiled. "Hormones will do that to us."

"I'm rethinking how many kids I want too. I don't want to put anyone through that much... pain. Or the possibility of it." He shrugged.

"Children are a gift. Whoever you're lucky enough to have children with will understand." She felt her heart flutter.

He nodded. "Another thing." He glanced around. "I might just volunteer for turtle watch too. I've been wanting to for a few years. I just don't like the idea of waking up that early."

She laughed. "That's the number one reason I only did it for one year."

She took his hand and started walking again. "Feel better?"

"Yeah, thanks. I was getting stuck in a debate loop in my head."

"Yeah, that'll happen with something like this."

"I meant it. You're good for me." He pulled her to a stop again. "Why don't we head back to your place? I'd like to hold you tonight."

"Just hold me?" she asked, feeling her body heat.

"For tonight." He nodded.

She smiled and felt her entire being melt. "I'd like that."

The next morning, waking in Damion's arms felt so right.

She almost told him right then and there that she'd move in with him. That night.

Instead, she waited until his alarm went off, then showered with him, dressed, and drove him into work, since his truck was still in the camp's parking lot.

Since she was early, she decided to swim a few laps while Damion cleaned the filters and scooped out grass, pine needles, and a live toad that she helped him catch. The toad was avoiding them as if he wanted to stay in the pool. But she knew from experience that it would probably end up dying if they didn't get it out of the water soon.

"Most impressive," he told her when she finally scooped the toad out of the water. It was as big as her big toe and seemed very content as it jumped away into a bush. "Most women are afraid of frogs."

"I'm not."

"Spiders?" he asked and she shook her head. "Snakes?"

There she nodded. "Yes, if that had been a snake, I would have been climbing that pole." She motioned to the flagpole.

Damion laughed. "We do have some dangerous ones here," he said, still scooping pine needles out of the water while she enjoyed her swim.

"I know. Each year we have to get trained about what to do in case of bears, snake bites, and other animal attacks. Remember the first time there was a black bear scare?" She laughed. "Zoey had to outrun it while Dylan locked himself in the cabin."

Damion laughed. "Dylan claims he was too small to fit out the window. I'm pretty sure Zoey didn't give him a chance."

"I hope she's feeling better this morning. When I go in to work, I was going to call and ask how she is doing."

"Once I'm done here, we can head in and grab a bite to eat before you have to work," he suggested.

"Sounds good." Even though she hardly ever ate breakfast, she still wanted to spend that time with him.

She climbed out of the pool, dried off, and pulled on the sundress she'd worn that day. Since she had known she'd wanted to go swimming, she'd worn her simple black swimsuit underneath. It was basically the same thing as a bra and underwear but were somehow far more comfortable.

She pulled her hair up in a messy bun and wished she'd thought to bring her makeup bag.

"You look sun kissed," Damion said, setting the net down on the hook and then walking over to her.

"I should have brought some makeup," she complained.

"You don't need it." He scanned her face. "There aren't a lot of women that have natural beauty like you do."

She smiled. "Buttering me up?"

He laughed. "Telling you the truth."

They ate breakfast with a group of other employees, and all talked about Zoey's recovery. She was already at home, resting, with Dylan and Paige. Schedules were shuffled around to help fill in for her and Dylan's missed time.

She ended up taking Zoey's spot at the next two sunset sails. The first one was in only two nights. As she went to work, she couldn't help but be nervous about it. She kept thinking of cancelling on Damion. Then they met for lunch, and he talked her into keeping the arrangements. After all, she'd done so well on the trip to St. George and back, except for that brief time where she'd had to stomach the waves.

But Damion practically guaranteed that if the water got too choppy, he'd keep the boat in the bay instead of heading to the Gulf.

After lunch, a rush of new guests arrived, and she was far too busy to rethink her decision. She was thankful that the Tribbertons had left. The man had creeped her out the night before. She'd been expecting him to hit on her, which he had, but thankfully, with the bar between them and McKenna filling his drink orders, it hadn't been too bad.

When Aaron had shown up and asked the man to follow him, she'd hoped it was to have him leave. Then she'd gotten Damion's text messages and had heard what had happened to Zoey. She'd asked McKenna to shut down the bar and had rushed to the hospital without a second thought.

Zoey had been the one to hire her, the first Wildflower she'd gotten close to. Now, she adored them all, of course, but she had a closer relationship with Zoey.

When the doors opened, she glanced up. Scarlett was following Zoey through the doors, berating her.

"What are you doing here?" Jules said to Zoey.

"I'm just..." Zoey started.

"She's just disobeying orders," Scarlett said sharply. "And if she doesn't turn around and go back home, I'm going to call Dylan. Or worse, Mom."

Zoey stopped short and glared at her sister. "You wouldn't dare."

"Try me," Scarlett said, lifting her chin in the air.

"Fine!" Zoey threw up her hands. "I'm going." She turned and looked at Jules. "Did they leave?"

"Yes," Jules answered, knowing full well who Zoey was asking about.

"Good. No matter what happens, don't refund them a dime," Zoey said.

"Over my dead body will they get any of their money back," Jules said and Zoey smiled. "Go home. We've got this. Rest."

"Thanks," Zoey said, looking tired suddenly. She turned to Scarlett. "Okay, take me home."

Scarlett took Zoey's arm and led her to the door.

The door had just closed when Hannah rushed into the lobby from her office.

"Did I just hear Zoey?" Hannah asked her, looking around.

"Scarlett's taking her back home," Jules assured her.

"Who?" Elle said, coming down the stairs.

"Zoey was just here," Hannah answered.

"What?" Elle asked, a hand on her back and one on her stomach.

"She was here all of two minutes. Scarlett is taking her home now. She just wanted to make sure the Tribbertons had left and that I'm not going to refund them a dime," Jules answered.

"Damn right we aren't," Hannah said firmly.

"I can't believe that we even cared what they thought," Elle said, leaning against the countertop. "I mean, I know the man owns one of the biggest travel magazines in the area, but damn, there's only so much a person can take to get a good review."

"Right," Hannah agreed, sitting in one of the chairs in the lobby area. "Who needs it. We're doing great without his help. We're booked solid for the next year and a half."

"As it is, we're thinking of building ten more cabins," Elle told Jules. "We'll have to clear some more land, but it's doable."

"I can help arrange all that," Jules suggested, already thinking of the steps that would have to be taken. "I helped, or well, sort of helped plan the last three cabin builds."

Elle smiled and then looked at Hannah. "We were hoping you'd say that."

"You were?" Jules held her breath.

"Yes. We were all going to talk to you about it this week," Elle answered. "There are some files on the drive you can look at and work on. I'll show you where they are." Elle moved behind the counter and, for the next hour, helped Jules familiarize herself with what they wanted.

Jules wanted to jump in to working on the plans with both feet but then things picked up again and she had to close everything down and focus on her current job.

Damion's normal workday typically ended almost two hours before hers since he usually arrived hours before she did. Which meant he was usually gone by the time she got off work. Today, however, he stuck around and waited for her in the employee dining room.

They had arranged to have dinner there together. Isaac's food was far better than most restaurants around town, and cheaper. Besides, they got two free meals a day and employee discounts on everything else.

She clocked out and shut everything down, then she headed to see Damion, only to come up short when she saw an image of the camp on the large flat-screen television that hung in the lobby.

Walking over, she turned on the sound and watched the news report. After listening for a few seconds, she rushed over, grabbed her walkie-talkie, and called Elle, Hannah, Scarlett, and Aubrey into the lobby area.

"What?" Elle asked when they were all there.

"That." She motioned to the television. She'd recorded the report and had it paused. Now, she hit the play button and they all stood around and listened to Joe and Lisa Tribberton trash the place.

They watched it a couple more times, and she noticed Damion walk in and watch it. Then there were more than a dozen employees all watching it.

"What does this mean?" someone asked.

"It means nothing," Hannah said firmly.

"Right." Elle nodded.

"So one rich couple with influence had a terrible experience. We all had to deal with them ourselves. I bet there isn't a resort or hotel they have been to that doesn't know just what kind of guests they are," Scarlett said. "Carter, you had to stop Mrs. Tribberton from whipping poor Charlie to death."

"No one whips my horses," Carter said in a low tone.

"And Andrea, you stopped Joe's massage halfway through when he exposed himself to you several times," Scarlett added.

"If I had wanted to see something so small and shriveled up, I would have put a sausage in the dryer for a few hours," Andrea said, earning enough laughs that the entire atmosphere in the room changed.

"We've been in business more than five years now and we're successful at it. One little news report about some spoiled rich asshat isn't going to change that," Scarlett said firmly.

But then the phone rang across the room, and everyone stopped to look at it. Then they turned to her.

She walked over and answered the call, even though she knew that the answering service would get it.

"River Camps, how may I help you?" she answered on the third ring.

"Yes, I'd like to cancel our reservations for the fifteenth of next month," a woman replied.

Before she could get the woman's information, the other line rang, and Jules's heart sank.

Half an hour later, after taking more than a dozen calls for cancellations, she switched the phones to night mode and shut her computer down.

"Shit," she said to the smaller group that had stuck around.

"We need an employee meeting first thing in the morning," Elle said. "We have to nip this in the bud."

"What we need to do is an interview of our own," Aubrey said.

"No, not yet. Not until we can all be there, and Zoey isn't up for it. Not yet," Scarlett added.

"Right," the friends said together.

"Does she know about this yet?" Jules asked them.

"No. Hopefully she won't until we can tell her. Dylan's assured us she's resting," Scarlett answered. "Go on home. We'll meet in the morning," she told Jules.

Jules looked over at Damion, who nodded. "We'll be in there having dinner if you need us," he said to the group. He took her hand, and she grabbed her bag and followed him into the other room to have dinner. But she was no longer hungry.

She hated that someone so mean could ruin more than a hundred people's lives because they were spoiled.

"Hey, shut it down for now. We'll figure something out. Not everyone listens to the news or cares what two people think," Damion said once they had their food.

"Those two people happen to be owners of one of the most successful travel magazines around. It's kind of their business to tell people what they think," she reminded him.

"I'm sure someone out there has had a run-in with them before. Right?" he said, and suddenly she got an idea.

"That's it." She snapped her fingers. "I need to make some phone calls." She started to get up.

"So, I'm guessing dinner is off?" He motioned to the food.

She looked down at the burger he'd gotten her and smiled. "No, bring it with us. Suddenly, I'm very hungry."

# CHAPTER NINETEEN

There was nothing Damion could do other than sit and listen and watch the group of women plot.

They worked into the night, compiling lists, names, and phone numbers. Both Hannah and Elle left shortly after ten to head upstairs to the apartment on the top floor to sleep.

Everyone else, however, stayed put. He made a few coffee runs, and had even grabbed some donuts, cookies, and a pie. He knew that Jules would need sugar to keep working.

They ended up calling it a night around one o'clock in the morning. Jules decided she was too tired to drive, and he drove them back to her place. He knew he could get away with wearing the same outfit tomorrow morning and guessed that she would probably want to change.

It felt as if they had just laid down to sleep when his alarm was going off.

He groaned. Jules groaned.

"Sleep," he told her. "I can come back and get you in an hour."

"No, I need to start making calls this morning." She rolled

out of bed. "I could use some sugar. Big fat frosting-covered donuts the size of my head," she mumbled as she made her way towards her bathroom. He smiled and followed her.

While he went to work outside, he knew Jules and the rest of the Wildflowers would be inside, hashing out their plan and putting it into action.

All around the camp, everyone was buzzing about the interview, employees and guests alike.

He overheard several guests talking about how much of a bitch Lisa was or how Joe had hit on someone and wouldn't take no for an answer.

He even overheard someone talking about how Lisa had basically attacked Damion during the entire sail.

"The poor guy was trying to push her away the entire trip. She just wouldn't take no for an answer. Spoiled brat is what she is. I wouldn't doubt that they set out to ruin this place from the get-go," the woman said.

The other woman responded. "This place is so amazing. I'm going to tell all my friends to book here. I'm even going to go in and see if we can come back in November."

Damion smiled and when he ran into Jules rushing towards Elle's office, he quickly told her what he'd overheard.

"Thanks." She kissed him. "You just made my day. Gotta go," she said, waving at him as she rushed into the office.

"Lunch?" he asked.

"Sure, bring it here though." She pointed to the office.

He doubted anyone else in the room would have time for lunch or had even thought of it. He strolled into the dining room and filled a tray with a variety of pre-packed lunches and desserts. Then he added a bunch of bottled drinks and sodas.

When he knocked on the door, Jules was on the phone and waved him in.

Aubrey stood up and helped him set all the food down.

"Wow, this is great. I was just going to make a food run." She grabbed a container and then raced to answer the phone when it rang.

Everyone else in the room—Aubrey, Elle, Scarlett, and Jules—were all on their cell phones, talking or listening to someone talk.

He set a chicken sandwich down in front of Jules along with her favorite drink, a bottled of unsweetened tea with lemon in it. Then he sat next to her and started eating his own lunch.

Between calls, she filled him in on how their master plan was going.

"So far, we have over thirty local resorts or hotels reaching out to the press against the Tribbertons. There are some who are actually in the process of suing the couple and their travel magazine for defamation," Jules said between bites. "A couple of staff members have claimed physical abuse. Brett is checking on police reports. Not that we can use any of that, but if lawyers were involved..." She dropped off. "We have a chance, I think. We're going to play host to a group of reporters who will do an actual piece on River Camps. Facts. Not opinions. We'll show them around, talk about the camp, let it speak for itself," she said quietly.

"We don't want the interview to come across as us, the owners of the camp, defending ourselves or our business, but rather a professional business standing up against the Tribbertons' character and their abuse of power directly," Aubrey said from across the room.

"There's enough evidence here to take them and their magazine down," Elle added. "If all of the other resorts stand together and stand up for ourselves."

"What does Zoey think of all this?" he asked.

Everyone glanced at each other for a second.

"We were going to tell her during lunch," Hannah said. "Which I suppose is now." She stood up.

"We'll take a break. I think we've gathered enough people to speak out. Enough evidence," Elle said. "Let's go talk to Zoey. Fill her in. Thanks Jules." Elle turned to Jules and smiled. "This was a really great plan."

Jules smiled and he watched her cheeks turn a slight pink. For as long as he'd known her, she hadn't been able to take compliments well. Normally, she shied away and ended up looking at her feet. Now, however, she smiled and held her head up high, even though her cheeks appeared to be burning.

The room quickly emptied, leaving Jules and him alone as everyone shuffled out.

"That was fun," he said. He finished his sandwich.

"It was." Jules turned to him with a huge smile on her lips. "I don't think I've ever enjoyed a morning more than this." She sighed and leaned back in her chair.

He ran his eyes over her and realized that it wasn't just her cheeks that were flushed, it was her entire body. She really had enjoyed the investigative aspect of what they had been doing that morning.

"Have you ever thought of being an investigator?" he asked.

"Like a PI?" She laughed.

"What you did last night and today, you obviously liked it," he pointed out.

"True, but I like my job here more. The freedom it gives me. Not to mention the people." She finished off her drink and then stood up. "Come on, let's take a walk." She took his hand in hers and pulled him out into the hallway. He made sure to shut the door behind him, since he knew that all the offices in the hallway were always locked.

"So, tell me what you've found out," he said when they stepped outside.

"I'd rather talk about us," she said, pulling him towards the beach pathway. "I've decided I don't want to spend my nights alone."

He stopped and turned to her. "You have?"

A slow smile crept on her lips, and she nodded quickly. "Yeah, so, I'm not sure how—"

He didn't let her get any further. He bent his head down and kissed her.

"I'll move in with you until your lease is up. I'm doing month to month on my place and there's only a few days left on the contract," he said quickly. "Most of my stuff my mother can sell. Whichever things you want, we can move over to your place. If you don't like any of it, I'm sure my mother can sell it all."

She laughed. "It's that easy?"

"It's that easy." He nodded.

"Okay." She hugged him.

"Okay." He kissed the top of her head.

Since he didn't have a sunset sail that evening, he spent his night boxing up his personal things. In the end, everything he wanted to keep fit in only four boxes.

The rest was items that his mother had filled his apartment with. Not that he was complaining. He liked the stuff. Enjoyed having nice furniture to sit on, to use. But he'd always wanted to make his own mark on his place.

When his new home was finished being built, he was going to make sure he and Jules chose every single piece that was put in it. He liked her style. Her place was filled with colors, patterns, things that drew the eye and made you ask questions.

His mother's style, although classy, tended towards natural colors, boring items, and repetitive patterns.

By the time Jules got off work, he was standing outside her apartment next to the stack of his boxes.

"What..." She stopped and then laughed. "You meant to start moving tonight?"

"Start?" He frowned for show. "You mean finish. This is it. Everything I own that I want. We can go through my place this weekend and move whatever other items you want to keep. My mom will have the rest moved to her store."

She was smiling as she shook her head and then dug in her purse and handed him a bright fuzzy green ball.

"What's this?" he asked.

She took his hand and placed the ball in his palm. It was then that he realized there was a key attached to the fuzzy ball.

"Your key." She smiled.

"Do I have to keep the green thing on it?" he asked.

She walked into his arms and held onto him. "You do for now."

He laughed. "Is this another one of your stipulations?"

"Call it a test," she responded with a laugh. "Now, I promised Tutu I'd come over for dinner. My aunt arrived earlier this morning." She looked up at him. "Let's change and head over."

His smile grew. "I'd like that." Then he took his new key and unlocked the door and held it open for her.

It took him less than five minutes to pull his boxes into her place. She had him move them to her walk-in closet for now.

They changed clothes, him into a pair of khakis shorts and a button-up shirt and her into a soft floral sundress. She'd tied the front of her hair back and put a white flower clip just above her ear.

"You look amazing," he said, kissing her. "We could stay in. Enjoy our first night officially living together?"

"Later." She wiggled her eyebrows and then kissed him.

As she drove to her parents' place, she filled him in on her aunt Rita.

"Rita is a professional hula dancer. She's very deep into preserving the Hawaiian traditions. Our heritage," she explained.

"And she's moving here to help your dad?" he asked.

"Yes. She's the oldest in the family. My dad was the baby." She smiled. "She's the one who taught me how to hula." She glanced over at him. "Just a warning, I'm not very good at it. She had her own studio teaching the younger generation. Her ex-husband took it in the divorce and sold it to her competitor."

"Did he dance?"

"No." Jules frowned at him. "He was a lawyer."

"Right," he said slowly.

"He took everything she had. She's been living with my aunt Rhonda for the past year. She's had to take jobs at some of the tourist spots just to pay her legal bills."

"What an ass. He took everything?"

"Yeah. If their kids were younger, he probably would have tried for full custody of them too," Jules said as she parked in her parents' long driveway.

He waited until she turned off the car and then asked, "And he's the one who cheated on her?"

"Yup." She nodded. "Now you know why my aunt was willing to drop everything and move thousands of miles away to help my parents. So, I'll apologize ahead of time if she seems... bitter."

He leaned over and kissed her. "Even if this goes south, which I'm hoping it won't, ever"—he smiled—"I can pretty much promise you that you can have all our shit."

She laughed and kissed him back. "Thanks, but are you willing to put that in writing?"

"Hell yes." He laughed. "Just don't take my boat."

Her smile slipped and her eyes turned dreamy. "Never." She kissed him again.

Jules's aunt Rita was nothing like he'd pictured. First off, she looked younger than he'd expected. If she was the oldest out of four kids and Jules's father was the youngest, he was pretty sure the rest of the family looked just as good.

Physically, she was, he imagined, exactly what a hula dancer should look like.

Even though Jules's father was having health issues, the man could easily pass for a man half his age. Rita was in the same boat, only she was in incredible shape. Jules's body style and shape were so much like her aunt's that they could have passed as sisters.

She also wasn't the depressed person Jules had made her out to be. Rita was a complete jokester. She was constantly telling jokes, laughing, or teasing everyone, including him.

It made him feel instantly accepted. He knew that her parents and Tutu had accepted him long ago.

The rest of her family, he'd never met. It mattered a lot what they thought of him only because she often talked about them. About their family trips to the islands and how important they were to her and to her father and Tutu.

They had just retired to the back deck after dinner when her father's entire attitude changed. He grew quiet first. Damion wasn't the only one who noticed. Jules's mother suggested that he head upstairs to rest, but Roni just shook his head and said he was fine.

About five minutes later, Roni stood up and shouted at Jules for no reason.

"Damn it, Juju, I told you to be home by ten," he said loudly, using his nickname for Jules.

Jules jumped slightly next to him. "Daddy?"

"Roni, I think it's time..." Amy and Rita said at the same time.

"Am, don't side with her." Roni pointed at Jules. "We told

her ten o'clock. It's..." He glanced down at his clock and frowned, then swayed.

Amy, Jules's mother, stood up and gripped him. "Why don't we head upstairs?"

Roni shifted, his eyes going around at each person. "Rita? What are you doing here?"

"RonRon, head on upstairs. Get some rest. It's been a long day," Rita said as Amy led Roni back inside.

Tutu stood up suddenly. "I'm going..." She motioned.

"Need help, Mom?" Rita asked.

Tutu walked over and kissed Rita on the forehead. The gleam in her eyes had gone out after the incident. "No, sit, relax. They'll be plenty of that in the future." Tutu turned towards them and smiled. "This is good. This, I like." She nodded. "Goodnight."

"Night," Jules and he said at the same time.

"Does that happen often?" Rita asked Jules.

"It's beginning to," Jules answered. "He tends to get violent and yell. I don't understand that because, growing up, he never raised his voice." Jules wrapped her arms around herself, and he saw the sadness in her eyes. "I think he was remembering the night I came back from prom half an hour late. My date's car had a flat tire. He knew this and never yelled at me that night. I don't understand why he's getting this way."

"I've done some of my own research," Rita said, taking Jules's hand in hers. "In some cases, people get confused, and anger is a direct result of that confusion. That's why I'm here. To help him through the worst of it." Rita smiled. "Now..." She leaned back and took another sip of her wine. "Tell me all about this weekend the two of you went on."

Damion knew that Jules's aunt was trying to lighten the mood again, but the damage to the evening was already done. Tutu and Jules's mother never returned outside. Less than half an hour after her parents and grandmother had disappeared inside, Jules and he drove away from the house.

"I'm sorry about tonight," he said softly.

"I'm the one who should be apologizing," she retorted.

"What have the doctors said?"

"Nothing new. Just... Alzheimer's. They're checking for something else. I forget the exact name. CJD. It's a brain-eating disorder... We won't know it that's what this is for a few more days." She sighed heavily. "I think my aunt is correct. My dad turns to anger because he's confused. It's just so strange. The only time I can remember him raising his voice was to cheer me on in sports."

The car was quiet for a moment, then he asked, "What sports did you play?" Jules laughed as she glanced over at him. "Don't leave me hanging. Now, I'm picturing you in..." He titled his head and bit his lip. "Not a cheerleader." She shook her head and her smile got bigger. "You are far too short for basketball."

"Hey now, short people can still jump and dribble," she said, acting wounded.

"Nope." He shook his head. "You're not the type. Soccer? Volleyball?" He saw her eyebrows arch up. "Oh, volleyball." He nodded. "Yeah, that fits."

"That sport requires jumping too," she pointed out with a laugh.

"We will just have to see how good you are at it. I challenge you to join in the next game I referee."

"Nope, I'll only show *you* my moves." She wiggled her eyebrows at him. "If I play against you, winner takes all."

"Challenge accepted." What he didn't tell her is that he, too, spent many summers playing beach volleyball.

This was going to be fun.

# CHAPTER TWENTY

After the day and night that she'd had, Jules was looking forward to a release. The moment they stepped into her apartment—*their* apartment—she pushed Damion up against the wall and basically attacked him.

She dumped her purse just inside the door and jumped on him. She didn't want to give him a chance to make the first move. Not here. Not now.

This was her time. Her wanting to take control. To see how he would respond. Would he let her? Would he enjoy it? It was a gamble, but she was going to take what she wanted. And she wanted a lot.

While she kissed him, she fumbled to unbutton his shirt. She was pretty sure several of the buttons popped off it in the process. Finally, her fingers ran over him, going lower until she removed his shorts.

She didn't even give him time to step out of them before cupping him in her hands. Feeling him grow hard, she knelt before him and took him fully into her mouth.

His hands went into her hair, pulling the clips out of it until it fell free so he could bury his fingers deep into it.

"Jules," he groaned but made no move to stop her. She wanted speed, but here, with her mouth wrapped around him, she took her time, enjoyed the taste of him, the feeling of his pleasure filling her mouth.

Her nails scraped down his thighs, and she felt the light dusting of hair that covered those powerful legs.

Then he moved. So quickly, she yelped and then laughed as he carried her into the bedroom. Her sundress was hiked up, her panties ripped aside and in one swoop he was in her. Filling her. Taking her to the edge and over.

"You can't just attack a man like that," Damion said moments later into her hair.

Both of their breathing had steadied, and their bodies had cooled off enough that she was thankful he was still covering her.

"My plan seemed to work perfectly," she said into his chest. "We both won."

"Yeah, but at what cost?" He glanced down at her. "I doubt my heart can hold out much longer if that becomes a standard occurrence."

She laughed and slapped him on the butt. "Get up, I need to use the bathroom."

He rolled aside and watched her walk to the bathroom. Since they weren't there in their relationship yet, she shut the door.

When she came back out, wearing shorts and a tank top, he was digging through one of his boxes full of clothes. He'd pulled on a pair of cut-off sweats and looked damn sexy. She already wanted to jump him again.

"I can move some things around and give you some drawers." She tapped the massive purple dresser she'd painted herself.

"That's cool," he said, finding what he was after, then stuck the neon alarm clock on her nightstand. "This side okay?"

She nodded. "I've never had to choose a side of the bed before," she admitted, sitting on the bed next to him. "I've never lived with someone before."

"Neither have I, which is why this means so much." He picked up her hand, and his fingers ran over hers. "Even though we've known each other for five years, this is new territory. Don't be afraid to tell me to fuck off if you need space."

She smiled. "I won't."

"Good. Also, I think we both know we're not messy people. But if I leave shit lying around"—he nodded to the boxes—"feel free to put me in my place. My mother never failed to do so."

She laughed. "I'm not as concerned about the décor as your mother is." She motioned to the brightly colored secondhand furniture.

"I like your style." He pulled her close.

"Eclectic." She looked around at the hodgepodge of items she'd collected over the few years she'd lived alone.

"Exciting, fresh, bright, and cheery," Damion said, turning to her. "And sexy. Everything that you are."

She smiled. "You have either blinders on or rose-colored glasses."

He shook his head. "Nope, just a simple boy who likes a girl and her style."

He leaned in and kissed her until her back was pinned on the bed again. This time, their movements were slower. Still fervid, but a ballet instead of the speedy mambo that had come before.

The passion was so intense that tears spilled from her eyes as his fingers danced over her skin. When his mouth slid over hers, she lost the last strings she'd been holding herself back with.

Everything she was now belonged to him. Every dream she had, he was now a side character in. There was no future without Damion in it.

In conclusion, she was totally screwed.

The days seemed to whisk by them. They would carpool to work each day, then spend their nights pleasing one another.

The first time she'd worked one of his sunset sails, she'd earned eighty dollars in tips. The second time, that amount doubled. Each time, she'd deposit the money into her account and immediately send a check off to her car loan. Whatever she could do to knock the payments down seemed to help her state of mind.

It wasn't the only bill she had, but it was the biggest and the one with the worst interest rate.

Damion suggested she keep it in a savings account, which she had every intention of doing after she knocked a thousand dollars or two off the car loan.

Her father's tests came back negative for the fatal Creutzfeldt-Jakob disease. As far as they could tell, it was an early onset of Alzheimer's, which would progress rapidly over the coming years.

At work, the Wildflowers had arranged for a huge media meeting where most of the local news stations, and some national ones, would gather at the camp on Monday. Several state press members had been booked in the cabins of those guests who had cancelled.

Next week's media meeting was going to be the telltale moment. The event would either return the camp to its former success or guarantee its demise.

Of course, with this news, all of the staff had been put on extra duties. The maintenance crew was working overtime touching up paint, cleaning in all the dark corners, oiling anything that squeaked, and repairing or replacing anything that was damaged or broken.

Employees were asked, if they had time during their normal hours, to walk the grounds and help spot anything that might need updating or cleaning. Most of them took it upon themselves to carry trash bags or even small containers of paint and brushes.

The signs along the pathways were all painted with the same teal colors in the camp's logo. The signs themselves had been carved and placed by Liam shortly before the camp had opened five years ago, as were all of the unique wood benches around the campgrounds. It was a game to some employees to guess how many benches there were. To her count, there were more than a hundred and twenty unique carved seats.

All of the bikes and golf carts had been taken in for a tune-up and or had been replaced.

Isaac's staff worked extra hours cleaning every inch of the kitchens and dining rooms, including the staff areas.

Jules had helped Andrea and Kara clean the massage rooms and pool house areas after Andrea had asked her for help. Damion had gotten a bunch of help scrubbing all the glass tiles in all three pools.

Most of the volunteers didn't mind the job since it entailed bathing suits and pool time.

By Sunday morning, the entire camp looked and somehow even smelled brand new. Every single employee currently on the camp's payroll would be present for the next few days.

Eight reporters would be checking in that day and staying for at least two nights. It was her idea to offer them a discount to fill the cabins abandoned after the Tribbertons' interview.

Jules stood behind the counter in a freshly ironed shirt with an embroidered camp logo and a name tag on the left side of her chest.

Her hair was tied up in a neat bun, and silver earrings that her mother had bought her for her last birthday dangled on her ears. A matching necklace, which had come the year earlier, was showcased just between the opened buttons on the pressed blouse.

The black slacks and low-heeled boots she wore showed that she was all business.

She might not look big city chic, but she could easily pass for classy.

When an older woman stepped into the lobby, Jules instantly knew who she was. She'd been watching Belinda Ness on the evening news for as long as she could remember.

Jules knew some of the basics about Miss Ness's personal life. Just enough to be a great hostess.

"Miss Ness, I hope your flight and trip to River Camps was pleasant," Jules greeted the woman.

The woman smiled pleasantly. "It was"—her eyes moved to the embroidered name— "Julie. Please, call me Belinda."

Jules's smile grew. "Of course." Jules put a note in the woman's screen. Each guest had their own page of data—their likes, dislikes, allergies, medical issues, or just their preferences.

Wants to be called Belinda, she typed.

"I show here you have the Hammock House for a two-night stay." She leaned forward and lowered her voice slightly. "One of my favorite cabins."

"This place certainly lives up to the camp in its title," Belinda said, glancing around the massive three-story wood-filled lobby.

"It used to be an elite camp for girls," Jules said easily.

"That's right." Belinda nodded.

Somehow, Jules doubted the woman didn't know that already. Was she being tested? Either way, Jules loved talking about the camp.

"When its previous owner, Joe Saunders, passed away, he willed it to the Wildflowers." Jules smiled.

"The Wildflowers?" This time Belinda's question was sincere.

Jules chuckled. "What the five friends called themselves back when they met at camp all those years ago when they were only eleven years old. Elle Saunders, now Elle Costas. Hannah Rogers, now Hannah Costas. Zoey and Scarlett Rowlett now Zoey Costas and Scarlett Walsh. And Aubrey Smith, now Aubrey Stark."

Belinda interrupted. "Smith, that is Harold Smiths' daughter?"

Jules's smile slipped ever so slightly, remembering how hard Aubrey had it because she was the very rich, very famous man's only daughter. "Yes."

"There seem to be a lot of Costas around now. I know all about the family. I even went on a date with Leo Costas once or twice," Belinda said as she raised her chin slightly.

"Leo comes around often now that his sons are... invested. His words," Jules said with a chuckle.

"Are the Costas... the other members, around?" Belinda glanced around the lobby. There were other guests walking around, some in bathing suits shopping in the gift shop, others heading into the dining hall, and one man sitting at a desk with his laptop on some sort of conference meeting.

"They are. They'll be happy to meet with you... later today. Let's get you settled in your cabin first. I will be showing you to your cabin and around the campgrounds myself." Jules turned to Beth and nodded.

She knew that the Wildflowers were probably all huddled around the computer, watching the interaction on the security system.

It had been decided that it would look better for the camp if the five owners weren't readily available straight out of the gate.

Jules had suggested showing Belinda around herself when the woman arrived since she was the most influential of the reporters arriving.

Dean appeared from behind the counter and easily picked up Belinda's luggage.

"Thank you, Dean," Jules said as if he helped all the time.

"I'll put this on cart number seven," Dean said with a smile.

"Charming," Belinda said after watching Dean leave through the front doors.

Jules smiled.

As she and Belinda walked out the front door, Jules talked about the camp's amenities. When they stepped outside, Jules pointed out key buildings.

There was a row of golf carts parked out front, as usual. Dean was just finishing putting the luggage on the back of the first golf cart, cart seven, which was known all around the grounds as Lucky Seven.

"If you need anything during your stay," Dean said to Belinda as she passed by.

"Thank you, Dean," Belinda said, reading his name tag.

It was standard that employees wore name tags. However, most of the time, they made up fake names, as a joke. This week all the fake names had been retired. Everyone was all business.

"This is certainly a unique place," Belinda said as Jules started driving the cart around the grounds.

"Yes, it is," Jules agreed and then continued with her planned speech about the grounds and the fun activities available to all guests—the horses, the boat activities, —and followed things up with the meals by celebrity chef Isaac Andrews, all while driving through the paved pathways that wound around the property.

"This is a very impressive facility. I'd like to see it all. Is there someone who can show me around after I get settled?" Belinda asked.

Thankfully, they had planned for this exact request. When they pulled up to the Hammock House, Jules knew instantly that the woman was impressed with the cabin.

Who wouldn't be impressed with the two-story wood-sided cabin. Large windows looked out over a small stream and, yes, four hammocks hung on large pine and oak trees along the water's edge.

Still, Belinda didn't say anything as Levi appeared from the pathway and offered to take the bag up to the cabin.

Four stairs led to the front glass door of the eight-hundred-square-foot cabin. Most guests were impressed their first stay at how spacious and quaint each of the cabins were.

After Elle had overheard a handful of guests talking about wanting to stay in each of the unique cabins, they had created a punch card of sorts for guests so they could keep track of which cabins they had already stayed in and which ones were their favorites.

Their return customers loved the idea so much there were now T-shirts and key rings claiming the number of cabins they'd stayed in.

"Shall I show you around?" she offered.

"Please." Belinda stepped inside.

Since this cabin was one of the newer ones that Aiden and his crew had built shortly before the camp opened, the inside was unique to the name it had. Small hammock designs were everywhere, from the knobs on the cabinets to small hammocks etched in the glass and mirrors.

Several large paintings depicted relaxing scenes of hammocks near the beach with palm trees, all from a local artist, of course. They were all for sale.

The bedroom was up a wrought iron spiral staircase and filled the entire loft above. Its views overlooked the treetops, giving a second layer of privacy to its occupants. There was a massive bathroom that Jules envied, as well as the sitting area and a small kitchenette.

All in all, the cabin, much like all the others, was homey and oozed comfort.

"This is your communications screen." Jules walked over to the touch screen installed in each cabin. "From here, you can see what events or activities are available." She swiped the screens to showcase several items, including yoga classes and massages. "If you wish to schedule, say a massage..." She clicked to the screen and hit an open slot. Instantly, Belinda's name filled the allotted time. "To cancel..." She swiped again and the name disappeared. "You can order meals from here to be delivered to your door, or to be ready when you arrive at any of our three dining locations—the dining hall, the outdoor terrace, or the main pool deck bar and grill." She scrolled to another screen. "This is your calendar. It will show you what you have signed up for, in case you forget. It will also show you what camp events are scheduled. Tonight's theme for dinner is Neon or Glow Night." Jules smiled. "If you didn't bring something neon, don't worry, they'll be plenty of glow sticks to go around." She shifted to look at Belinda, who was taking it all in. "I suggest attending at least one themed event during your stay. You won't regret it. You can also download the app with access to all this by just scanning this QR code and logging in in with your cabin name and the last two digits of your credit card. Then you'll have access to everything I just showed you, directly from your phone."

Jules stood back and glanced around. "This is Levi, he's going to show you around once you feel settled."

"I'm ready now," Belinda said eagerly.

Levi smiled. "Shall we take the golf cart?" he asked her.

"No, I'm ready for a walk. Let me just change my shoes," Belinda answered.

"I placed your bag up the stairs on the bed," Levi said. "I'll be waiting just outside."

"Thank you." Belinda turned to Jules and, after digging in her bag, placed a fifty-dollar bill in her palm. "I don't think I've ever been shown this much attention in my entire life," she said with a wink. "You're off to a very good start."

Jules smiled. "That is the joy of this place. To us, this is our standard, every day. It's one of the reasons I love working here. Have a pleasant stay. If you need anything"—she motioned to the screen— "I'm only a button away."

# CHAPTER TWENTY-ONE

Damion and the other guys had been put in charge of showing the handful of journalists around the camp. He'd gotten a very stocky man in his late fifties by the name of Brian Clint. He'd never seen the guy on television, but he had heard his name before.

After helping the man get settled in one of the closer cabins —due to health issues, he required a cabin with no stairs— Damion drove the man around the grounds in a golf cart.

The guy actually took notes as they went along. He asked a ton of questions, none of them really about the camp. But he still noted each of the activities or events that were planned.

The questions were more about the employees, the owners, and the job he had been hired to do.

When Brian found out that Damion was, as he put it, nothing more than a pool boy, Damion's next stop was to head to the boat house.

At first, Damion believed the man was never going to loosen up. But when they arrived at the docks, the guy did something that shocked Damion.

"I love to sail," Brian admitted. "I'd love to take a closer look at her."

Damion parked the golf cart and motioned. "Be my guest. We're taking her out tonight for a sunset sail. There are a few more seats available. I can block one out for you."

Brian frowned. "I haven't been sailing in... oh, too long."

"There's nothing stopping you now. The cost is included in your stay," Damion said as the man stood on the dock, looking eagerly at the boat.

Then Brian ran a hand over his large belly. "I... wouldn't want to make anyone feel uncomfortable. I don't even fly anymore..."

Damion stopped him. "The *Wind Chaser* is not an airplane. There would be plenty of room and"—he motioned to the sailboat— "I think you'll agree there is nothing like the wind in your face."

"No." Brian sighed and then Damion watched a smile creep on his face. "Okay, what the hell. Sign me up."

After that, Brian put away his notepad and talked more freely. He even joked with Damion about a few past sailing trips he'd taken and how he'd found his wife, Karen. He had been sailing around and she'd been surfing with a friend when he'd noticed two girls screaming about a shark.

"So naturally, I sailed over and picked them up." He smiled. "We were married two weeks later and have been happily married for almost thirty years now."

"Wow, congratulations," Damion said easily. "Why did you stop sailing?"

Brian frowned. "I sold the boat to buy a house after we found out Karen was pregnant with our first born. I never went sailing again, sadly. I got a desk job at the newspaper and..." He rubbed his belly. "Gained so much more in life that anchored me in place."

"You should come back and bring Karen when you can. Take her sailing again," he suggested.

Brian sighed. "If it wasn't for the company putting me up, I'm not sure we could afford it."

"We have blocks of discount dates available. You'd be surprised at how cheep the costs are. Less than a hotel in some cases," Damion explained.

"Really? I..." He shook his head. "She'd like that. Our thirtieth anniversary is coming up next year."

"Talk to Jules at the front desk. She can get you a bigger discount for your anniversary." He smiled and knew that he'd won the man over.

By the time it was ready to load up and head out for the sail, Damion was thankful he'd taken an extra couple of cookies and a soda after lunch. He needed the extra push to get him through the evening. After the sail, he was supposed to head back up to the dining hall and help finish up at the dinner.

Thankfully, Jules was there to help him through the sail. Besides, he was really enjoying Brian's conversation. The man came completely out of his shell the moment they set off.

He knew the guy was nervous about his weight and putting other people on the sail out because of how much room he took on deck. But the nice thing about the *Wind Chaser* was that she was plenty big enough for people of all sizes.

Brian had a comfortable seat next to him for the entire trip. Damion even let him steer for a while. He could have sworn he saw tears in the man's eyes as they docked.

Both Jules and he rushed to the dining hall the moment they had locked up and made sure everyone was off the boat. After a quick change, they stepped into the dining hall together.

"See you later." Jules kissed him and headed to help out behind the bar.

He was on clean-up duty—bussing the tables, making sure dirty dishes were put in the dishwashers, even refilling waters or delivering drinks. For the next three hours, he did whatever was needed.

He didn't know all of the journalists that were staying at the camp, but he did spot one that he knew. Belinda Ness. He'd had such a crush on the news anchor when he was younger.

The woman was a legend, and still sexy as hell even now that she was in her late sixties.

When he served her the wine she'd ordered, she took his arm. "You're Damion, right?"

"Yes." He nodded. "May I just say, I'm a huge fan."

Belinda smiled and motioned to the empty chair next to her. "Do you have a moment?"

He sat down quickly, putting the empty tray on the table. "For you, I've got the rest of the night." She chuckled and took a sip of her wine. "Sorry, did I mention I'm a huge fan?"

"You did." She nodded and smiled. "Rumors have it that you and Jules are an item?"

He glanced over at Jules, who was pouring a glass of wine. "Yes," he said, without taking his eyes off Jules.

"Wow, if I had a man look at me like that, I wouldn't have divorced four times," Belinda joked.

"She doesn't know it yet, but I'm buttering her up to marry me within the year," he said easily. He'd been thinking about it since their trip to St. George Island. There was no point fighting it. She was what he wanted, and nothing would change his mind.

Belinda sighed and leaned back as she ran her eyes over him. "The pair of you have been working here since the doors opened?"

He nodded. "I went to school with Elle and a handful of other people working here."

"Those handful of people—Aiden Stark, Levi Walsh, Dean Wallis, and a few others—have also been here from day one." It wasn't a question, but a statement. Still, Damion nodded again. Belinda took another sip of her wine. She'd obviously done her homework. "That says a lot about an employer. Having friends stick around that long. I've talked to each one I just listed, and they all seem more than content."

"Why wouldn't they be?" He shrugged. "This place is..." He looked around the massive room. His eyes ran over the crowd and yet he somehow ignored all the happy guests and instead focused on his friends and all the workers. Each and every one of them had a smile on their faces. Some laughed and joked with guests, while others practically glowed with joy. "Magical," he finished, looking back at Belinda. "Have you danced yet tonight?" he asked her.

That question seemed to take her aback. "No, I'm here alone."

He stood up and held out his hand. "Allow me?"

She paused for a moment before taking his hand. He led her towards the empty dance floor.

"Are you sure?" Belinda challenged. "You seem awful young..."

He didn't let another word out as he spun her easily. She came back to him, laughing.

"Oh, I like a challenge," she said, her chin going up.

"One of the first reports I remember seeing you in was when you interviewed Carl Steinburger." He smiled. "I begged my mother to teach me how to dance after seeing you and Carl glide across the dancefloor. Later, an ex-girlfriend convinced me to take classes with her. Best thing I walked away with out of that relationship was to learn how to dance."

"That interview was... too many years ago." Belinda laughed.

At that moment, music filled the room and the lights lowered.

For the next few minutes, Damion led one of his idols around the floor in a dance he'd learned because of her. She laughed. He laughed. Other couples filled the dance floor around them.

When the song was over, everyone parted and stood around them, clapping.

"I'm afraid I only have one of those in me." Belinda smiled at him. "You should dance with your girl. I think I learned all I needed tonight."

He lifted her hand to his lips. "It was a pleasure."

"Thank you for making an old woman feel young again. Even if for a moment." Belinda turned and went back to her table.

He felt a tap on his shoulder and turned to smile down at Jules.

"Is this dance taken?" she asked him.

He pulled her into his arms. "I'm all yours," he said into her ear and meant it deeper than she knew.

The following morning at exactly ten o'clock, a large group of journalists, including the ones that were currently staying at the camp, gathered around the front courtyard.

The Wildflowers and their spouses stood on the front steps of the main building. A handful of employees, ones who could be spared during the press conference, stood behind them.

He stood next to Jules, holding her hand in his.

They were all nervous. He felt Jules's palms grow damp and she wiped them several times on the skirt she was wearing.

It had been decided that Zoey would open the press conference. The friends had a written speech that they would each take part in before they opened it up to questions. Then they would give a tour of the campgrounds to any journalist who wished to look around.

Before Zoey stepped up to the microphone, a ton of photographs were taken of the large group. He remembered the days before the camp had opened, when there had been a handful of travel guides and magazines that had interviewed the friends. This was nothing like that.

Currently about triple the number of people were snapping photos. Besides, during those first photos and interviews, no employees had taken part. Now, everyone here stood in solidarity with the five friends.

Zoey walked up to the microphone and a hush fell over the group.

"Hello, and welcome to River Camps. I'm Zoey Costas. In a few minutes, you'll get a chance to meet all of the River Camp owners. But for now, you're stuck with me." Zoey paused as a few chuckles filled the air. "I'm going to walk you through the basics. River Camps was originally opened more than fifty years ago by Joe Saunders, who purchased the land and built the property as an elite summer camp for girls, in honor of his daughter. Elle is Joe's granddaughter." Zoey turned to Elle, who waved her hand and then put it back on her growing belly. "Elle, Hannah, Aubrey, my sister Scarlett, and I all met here when we were eleven years old. We have remained friends all throughout our lives. When Joe died, he left the property to us." Zoey motioned to Elle, who stepped forward as Zoey stepped back.

"It was my crazy idea to turn River Camps into what it is today." She smiled. "With a little help, okay, a lot of help"—she rolled her eyes— "and a lot of favors, we accomplished the goal within a year."

Hannah stepped forward this time. "I pulled a lot of strings and managed to get Isaac Andrews to agree to become head chef and take over the kitchens here. You will all get a chance to enjoy a specially made lunch after the press conference." This brought several cheers.

It was Scarlett's turn to step forward. "For those of you who are feeling a little more adventurous, follow me on a tour of the grounds, where I'll show you our custom-built zip lines. You can visit our barn filled with more than a dozen rehabilitated horses that guests can enjoy. We also have our very own sailboat complete with owner and captain Damion"—Scarlett turned to him, and he stepped forward and waved, as requested — "to fill those summer nights and take you to see some of the best sunsets Florida has to offer."

Aubrey stepped forward next. "You can join me in a class—tai chi, judo, yoga, self-defense. You name it, we teach it. If you're not into that much physical strain, grab a free five-minute massage from one of our certified masseuses." Aubrey motioned to Andrea and Kara who both waved. "Or take a dip in one of our three swimming pools or sit back and enjoy our very own private beach." Aubrey finished up as Zoey stepped forward.

"As you will see for yourself today, River Camps has something for everyone's inner child. The staff and the grounds, including all of the amenities, are yours for today's enjoyment. We will take questions at this time before we break into tours."

At this point, several questions were thrown at them. Zoey looked slightly taken aback and held up her hands.

"Please." Zoey turned to Jules, who stepped forward and took the extra microphone and started walking around picking people to ask questions.

Damion pretty much zoned out at this point but came shooting back to focus when he heard the question thrown at Zoey.

"Is it true that you personally aborted your living baby a few days ago right here on the campgrounds?"

Damion saw Jules jerk the microphone away, as if she wanted to hit the woman over the head with it.

Several gasps filled the air while more pictures were taken of Zoey.

Dylan stepped behind Zoey and wrapped a protective arm around her waist. Zoey looked as if she had been shot. Damion was almost sure her face was as pale now as it had been when he'd caught her on the docks.

"Please keep your questions focused on River Camps. Next question please," Dylan said firmly.

# CHAPTER TWENTY-TWO

Jules was steaming. She wanted to smack the blond woman who had asked the question to Zoey. She wanted to correct her. To tell her exactly what had happened. But it wasn't her place.

Instead, she continued to walk around and hold the microphone for a few more questions before everyone broke up and started being ushered around the grounds.

Jules did note that the blonde left right after the press conference portion.

She wanted to go and make sure Zoey was okay, but Dylan was there with her, and Jules had a job to do. She, along with a handful of other employees, were tasked with showing around anyone who asked to see the grounds.

After an initial shuffling around, she was put in charge of three journalists and their photographers. She answered questions, showed them the stables, the boathouse, the pool house, and the beach before heading back to the main building and dining hall so they could enjoy their free lunch.

The plan was that the visiting journalists would all leave

the campgrounds before dark. For the most part, all of them followed the rule. However, there were a handful that asked to speak with the owners one more time because they had new questions.

Jules arranged for the smaller group to meet with the Wildflowers at the base of the main staircase inside.

This time, almost all of the questions were asked to Zoey.

"Is it true that you attacked Lisa Tribberton?"

"No, it's not true," Zoey answered.

"Did you know the Tribbertons before their visit?"

"Not personally. My father and Joe Tribberton were... business partners at one point."

"What motive do the Tribbertons have to take your business down?"

"You'd have to ask them. All we know is that they were asked to leave after... an incident."

"What sort of incident?"

Dylan stepped forward. "My wife was attacked."

"By whom?" several people asked.

"Lisa Tribberton."

"Can anyone corroborate this?"

"I can." Damion stepped forward.

"We have footage of the incident, which was turned over to the police," Brett said, stepping forward.

"Who are you?"

"Brett Jewel. Head of security at River Camps," Brett answered.

"The same Brett Jewel who was shot saving the tourists last year?"

"Yes." Brett nodded.

"You were police?"

"Yes," he answered with a sigh. "Now I'm head of security here."

The room grew quiet.

"Can you share the tapes?" someone asked.

"No, the police have them. There is an ongoing investigation at this time."

"Are you saying that Lisa Tribberton is going to be charged with a crime?"

"No, I'm not saying—" Brett started, but Zoey put a hand on his arm.

"At this point, we'd like to thank everyone for coming today. Are there any other questions about the River Camps facility?" The room remained silent. "Thank you all again. Brett will show you to the parking lot. Feel free to stop by the front desk where Julie or Beth will be happy to book you and your spouse a stay here at River Camps so you can see firsthand how enjoyable it is to let your inner child out."

She didn't even wait a second before turning around and walking back down the hallway towards her office, along with the rest of the Wildflowers, who all wrapped their arms around Zoey as they went.

"That is one strong woman," Damion said under his breath. "It looks like you're up." He motioned to the front desk. Sure enough, there were two people standing there. One woman was talking to Beth, who was scanning the computer screen as if looking for availability of a date. The other woman was looking at a brochure.

Jules stepped behind the counter and smiled. "May I help you?"

The woman ran her eyes over her slowly, then practically sneered.

"Yes, I hope so. I'd like to look at booking a cabin for my family and I." There was a slight accent in the woman's smooth tone. New York? New Jersey?

"I'm sorry, but River Camps is an adults only camp. Unless

your family party consists of all twenty-one-year-olds..." Jules dropped off as the woman's eyes narrowed.

"It's too bad, really." The woman set the brochure down. "You'd make a killing if this was a family facility."

Jules smiled. It wasn't the first time Jules had heard the complaint, nor, she doubted, would it be the last.

The fact was, this worked, and it worked wonderfully. With children, Jules knew, there were a whole new set of issues. Not only would the camp's insurance spike, but there would have to be major updates to the grounds. Each of the pools would have to be fenced off for safety. Every single cabin would have to be retrofitted to house more than two guests, sleeping in just one bed.

At this point, there wasn't even a two-bedroom cabin on the grounds besides River Cabin, but that was only rented out about twice a year.

"I'll make sure to pass on your suggestion. Would you like to book a getaway for your significant other and yourself instead?"

The woman's eyes narrowed even further. "No, I think I've learned enough about this place."

The woman spun on her heels and walked out the front door without another word.

Beth had better luck with the other woman, who booked a full week stay in three weeks.

Thankfully, after that, things slowed down. They were still playing host to the nine journalists until tomorrow, but everyone is that group had been won over the night before.

Belinda seemed happier and more relaxed than she had been when she'd arrived. About an hour before dinner, she stepped into the lobby and made a beeline towards Jules.

"There you are. Jules." She narrowed her eyes and titled

her head. "That nickname fits you much better than Julie," she added with a wink.

Jules smiled. "How can I help you this evening?"

"You, my dear, can book me another cabin. I want to do that wheel thing your man was talking to me about." Belinda waved her hand towards the doors.

"Wheel of Cabins?" Jules smiled.

"Yes. I go on a writing retreat twice a year. One in June and one in September. How far out can you lock in a new cabin for me?"

Jules smiled. "How far out do you want to go?"

Belinda's smile grew. "How many cabins do you have?"

"And then she booked out a week in a new cabin for the next fifteen years," Jules said as she leaned her chin against Damion's chest later that night.

Damion laughed. "I like her."

"From the looks of it, she really liked you too," Jules joked.

Damion's smile grew. "I can cross that item off my bucket list."

"What?" She leaned up and looked down at him. "Dancing with Belinda Ness was an item on your bucket list?"

"Hell, yes, it was." He reached up and touched her face, brushing back her hair.

Jules relaxed back and thought about her own bucket list. There weren't a lot of items on it, but still, some she could cross off herself. "What else is on that list of yours?"

His fingers lazily circled her bare shoulder. "First, what's one of yours?"

"Mine are boring," she said, trying to hold in a yawn.

"Nope, spill," he said as his fingers stopped.

She glanced up at him. "Mind you I made most of these when I was in sixth grade," she warned.

His fingers started moving against her skin again. "Okay, shoot."

"Item one was to kiss a boy," she said, feeling her face heat.

"Check." He made the motion of putting a check mark on her shoulder. "Go on."

"Two was to dye my hair blond." She remembered the hours she'd spent in the salon chair to get her dark hair to lighten up that first time.

"Check," Damion said. "And by the way, I like it. Of course, I liked your natural color, too."

"Three was to spend a weekend sailing with a handsome man," she lied, and he laughed. "I've told you two of mine." She nudged his ribs. "Your turn."

"Hawaii. I've always wanted to sail to Hawaii."

"From here?" She jerked up.

He chuckled. "Yeah, it's a trip, but..." He shrugged.

"You think?" She shook her head.

"It's not as bad as you think. Straight down the Gulf, through the Panama Canal, then it's pretty much a straight shot out to Hawaii. About three weeks of sailing, in good weather, with a few stops."

"It's the bad weather I'd be concerned about," she said. "Have you taken any trips that long before?"

"I've been to the Keys plenty of times, to Jamaica twice, and Puerto Rico three times."

"Alone?"

"No, I usually talk my dad or a friend into going with me. Dean and Carter have both gone out with me before."

"Yeah, they would. They're like your besties," she said with a chuckle.

"Yeah." He shifted under her. "You and Zoey seem pretty close."

"She has her Wildflowers. But, yeah, she's cool. Out of the

five friends, she's the one I feel the most closeness with. Her and Lea. We get each other." She smiled.

"You got pretty pissed at the journalist who asked Zoey about her miscarriage today," he pointed out.

"Yeah, you did too. I saw the fire in your eyes." She glanced up at him.

"I was there. I saw what Zoey and Dylan went through. They wanted that baby. Loved it as much as they love Paige. I can't imagine going through something like that." He locked eyes with her. "It would kill me to see you in that much pain. Both physical and emotional."

She reached up and cupped his face. "Same." Her heart melted. Damion was more than she'd ever expected.

Living with him was so easy, she wondered why they had been fighting their attraction all those years.

"Do you think today helped?" she asked him.

"Yeah. I think that tomorrow morning, we're going to be surprised at all the calls." He kissed the top of her head. "Goodnight."

"Goodnight." She leaned up and kissed him.

She heard him fall asleep quickly. She'd learned he dropped off within seconds. If only she could do that. Instead, she lay there, listening to him breathing, feeling his chest rise and fall, and thought about the day. Her mind refused to shut down until finally, sometime after midnight, she slipped into a light sleep.

Damion was correct, that next morning, there were a ton of calls. Most were reservations, however, there were a strange number of calls from people shouting into the phone about the camp supporting the killing of babies, and some about drugs or illicit affairs going on there that the camp was privy to.

Whenever she or Beth answered those calls, they hung up.

Shortly before noon, the police arrived. At first, Jules

thought it was just some of Brett's friends coming to meet him for lunch, which they did often enough. But then they asked to see Zoey.

Jules called Zoey and then sent a text message to both Dylan and Brett.

The three of them entered the lobby at the same time.

"Larry, Troy." Brett nodded to the officers. "What brings you here today?"

"We've got a complaint we're following up on," Troy, the older man said, stepping forward. "Is there someplace we can talk?"

"Here is fine," Zoey said, holding her head up. "If this is about Lisa Tribberton, I've already—"

"It's not, ma'am," Troy interrupted. "You're Zoey Costas?"

"I am." Zoey nodded.

"We need to ask you a few questions about..." He looked around. "Are you sure there isn't someplace more private we can go?"

Zoey glanced around. At this time of the day, most guests were enjoying lunch. The lobby was completely empty, except for Jules. Beth had taken her lunch a few moments earlier.

"Here is fine," Zoey said.

Troy nodded. "We're here to ask you about a rumor that you had an abortion."

Everyone was quiet. "She didn't," Dylan finally spoke up. "Her doctor, Lea Val, can confirm that."

"Yes, well." Larry cleared his throat. "Miss Val's—"

"Dr. Val," Brett broke in. "She's a doctor."

Larry sighed heavily as if annoyed about the interruption. "Her credentials are under investigation as well."

"Why?" Zoey asked.

"As you know," Larry started. Jules noticed that the

younger man's eyes were burning into Zoey's. "The state of Florida prohibits—"

"We all know the new laws," Brett barked out to Larry, who glared back at Brett.

Jules knew instantly that the two men didn't get along.

Since no one was paying attention to her, she picked up her phone and shot a 911 group text to the Wildflowers.

"Cops in lobby. Zoey needs backup. ASAP."

"We'd like you to come down to the station to answer a few simple questions about what happened," Larry continued.

"She had a miscarriage." Dylan almost shouted it. "We lost our baby."

Zoey placed a hand on his arm.

"If you have nothing to hide, then you won't mind coming down to the station to answer some questions," Larry sneered.

Brett stepped forward. "You'll have to go through their lawyer, who will provide any statements or evidence you need."

Just then the rest of the Wildflowers showed up. Aubrey actually ran into the room wearing yoga pants and a sweat-soaked top.

"What is this all about?" Elle asked, holding her hands on her protruding belly.

"You can come to the station now peacefully, or we can handcuff you." Larry stepped forward, reaching for his handcuffs.

"Troy, rein in your dog," Brett warned, taking a step between Larry and Zoey.

"Step back," Troy said to Larry. "Mrs. Costas has the right to retain her lawyer. We'll expect you and your lawyer to appear in the station by tomorrow morning," Troy said to Brett. He turned to Larry and barked, "Wait for me in the car."

The man glared back at Brett, then Zoey, before turning and leaving.

"Sorry to do this to you, but the law is... well, you know," Troy said to Brett.

"Son of a... She had a miscarriage, Troy. They are grieving like any loving parents. Let them just grieve." Brett ran his hands through his hair.

"Normally, I wouldn't think twice, but this is coming from pretty high up. Apparently, we got a call from a reliable source that claims Zoey did something to harm herself and end her pregnancy." Troy shook his head. "This all sucks if you ask me," he said as he turned around.

Zoey, who had been standing rod still, not speaking, fell into her husband's arms the moment the front doors were shut. Dylan lifted her in his arms and marched to the sofa where he held her while she cried uncontrollably for almost five minutes straight. All of her friends gathered around her, holding onto her tight.

A couple came strolling into the lobby, but Jules rushed over and asked if they could come back later.

Then she too stood over Zoey and silently cursed the powers that were making her friend go through more pain. As if losing a baby wasn't painful enough.

# CHAPTER TWENTY-THREE

It had been decided that, since Damion had been a witness to the event in question, he should be present as a witness. The following morning, at nine o'clock sharp, he, Zoey, Dylan, Dr. Val, and a very scary looking lawyer by the name of Steinbeck, who was dressed in a suit that looked like it was as expensive as the *Wind Chaser*, walked into the lobby of the police station together.

They were shown into a small conference room where Lea laid out a few folders that the lawyer had already looked over and approved.

Two officers in plain clothes stepped into the room—a woman no older than he was and an older gentleman who resembled a lawyer more than an officer.

"Good morning," the gentleman started. "I'm detective Hobbylark. This is detective Romero." They sat down. "Romero will be conducting this investigation, as situations like this require a delicate hand. I'm here strictly to observe." He nodded to the female officer, who was opening a laptop.

Zoey introduced herself, then her lawyer, who finished introducing everyone else in the room.

"I don't really think this interview warranted a lawyer and a witness," Detective Romero said sharply.

"I don't really think this situation warranted police questioning," the lawyer countered.

The detective nodded and then opened a file she had set on the table.

"Miss..."

"Mrs.," Zoey corrected. "Mrs. Costas."

Detective Romero typed something on her laptop. "Mrs. Costas. When did you know that you had become pregnant with your second child?"

Lea opened her mouth to speak, but one look from the detective and the lawyer had her sitting back.

"The first time I suspected was..." Zoey opened the folder Lea had set in front of her, and then rattled off the date and time.

"Do you always let your doctor keep your replies handy?" Romero asked.

"When she is my close friend and the woman who birthed my daughter, yes," Zoey answered easily.

"You have currently had one live birth?" Romero asked, looking at the paper in front of her.

"Yes," Zoey said, but Damion could tell she was grinding her back teeth.

"Did you knowingly drink or take any illegal substance after finding out about your second pregnancy?"

"No," Zoey answered.

"Did you willingly do anything to harm your second baby?"

"It wasn't a viable..." Zoey started, but Romero jerked her head up.

"Mrs. Costas, I don't think you understand the gravity of

your situation. The accusations brought against you are enough to have your daughter"—she paused and looked at her screen—"Paige put into foster care until this matter is resolved."

Everyone in the room tensed and both Zoey and Dylan gasped and held onto one another.

"A yes or no answer please," Romero said sharply.

"No," Zoey answered. "No, I didn't do anything to harm anyone. Myself or any child."

Damion wanted to yell and scream at the woman. Instead, he sat there and waited for his chance to talk. To defend his friend.

"Are you willing to testify to these facts?" Romero asked.

"Yes." Zoey looked at the lawyer.

"My client would like to provide you with proof of her situation." The lawyer slipped a USB drive across the table. "As well as a witness." He motioned to Damion.

"What is this?" Romero asked, holding up the drive.

"Security camera footage," the lawyer answered.

Romero shifted, her eyes narrowing. She set the USB drive down on the table, as if offended she had been handed it. After a moment of silence, Romero shifted in her seat, then straightened her shoulders and placed the USB drive in her computer.

Damion knew what was on it. After all, he was the one who had suggested they look at the footage to see if they caught everything that had happened. They had turned copies of the video over to the police as evidence when Lisa accused them. It only seemed right that the rest of the video would be proof that Zoey had done nothing to warrant this questioning.

The entire incident with Lisa Tribberton was center screen. Though you could barely make out what was said on the sailboat, when they moved to the dock, every word was crystal clear.

So was the moment Zoey slumped against him. When he

lifted her up, the blood dripping down her legs. Him yelling to call 911 and disappearing off screen. They had spliced together video of him running through the camp. Brett pulling his car up, him gently putting Zoey in the back. Lea climbing in after them, and Dylan jumping into the front seat.

"From there"—Lea shoved her folder forward towards Romero— "you can read what happened in my official medical report. This is all the medical evidence you need right here."

The woman looked up and Damion knew they had won. What would make a person be so full of hate?

"I think this is enough to close this case." Detective Hobbylark stood up. "Thank you for your time. I'm very sorry for your loss." He held out his hand towards Zoey, who ignored it.

"I want to say something. On the record." Zoey narrowed her eyes at the other woman. "My heart was broken when two doctors I trust with my life and the life of everyone I love informed me that my pregnancy was not viable, according to several scans. What was growing inside me had no heartbeat. It had no chance of survival. I was lucky, having proof that backed up my story. How many women will be so lucky?" she asked. "How many will wake in the middle of the night, alone or next to their mates, covered in blood, knowing that the baby that they loved, the hope that they had for the future, is gone? Their physical and emotional pain won't be a drop in a sea compared to what you or people like you will put them through. What will you do, detective Romero, if the unthinkable happens to you? Will you be lucky enough to have people like these to stand behind you?" Zoey motioned to the people that surrounded her. To Damion. "Caring people who will back up your story that you didn't willingly or knowingly do anything to harm something no bigger than a bean. Something that, even though it's small, you loved more than your next breath. Yet, somehow, its rights were more important than your own. Using it as a reason, your name and your life are dragged through the mud." Zoey slowly stood up. "Think about that the next time you sit in that chair and talk to a woman who has just gone through the unthinkable."

With that, Zoey turned and left the room with the rest of them following behind.

He wanted to shout and cheer that they had won the battle. However, the moment he stepped outside into the heat of the day, he saw Zoey and Dylan hold onto one another. Then it hit him that they were still grieving the—as she had put it—unthinkable. It had still happened to them. In the past week, Zoey had not only had to suffer through something so physically traumatic—he'd watched her almost bleed out in his arms—she'd also lost something she had already grown to love. And then she'd had to stand up for her business, her own name, and her family.

How was it that a woman could be attacked from all sides and still hold on? How could she still stand up straight with all that pressure on her shoulders?

He walked over and, without thinking, wrapped his arms around the couple. He felt Lea come up and do the same. The four of them stood on the steps of the police station in the growing heat of the day and just held on to one another.

He wasn't scheduled to work that day because he was closing on his land around three o'clock, but he still showed up just before lunchtime. Jules agreed to take lunch with him, and he'd arranged for them to have lunch out on the water.

Instead of taking the *Wind Chaser*, he pulled the biggest rowboat they had onto the water. He put two to-go lunches in a basket and waited for Jules to arrive.

"What's this?" she asked with a smile.

"A celebration of sorts, if you can call it that." He shrugged.

"I heard. We all did." Her smile slipped a little as he helped her into the boat.

"Yeah, and yet I feel just as angry as I felt this morning," he admitted as he kicked off from the dock.

"Most of us do." She nodded in agreement as she leaned back on the pillows he'd tossed in the boat for comfort.

"How's Zoey doing?" he asked her.

"Dylan and the rest of them convinced her to go home. She's spending time with Paige and Dylan for the remainder of the week," Jules said with a sigh. "I can't believe she tried to work today."

"I can. It helps keep her mind busy. Off her pain." They grew silent for a while. "You should have been there and seen Zoey. It was like one of those scenes in a movie, near the end when the character makes the speech, the kind that gives everyone in the audience goose bumps." He shook his head. "If I didn't already know she was amazing..." He thought back to how she'd stood up for herself. For other women who might come after her.

"All of them are strong. To think that they created all this..." She motioned to the grounds beyond the calm waters.

The beach was just coming into view. There were guests lounging on the chairs, lying in the sand, or playing volleyball.

"They did this together. I arrived before opening day and saw the mess they had to deal with to rebuild this place," she added.

"Yeah." He nodded as he thought back to the first time that he'd stepped foot on River Camps. "They pretty much had to do a full overhaul on the place. Still, I can't imagine working anyplace else."

"Me either." She laughed. "Can you imagine us hobbling down the pathways with walkers?"

He smiled. "Better yet, in those go-cart things? We can race." He wiggled his eyebrows.

She sighed and leaned back again. "I don't even need food. The sunlight feels so nice today. I could just nap right here for my entire break."

"Are you sure? I brought your favorite?" He stopped rowing and pulled out the containers.

"Pizza?" she asked, sitting up slightly.

He laughed. "I was close." He opened the lid to one of the calzones he'd grabbed.

She hungrily took it. "Okay, food, then a quick nap." She took a bite.

After lunch, he walked Jules back to the main building and went to find Brett. He had another idea that might get him in trouble, but he didn't care. He wanted more than anything to teach Lisa Tribberton a lesson. The woman had hurt people he cared for. It was time she knew how that felt.

"Got a sec?" he asked, knocking on Brett's door. Since the man had taken over security for the camp, he and Damion had gotten closer. They'd grown up together. Had known one another since grade school. Brett had turned to the law; Damion had turned to the sea.

Now that Brett was almost one hundred percent back to his pre-getting-shot self, he had started hitting the gym more often, joining Carter, Dean, and Damion during their three-times-a-week workout ritual.

"Sure." Brett shut his computer down and motioned for Damion to sit down.

"How bad would it look for you, and the camp, if footage of Lisa Tribberton attacking Zoey was leaked?" he came right out and said.

Brett looked slightly shocked. Then he tilted his head and started laughing.

"It would serve her right," Brett admitted. "I'm not too sure about the backlash for the camp. If there would be any." Then he frowned. "We'd want to talk to Zoey and Dylan first. Get their okay. We do own the rights to the footage. Guests agree to the security measures when they check in. So legally..." He dropped off. "I'll still want to check it out with the lawyers."

"Seeing what Zoey and Dylan went through this morning makes me want Lisa Tribberton to squirm," he admitted.

"Hell, yes." Brett nodded. "Seeing Robert Dixon, Sr., being hauled out of the courtroom in chains was the reward I needed, so I understand. It didn't undo the horrors Lea had to go through, but it helped."

Damion nodded. "Knowing that Lisa Tribberton would have to explain her actions would help. When do the news reports go out on the camp?"

"Elle told Lea the first one went out this morning. Jules and Beth have been busy vetting calls," Brett said as he typed on his computer. "Sent a query to the lawyer. Do you want to ask Zoey and Dylan yourself?"

Damion thought about it, then nodded. "Yeah." He glanced at his watch. "I'm closing on my land in an hour. I'll head over to their place first."

Brett smiled. "Finally. I thought you closed last week."

"No, there were some issues with the property line. The place hadn't been surveyed in fifty years."

"I hope it all worked out."

"It did. I got five more feet on the left side than I thought I'd get." He smiled. "Which means the price went up slightly, but bank of Owen assures me that he's good to cover the cost. I'll probably be working it off for the rest of my life, that and the house Aiden's going to build for us."

"Us?" Brett's eyebrows shot up.

Jules and he hadn't told anyone they were living together.

They were pretty sure several people knew, but everyone had been so focused on saving the camp that there hadn't been time to share the good news.

"Yeah, Jules and I moved in together last week," he answered with a smile.

"Hell, congratulations." Brett laughed. "Of course, for the bet, we'll need to know the exact date."

"Shit, there was a bet going around?" Damion shook his head.

"Yeah, I won the one about you asking her out." Brett smiled. "I had last Tuesday down as the day you'd move in together. Lea had next year." He laughed.

Damion rolled his eyes. "There is no such thing as a personal life around here."

"Nope," Brett said with a smile. "But I'm really enjoying that aspect."

"Yeah." Damion stood up. "So am I." He thought back to Zoey's speech earlier that morning.

One thing was crystal clear—the people that worked at River Camps stood up for one another. They weren't just employees, they were family.

# CHAPTER TWENTY-FOUR

"My plan is tricky," Damion told Jules later that evening.

They had gone to his parents' place to celebrate the closing on his land.

She enjoyed his parents a lot. Almost as much as she enjoyed time with her own folks. It was a relaxing dinner. One where Jules hadn't feared the outbursts that she'd grown accustomed to from her father.

They were back at their place, sitting on the sofa and eating some of the ice cream they'd gotten at the grocery store during their first official shopping trip as a couple. She'd learned that grocery shopping could be fun, with the right person.

"Plan?" Jules asked.

"I've run it by everyone—Zoey, Dylan, Brett, and the lawyers." He glanced over at her on the sofa. "We're going to leak the video of Lisa Tribberton attacking Zoey on the *Wind Chaser*."

Jules first gut response was to laugh, but then she thought about it. Really thought. Then she smiled.

"That's an amazing idea." Jules set her spoon down and leaned forward. "When?"

Jules knew that the first of many news reports had been released on the camp. The rest of the articles were scheduled to start going out to the public tomorrow. The impact from the article releases would be much more massive than the first one released that morning from the local station.

"Tomorrow, the same time the reports about River Camps will go out," Damion answered.

Jules's smile grew. "What a wonderful idea." She leaned over and kissed Damion.

"You know this means that you and Beth are going to be much busier tomorrow answering phones," he joked.

She laughed. "Yes, I bet. Who cares. I can't wait." She hugged him again.

"I thought you would say that. We've decided to send the file to Belinda in the morning."

The following morning, a large group of them met in the employee dining room over breakfast.

Zoey and Dylan were there with Paige. Normally, they didn't have their daughter on the campgrounds, but since Zoey's mother Kimberly and Reed Cooper were there as well, they brought her along.

All of the employees gushed over the little one-year-old. Jules had spent many hours with the little girl, sometimes even babysitting her when Zoey and Dylan wanted a night out. So naturally, Paige reached for her and sat in her lap while everyone talked.

The girl dribbled all over Jules's fingers and sucked on her bottle and then fell asleep in her arms.

Jules wanted to stay right there for the rest of the morning, but duty called. The email had been sent from Brett's account.

If anything went down, Brett figured he should take the fall, since he was head of security.

When Jules finally reluctantly handed Paige over to Dylan and returned to the front desk, Beth was waving her to hurry up and answer the other ringing phone.

After answering a few questions about bookings, Jules blocked out the dates, took the credit card number for deposit, and then hung up.

Beth had just hung up the phone as well.

"It's been crazy. Booking after booking." Beth did a little booty dance. "We're back, bitches." She high-fived Jules.

"Nothing negative yet about the Tribberton video?" Jules asked.

"No, let's check online." Beth pulled out her phone and went to social media. "Holy shit." Beth showed her the screen.

The video had gone viral on several social media platforms. Some had even dubbed music to Lisa's fall into the water, titling the video "Karen gets what she deserves." Others had compared her theatrics to a couple of terrible actor moments in movies. There were news reports, which they watched in between the calls.

Then, just before lunch, they noticed a few videos that highlighted Damion in them. Someone had slowed down and zoomed in to the part of him climbing the ladder out of the water. The way his white camp shirt had stuck to his skin. How he'd shaken the water drops off his hair. Even though the images were grainy, people were asking who he was and, more important, if he was single.

One video zoomed in and played sexy music, then added a woman biting her lip while watching him. "Damn, sign me up for swimming lessons." She wiggled her eyebrows at the camera.

Jules felt her body heat. *Yeah, I know how you feel sister. But hands off.*

They decided to eat lunch with everyone else that day, so they could discuss how things were progressing. When Damion walked in, Beth whistled and cheered.

Jules knew that he'd found out about the videos because he actually blushed.

"Yeah, yeah." He shook his head. "Hungry?" he asked Jules.

"Is she ever," Beth taunted.

"Get a boyfriend," Damion joked back with Beth.

"I'm trying, but nobody looks as good wet as you do." Beth leaned on the counter and ran her eyes up and down Damion.

"Put your eyeballs back in their sockets," Jules joked, knowing Beth was just teasing Damion. Beth had a thing for Aaron, though she was still mixed up with her ex. From what Jules understood, it was very sticky.

As they walked towards the dining room, Beth beatboxed a sexy beat. Damion laughed.

"I'm never going to live this down. If I would've known that I'd get this reaction, I would have had Brett cut that bit out."

"I think the video has done what it was intended to do," Jules said.

"Yeah," Damion nodded.

But the second they stepped into the employees dining room, they were greeted with jeers and catcalls.

Damion groaned and took her hand and almost walked out.

"No, I want to hear what others have found out," she pleaded. "Can you manage to deal with being the center of attention for a few moments? I'm sure they'll bore of it soon enough."

Damion sighed and nodded, then allowed her to pull him to the food line.

She had been so preoccupied with Paige that morning, she'd barely touched her food, and now she was starving.

Today's top menu item was Isaac's famous grilled cheese sandwiches. They were nothing like the grilled cheeses she grew up with or made for herself. For starters, the things were bigger than her head and made with at least six different kinds of cheese. You could get them with different proteins too—ham, turkey, bacon—along with tomatoes, jalapenos, and even her favorite, avocados. You name it, Isaac would put it in.

Since she knew she could never eat a full one, she convinced Damion to split one with her.

Normally, everyone would sit at their own tables, breaking up into smaller groups. But today they had pushed all the tables together and were all talking over one another.

Damion found them two chairs and pushed them up to the giant table.

When they sat down, Dean make a comment about Damion and the videos.

Damion's comeback stopped all the jeering.

"If you don't knock it off, I'm going to secretly create a River Camps calendar with every single one of you on it. There isn't a person here who is safe from my spy cameras." He looked around the tables.

"You know, that's not a bad idea." This came from Elle. "What?" she said when everyone turned to her. "Of course, it would be a voluntary thing." She shrugged. "We could sell it in the gift shop. Maybe have the proceeds go to the police fund or the firemen's fund."

"What about the women's shelter in town?" someone suggested.

For the next few minutes, she and Damion ate while everyone else plotted and joked about a River Camps calendar.

"You did that on purpose?" she said to Damion.

"It was your idea. You mentioned it the other night. I just..."—he waved slightly— "got the ball rolling. And the conversation away from me."

"Yes, but I never planned on telling everyone about the idea." She sighed.

"It was a good one." He took her hand. "If you want, I will give you full credit." He opened his mouth, but she laughed and quickly covered it with her hands.

"No, thank you." She laughed. "You can keep the credit for this one."

He shrugged and went back to eating.

The group's conversation grew quiet when someone went to Lisa Tribberton's social media page and saw the live video she was posting.

Everyone listened as the woman half-heartedly explained what was in the video. She actually blamed Zoey, once again. Then she said, her eyes full of tears, that Damion wouldn't leave her alone. That he was harassing her.

The woman looked crazed. Off. Desperate.

"The video doesn't show what happened before. The man's hands were all over me. He wouldn't let me go. Then that woman stepped in and, because she owns like one-fifth of the tacky camp, she starts yelling and pushing me. I was only defending myself." Lisa sniffled. "My husband wasn't there. He couldn't defend me. We're thinking of suing the camp." Here her eyes dried up. "That place should be closed down. It's a known fact that Zoey Costas had an abortion. The Costas are baby killers. Each and every one of them. They probably sell drugs that caused her to lose her baby."

"She fucked up now," Liam said getting everyone's attention. "Defamation is no joke." He touched Elle's shoulder. "I'm just going to slip out and make a call." He winked at her.

"Go get 'em, honey," Elle said. "I'm going to finish your cheese sandwich. Babies are hungry."

"Can you believe that woman?" Jules asked Damion.

"Yes." He nodded to Brett. "Go ahead and initiate plan B."

"We have a plan B?" she asked, looking between the pair.

Brett smiled. "Yes, we do." He got up and disappeared through the doors.

"You're going to release the whole video?" she asked.

"Up until Zoey passes out in my arms. We don't want her to have to relive the rest," he said softly. "But the truth is there for anyone to see."

"Why do people like her get such a big following?" Jules asked after looking at the woman's social media page. "She has three point eight million followers. I have ten." She showed him her screen. Jules scrolled through her timeline and then stopped. "She has a couple videos here of before the incident." She played one.

Lisa was sitting by the pool in a barely there bikini, a drink in her hand as she talked about how wonderful this little camp was and how they were comping her and her husband's stay for the entire trip. Then she stilled and bit her lip. "Yowzer. Look what just strolled in." The camera flipped and Damion walked into the pool area and took the net and started cleaning the pool. "I think I've found my next boy toy. Stay tuned followers. I'm going to bag me a real live pool-boy toy." The camera flipped again, and Lisa wiggled her eyebrows before the video ended.

"There are three more of those," someone said.

"She was basically stalking you," Carter added, holding up his phone. "In each of these, she talks about winning you like you were some sort of prize."

"If she only knew," Dean joked and got a few laughs.

"I can't believe she's not smart enough to pull these down," Jules said.

"Quick, do a download," someone suggested. "Proof."

"I'd better get back to work," Jules said a while later. "The calls have been nonstop."

"I'll walk you." Damion dumped their trash and put their trays away. Then he took her hand and they started walking back down the hallway. He stopped and pulled her into his arms and kissed her. "I don't care what others think of me. Only you." He rested his forehead against hers. "All this attention is nerve-wracking and embarrassing. Plan B should clear things up."

"I've seen the whole video. Trust me when I say that the attention on you will only get better. You stood up for Zoey, a pregnant woman, your boss. Then you jumped into the water and saved a woman that didn't deserve it, in my opinion. Follow that up with that ladder climbing and wet clingy shirt." She ran her hands over his chest and smiled. "Yeah, that bit we'll have to replay later tonight, when we're alone." She bit her bottom lip. "Then you hoisted Zoey up as if she weighed nothing. Trust me when I say that a man carrying a woman is one of the sexiest things ever. Every woman's fantasy come true." She shook her head and took a deep breath. "I'm just thankful I got my hands on you first." She lifted on her toes and kissed him, then laughed when he lifted her up and spun her around.

"Tonight," he growled softly next to her lips. "I'll show you how much I want you."

Someone cleared their throat, then said, "Get a room."

Jules didn't even bother looking to see who it was. Her eyes were locked on Damion's. She wanted so badly to tell him how she felt about him. Right there in the hallway, feet from where she worked. But she held back. There had to be a better time, a better place.

She swallowed the words she was about to say, her feelings, and took a step away from him.

"I was going to swing by my parents tonight. My mother said there was some news on my dad." Her mother had texted her earlier that morning a very encrypted message.

"Want me to tag along?" he offered.

"No, it's okay. I know you're tired. Go home, rest. I'll be home before dark." She kissed him again. "Want me to pick us up some dinner along the way? Li's is right by my parents. Feel like eggrolls and noodles?" She knew they were among his favorite foods.

He smiled. "Sounds good. But later, we're going to finish this." He waved a finger between them.

"Promise?" she purred, then turned and went back to work.

# CHAPTER TWENTY-FIVE

There was so much that Damion expected to happen after the video, the full video, was released. What he hadn't expected was an influx of personal attention, social media, email, and even messages. His name had been leaked. Someone he knew had connected him with the video.

His social media accounts were flooded with new follows and friend requests, all of which he ignored.

He doubted it was anyone at the camp. It wasn't as if he was trying to hide. After all, everyone know who Zoey and Lisa were. Aaron's name had yet to be connected to the video, though, which meant most likely someone had gone through the camp's employee roster and tagged him. Being one of the four black people working at the camp, he was probably easy to find.

Then again, he knew Aaron's past was... guarded. Maybe he was a little harder to pin down than Damion had been?

By the time he walked into the apartment, he had shut off his phone. He was tired of all the messages. He'd sent Jules a message telling her he was going to shut down for a while.

He had hit the gym with the guys before leaving the campgrounds. Since he knew Jules would be stopping off and grabbing dinner, he held off on eating anything when he got home. Instead, he landed face-first on the couch and fell fast asleep.

He woke to someone pounding on the door. There were three loud bangs, then the door was busted in as a group of men in all black stormed inside, shouting at him to get down.

At first, he thought it was a dream. But then he was shoved into the sofa, his face held into one of Jules's brightly colored pillows as things were shouted at him.

"Are you alone?"

"Do you have any weapons?"

"Stop resisting."

He lay there, completely lax as his body was forced into an uncomfortable position.

"Answer the questions," someone shouted in his ear loudly enough that his ears rang.

"I'm alone. No, no weapons," he said.

Then he was jerked up. "Damion Wells?"

"Yes," he said, blinking as a bright light was shown directly in his eyes.

"Are there any drugs or weapons on the premises?"

"No," he said, blinking. "Has something happened to Jules?" He glanced around, hoping to figure out what time it was. Had he slept longer than he'd expected? Shouldn't she be home by now? Worry flooded his mind. So much so he was no longer listening to the questions yelled at him.

Finally, after what seemed like hours had passed and a million questions had been yelled at him, the energy in the room settled.

Damion recognized one of the officers who had come to talk to Zoey shortly after she'd lost the baby. Larry walked right up to Damion and stuck his face in his.

"You've done it now, boy. We've got you," Larry spat.

"May I ask what this is all about?" Damion asked, trying to remain calm.

It wasn't Larry who answered, but another officer who stepped forward. "We had a tip that you personally, mentioned by name, were dealing drugs out of this apartment. That you were supplying guests and employees at River Camps with drugs."

Larry got back in his face. "So, I'll ask you again, are there any drugs in the apartment?"

"No. I don't do or deal drugs." Damion sighed and knew instantly what was happening. "You've got some bad info. I'm wagering your tip came from all the attention I've been getting today after the video was released."

Larry's eyes narrowed. "Do you think you're a hotshot? Above the law?"

If Damion wasn't sitting on his sofa, handcuffed and not making a move, he was pretty sure Larry would be striking out at him. Instead, Damion remained calm and spoke as if talking to a wounded animal.

"No, sir. I don't. I believe someone is striking out to hurt me and the camp because they are hurt or just sick. I don't deal drugs. Never have. Never will. Search the place. I'll cooperate fully."

It was then that Jules rushed in the front door. "What is going on here?" Her eyes moved from Damion to Larry to all the other officers searching through her things.

Two hours later, Damion sat on the same sofa across from his parents, Owen Costas, and Steinbeck, the lawyer who had gone to the station with Zoey. The lawyer was looking over the warrant he'd been given that had allowed the police to search the apartment.

Jules was holding his hand, and he could feel her vibrating with anger.

His parents looked worried and angry at the same time. This was his first brush with the law. He'd never even been pulled over or gotten a speeding ticket, but he'd been prepared for it. Every black man he knew was.

"They said they were going to search the camp," Jules said with a worried tone.

"They will have to obtain a warrant first," the lawyer answered. "They haven't filed for one yet. I'll keep on top of it. Most likely, it was a scare tactic."

"We all know what this is about. The Tribbertons are lashing out," Jules said.

"Do you have proof?" Steinbeck asked.

"No," Jules sank back on the sofa. "They busted my door in. Our neighbors are going to look at us like we did something wrong." Damion wrapped his arm around her. She leaned her head against his. "It doesn't matter what they think. I'm just thankful you're okay. Things could have ended much worse."

His arms wrapped harder around her. He knew. Knew all the other black people who hadn't been so lucky. If he had fought back, even for a second, things might have turned. His eyes met his father's and he understood he was thinking the same thing.

He was thankful he'd been asleep. Maybe if he'd been awake, without the cops yelling police, which thankfully, even in his fuzzy mind, had registered, things could have turned bad.

"Let's just get through this," he told the room. "They didn't find anything, nor will they. I've been clean my entire life. Haven't even smoked a joint. My parents' influence." He smiled over at his parents.

"Well, they aren't charging you with anything. Yet. Someone is out to tarnish your reputation since the video of the raid went viral moments after. They targeted you. Personally," Steinbeck said.

"Do we know who posted the video? Who posted it first, that is," Damion's father asked.

"No, but we can work on it," Steinbeck answered.

"If it was the Tribbertons, what can we do?" Jules asked.

"We've already got a defamation case against Lisa Tribberton for slander in her online video. She screwed up when she posted it to not only to her timeline, but also to her husband's business's social media pages too," Owen answered.

"For now, let me work a couple different angles," Steinbeck said, standing up.

"I've cleared it with everyone. The two of you are welcome to stay at River Camps. River Cabin is all yours for as long as you want it, if you want it." Owen stood up along with the lawyer.

River Cabin was the largest of all the cabins. Zoey and Scarlett's mother, Kimberly, used to live there. Before that, it was the original home on the land before Elle's grandfather purchased the land and turned it into a camp.

It normally wasn't rented out like the other cabins. Mostly because it could sleep six people and was farther off the pathways.

Jules looked up at him. "It's up to you," he told her. "I've only got four boxes of things to move," he reminded her with a smile.

She sighed and then turned to Owen. "Thanks, I'll let you know in the morning. Something tells me this won't be the last time something like this happens. On River Camps, at least we'd have the added security."

Owen nodded. "It's yours if you need it."

Damion stood up and shook the other men's hands, then watched them leave.

His father stood up. "We can stick around and help you try and fix the door," his dad offered.

"Don't bother. The building's got maintenance coming soon to replace it," Damion said.

"Do you need help cleaning up?" his mother asked Jules.

"No, I'm going to leave it all until the morning. I'm hungry and tired," Jules answered.

"Want us to get you something to eat?" his mother asked.

"No, I stopped off and got us some dinner. It's in the car. Thanks," Jules said.

His mother walked across the room and hugged Jules. "I'm so sorry you're going through this. We're here if you need anything."

"Thanks."

After his parents left, he turned to Jules and just held onto her. "I am so sorry," he said into her hair.

"For?" She jerked back and looked up at him.

"If I hadn't moved in with you, your—"

"Don't you dare," she said, dropping her arms from around him. "This is not on you. This is on them." She pointed to the door just as a maintenance guy stepped up and knocked.

"I've got a new door," the man said, looking at the shattered pieces of the door the police had broken in.

"Thank you," Jules said.

"It'll take me a while." The guy looked at the hinges of the door.

"I'll go get the food out of my car," Jules told him.

He nodded, not knowing what to say to her. This was his fault. Her things had been gone through, not his. His four boxes of clothes and personal belongings had gone untouched while all of her things had been handled and tossed around.

After Jules stepped out, Damion bent down and started picking up items the police had thrown around the apartment.

"Yeah, the cops never clean up after themselves," the maintenance guy said as he started unscrewing the broken hinges. "They raided my place a few years ago after my ex called in that I was selling drugs. In truth, she was pissed that I got full custody of our daughter." He shrugged. "She's an addict who is now living on the streets in Seattle."

Damion set a picture of Jules and her parents down on the end table where it normally sat.

"The truth is, anyone can make a call and get someone to do harm to you or your reputation," the guy added. "I had to go to court to get my daughter back." He shook his head. "But you get through it." He finished removing the hinges.

Just then, Jules came back, a bag of Chinese food in her hands.

She had pretty much held it together when the police were there and when Owen showed up with the lawyer after he'd made a call. Now, however, he could tell she'd gone out to her car and had cried. Her eyes and the tip of her nose were red.

Walking over, he took the food from her hands. "We're going to go eat this outside. You good?" he asked the guy.

"Sure thing. I'm really sorry this happened to you, Julie," the man said.

"Thanks, Rodrigo." Jules smiled.

Damion walked over and grabbed a couple of beers from the fridge, then led her down the stairs and out front. There was a small park across from the apartment complex.

During the day, there would be dogs running freely in the chained grassy area. Now, however, they were alone and sat on the bench and ate their cold food in silence.

"I know you don't want to hear an apology," he said once his stomach stopped growling angrily. "But I'm going to give you one. It'll make this weight on my chest feel lighter."

She set her chopsticks down and turned to him slightly. "Okay, but it's not necessary."

He moved his container of food aside, then took her hand. The truth was, he'd been thinking about this since the moment he'd seen her standing in her doorway, looking worried and concerned.

He should have prepped her. Prepared her for what it was going to be like being in a relationship with a black man in the south.

"I should have warned you," he started.

She stopped him by lifting her hand in the air. "First off, if you start the whole bullshit that this happened because you're black, you can stop right there. This had nothing—nothing—to do with the color of your skin. This was because you were a man who stood up for himself. Lisa Tribberton didn't hit on you because you were black. She hit on you because she looks at men as toys that she can buy with her husband's money. And when she can't get her hands on what she wants, she lashes out like a child. Her videos are proof of that," Jules said firmly. "The police would have raided anyone's apartment with the tip they received."

Damion thought back to the maintenance guy's story. Sure, he was Hispanic, but yeah, Jules was right. This wasn't about the color of his skin. At least not this time.

"Fair enough." He nodded. "So then I'll just apologize for being so damn sexy that crazy women end up starting shit over me." He smiled and relaxed when she smiled back at him. "If you want, we can move into River Cabin."

She shook her head. "No, this is our home for now. I won't be run off like we did anything wrong." She squeezed his hand. "But I am going to do some posting of my own." She pulled out her camera. "The good kind that will drive Lisa Tribberton nuts. We're going to show her that we are stronger than her tricks. We're going to prove to her that nothing she says or does can get us down." She held up her phone and after finding the latest funny filter trending on social media, filmed them laughing and joking as their faces turned into animals. At the end of the clip, Jules added:

"This one goes out to our friend, Lisa, whom we want to thank for an entertaining evening. Bite me, bitch." Jules shut the camera off.

"Damn, girl. Remind me to never cross you." He kissed her.

## CHAPTER TWENTY-SIX

The following day, Damion talked Jules into going into work while he cleaned the apartment. He had the day scheduled off, and she had a full day's work planned. She was working that evening's themed dinner party for extra tips. Besides, the theme was an evening under the sea, which was her favorite.

She tucked her outfit for dinner in her bag and headed out to work, leaving Damion to clean up the mess the police had made. They had cleaned their bedroom and bathroom last night since she wasn't able to sleep in such a mess.

She worried about leaving him home alone after the previous night. What other tricks did Lisa have up her sleeve? She knew she probably shouldn't have antagonized her with the video, but hell, she had to do something.

When she checked her phone after arriving at work, her video had more than a million views and she had a million new followers. Most had even gone through her old videos of the camp, the funny videos she made with Beth or one of the other employees, her parents, Tutu, and even the videos she and

Damion had made during their relationship, starting back with that first weekend sail.

Most of the comments were nice, friendly, fun. There were a handful of hateful ones that she didn't even bother reading. She either deleted or reported those comments.

"Girl, you're kicking it," Beth said when she came in. "Have you seen all those comments?" Beth set her stuff down and then walked over to hug her. "Sorry about the raid. Do you need anything?"

"No, we're good." Jules smiled.

"Posting that video of you and Damion was wicked. Nice slap in Lisa's face. If she's the one behind all this."

"Oh, I'm sure she is."

"Did you see what she posted this morning?" Jules took out her phone and showed Beth the short video that Lisa had made with her husband. It appeared to be an older video, since her hair was a lot longer and darker colored. Her husband appeared to be younger too. The happy couple was lounging in Italy on a private island resort and looking very much in love. Lisa did a voice-over explaining how strong her and Joe's relationship was. How they didn't need other people in their lives to be happy.

"A weak attempt if I've ever seen one." Beth shook her head. "My ex played games like that with me for a while."

Beth didn't normally talk about her ex. Jules didn't even know his name. She'd asked once, but Beth just said it was "he who shall not be named," so she'd left it alone after that.

For most of the day, the gossip carried on. She sat with Elle, Hannah, and Aubrey during lunch, and they all scrolled through social media or articles that had been released about the camp. Only one article from all of the press visits came back with any hint of negativity.

It was the blond woman who had asked Zoey about her miscarriage. The article went into a crazy conspiracy about how the camp provides not only drugs to its guests but morning-after pills. The author of the article, a Nikki Fields, went on to claim that was the real cause of Zoey's miscarriage on the infamous video.

"It's one article," Elle started to say but then Aubrey gasped.

"Nikki Fields is Lisa Tribberton's sister. I thought she looked familiar." Aubrey showed them a picture of the two women hugging with identical smiles. "No wonder she was a bitch."

"That totally makes sense," Jules said. "Can we use this to expose her article as a fraud?"

"I'll get on it." Hannah started to get up, but then sat back down. Her face changed from determination to worry. "I... I think my water just broke."

Everyone jumped up at once. Jules shot off the group emergency text. After Zoey's surprise baby-shower birth, they'd created a group message. She sent the "Hannah's water just broke in the dining room and it's happening now" text to everyone who needed to know.

Then she helped Hannah out to the front of the building where Liam was waiting in a golf cart to take her to the parking lot. Owen was working in his Destin office that morning and would meet them at the hospital.

Jules, unfortunately, had to go back to work since all of the Wildflowers were now heading to the hospital.

After the excitement of lunch, the rest of the day dragged on. Everyone was glued to their phones, waiting for news of the new arrival.

She changed into her sequined mermaid top and skirt after work and stood behind the bar serving drinks, but her mind was on her friend, waiting for news of another baby's arrival.

What she wanted more than anything was to be at the

hospital with her other friends, waiting to get the news first-hand. To visit and hold her friend's son herself.

She'd always loved babies. Had always dreamed of having a couple herself. She didn't care if they were boys, girls, or one of each.

As she thought about it that day, she realized that, when she thought about her children, she was certain they would look like Damion.

She'd been building up the nerve to tell him how she felt. But then things had gotten busy with the Tribberton mess and the social media attacks.

Maybe tonight was the night? She glanced down at her silly attire and sighed. Okay, maybe not. Maybe they could take another long weekend sail? Or she could arrange a dinner on the beach? Someplace romantic.

Someone sat in front of her at the bar, and she realized she'd been so preoccupied with her thoughts that Lisa had gotten this close to her without her alarm going off.

"Well, well, who would have thought that such a little insignificant girl like you would cause so much trouble," Lisa purred.

Lisa was wearing a sleek black dress that hugged all of her perfectly proportionate curves. Jules instantly felt like a child in her sequined outfit.

"I thought you and your husband were banned from River Camps?" Jules said, glancing around.

"Oh, Joe's not with me tonight. I'm here with someone... else." She smiled as her eyes ran up and down Jules.

"Why are you here?" Jules asked.

Lisa's smile grew. "You're smarter than you look. I think Joe underestimated you. He was under the assumption you were just a floozy. A skirt to chase." She shifted. "A glass of your best chardonnay first. Not the crappy stuff you're serving everyone else," she warned as Jules moved to get the drink. Not that she wanted to wait on the woman, but she wanted to get to the bottom of why she'd come back here. Why she was making a point to hunt Jules out. Or had she? As Jules opened and then poured the wine, she questioned Lisa's motives. Did she know Jules would be working that night?

Jules had posted a video of her in her outfit talking about tonight's event on her social media. It was a gut instinct to brag about her work. She loved the camp, loved the job and the people. Naturally, she would want to showcase it in her life.

Okay, so was Lisa here for her?

Turning, she set the glass down in front of the woman.

"Why?" she asked again.

Lisa took a sip and then made a face as if she'd tasted something foul. Jules knew full well the wine she'd served the woman was top notch. One of their most expensive bottles. She had every intention of charging the woman for it.

"I'm here to tell you that this stops here. The little game you are playing." Lisa shifted her gaze slightly. "Trust me when I say you are way out of your league."

"What are you talking about?" Jules wanted to hear every word of what she was threatening directly from the woman's mouth.

Lisa's blond eyebrows rose slightly and for a split second, Jules saw a hit of madness in the woman's eyes. "Fine, let me dumb it down for you. I will squash you, personally and professionally. I know all about your family." She smiled. "And I will use their lives to my benefit to stop you."

"Stop me from what?" Jules shook her head, unsure. At first, Jules had believed this was just about calling the woman out in the video the night before. Now, however, the way she was talking, Jules was unsure.

Lisa's eyes narrowed. "You are to never talk about me or my

husband again. Anywhere. You are to remove that tacky little video immediately. Plus, you'll get your little friends"—she glanced around as if expecting them to pop out of the shadows magically— "to stop their attacks on me and my husband's business. I expect them to make formal statements that confirm everything I have said about this camp."

Jules laughed. "That's not going to happen."

The woman's eyes narrowed. "Oh, I think it will. I have all the power here. You are nothing. This place is nothing." The woman's voice had risen slightly. Jules saw Brett start heading towards them.

Jules was fully aware of the woman's tactics. She was trying to gain attention. Behave as if she was a victim. After all, she'd not only watched the video of what had happened at the boat dock more than a hundred times, she'd watched every video the woman had posted on social media. There were so many Karen moments where she demanded something from someone all while berating or tearing them down.

"I believe you're the one who started all this," Jules said calmly as Brett was stopped by someone halfway across the room.

Jules's statement seemed to piss Lisa off. She jerked quickly and gripped Jules's arm. Her long fingernails dug into Jules's skin, no doubt leaving marks.

"Do you really think you can go up against me?" Lisa's eyes moved over Jules again. "The lot of you will stop harassing me and my husbands' business or we will sue."

"Aren't you and your husbands' business getting sued already?" Jules said with a slight smile of satisfaction.

The woman's words had confirmed one more thing. Lisa wasn't here necessarily for her. She just happened to be the only one here because everyone else in Lisa's scope was currently at the hospital, waiting for Hannah and Owen's new baby to arrive.

"That will stop too. I know all about your friends' lives. They won't want what I have exposed, and I will make sure to rip their quaint little lives wide fucking open." Lisa's tone turned strained.

Jules could tell she was nearing the end of her composure. The woman's eyes had even changed color. Instead of a calm blue, they were now almost fiery turquoise. Her fingernails dug even further into Jules's skin.

"Release me," Jules said calmly. "It wouldn't do you any good to cause another scene. After all, there are cameras everyone on the campus."

Lisa jerked her hand away from Jules's arm just as Brett rushed up beside her.

"You're done here," Brett said, taking hold of the woman.

"This is your one and only warning," Lisa said to her as Brett tried to get her to leave.

"That'll be thirty-two dollars. For the wine," Jules added with a slight nod.

Lisa's eyes narrowed as she jerked her arm free of Brett's or at least tried to. "Charge it to—"

"I'm sorry, all non-guests have to pay in either cash or charge," Jules said peacefully.

Lisa glanced around and wiggled her finger at an older gentleman. Jules couldn't remember the man's name, but she knew he was a guest.

"Is there a problem here?" the man asked Lisa.

"She's leaving," Brett said firmly.

"Byron, pay the woman for one of the worst glasses of wine I've ever tasted. I'm going to powder my nose," Lisa said, as if it was her decision to be tossed out.

Byron watched Brett walk Lisa out the door then turned and picked up the glass and took a sip. "That's good," he said, nodding. "Give me two more glasses of it. My wife is going to love this."

Jules wondered if it would piss Lisa off knowing that she was, in a way, responsible for her biggest tip of the evening.

When she walked into the apartment after work, she was happily surprised to see the place cleaner than it had ever been. Damion had set her little kitchen table and had two candles lit with a bottle of wine chilling.

He was wearing a nice pair of pants and a button-up shirt.

"What's all this?" she asked, tossing down her bag.

"I figured I owed you a dinner." He took her hand and led her to the table. Then he pulled her chair out for her and she took a seat.

Damion disappeared into the kitchen and brought back a covered plater and set it in front of her. Then he set the other in front of him and took a seat.

"I hope you like it. Isaac gave me the recipe," he said when she lifted the lid.

"You cooked this?" she said, looking down at the beautiful chicken cacciatore with two slices of garlic toast.

"Yes," he said as he poured her a glass of red wine.

She picked up her fork and took a bite and melted. The rich taste of the red sauce, the zip and tingle of the seasoning. Closing her eyes, she allowed the smell, the taste, the warmth to spread through her.

"You could give Isaac a run for his money. I'd say it's better than his." She took another bite.

Somehow, Damion had known exactly what she'd needed that night.

Reaching across the table, she took his hand and as she opened her mouth to tell him how she felt, they said the three words at the same time.

Her eyes locked with his and then they laughed.

"Damn, I wanted to say it first," he joked.

"It's a tie." She smiled. "I like it better this way."

He walked over to her, lifted her to her feet, and kissed her.

"So do I," he said against her lips.

"I should be wearing silk, not sequins." She laughed.

"I like it. My little mermaid." He looked down at her. "I feel like a prince when I'm around you."

She cupped his face and brought him back down to kiss her. "You are my prince."

# CHAPTER TWENTY-SEVEN

James Oliver Costas was born at a quarter past one in the morning. He weighed all of six pounds, eight ounces. And according to his father, he screamed bloody murder until he got his first meal.

"With those lungs, I'm surprised he didn't wake the entire hospital wing," Owen said, as he looked down at the small bundle in his arms.

Damion had always thought that newborns were ugly. They were usually bright red or pale white with pudgy little faces and eyes that were just little slits. Not to mention the lack of hair on their shiny cones.

But he had to admit, James was the exception. The kid was downright cute. He had a mass of dark curls on top of his head. His wide eyes seemed to look all around the room and follow whoever was talking. But he returned his gaze to his father and mother each time they spoke.

"How are things at work?" Hannah asked Jules.

Everyone else had left the family sometime earlier that day.

Hannah and baby James were scheduled to be released to

go home the following morning. Everyone else was back at work. Jules had the day off and he'd gotten Dean to fill in for him on his day off.

They had stopped and purchased the new family a small gift before stepping into the hospital.

Damion really liked shopping for the baby. He kept thinking of what their kids would look like while he checked out all the little outfits.

Thinking about kids had him thinking about marriage. He already knew Jules was the woman he wanted to spend the rest of his life with. What he didn't know was how soon was too soon to ask her to marry him.

They had technically been dating for less than a month. But they had known one another for almost six years. He knew more about her than he knew about anyone else he'd been with before. And he'd dated Regina for over a year.

How did he go from where they were now to where he wanted them to be?

He'd planned last night's dinner just on a whim. But in the back of his mind, he'd known that it was past time he told her how he felt. It had been a happy surprise when she'd told him at the same time.

It was the first time he'd said those word to any woman other than his mother and grandmother. He meant them more than he imagined he ever could. What he felt for Jules went beyond what he'd imagined love was.

"Here," Owen said, walking towards Jules. "You can hold him."

Jules easily took the small bundle in her hands, and he watched tears form in her eyes as she looked down at James.

"Hi." Jules smiled down at the baby. "You don't know it yet, but I'm going to be your favorite person." She leaned down and whispered, "I'm going to spoil you rotten."

Damion smiled and felt his heart melt. Then Jules moved towards him, and he looked down at the tiny bundle and felt his heart completely liquify.

"We heard from the lawyer this morning," Owen said. "The defamation case against the Tribbertons is moving along. We're set to go before a judge next week. I'll need both of you there. The lawyer will be contacting you later today."

"Sure," he said quickly.

"Oh, that reminds me." Jules walked over and sat down, still holding James. "Lisa showed up last night at dinner. She was a guest of Byron Gibbons."

"What?" He frowned. "Why didn't you tell me last night?" he asked, and then he remembered how dinner and what came after went.

Jules's eyebrows shot up and he knew she was thinking the same thing.

"What happened?" he asked quickly.

"She pretty much threatened me." She shifted the baby in her arms. "And gave me these marks before Brett kicked her out."

Owen walked over and carefully took James from her arms so they could all see red marks on her arms clearly from fingernails.

"We need to call the police," Damion started.

"No, I'm fine," Jules said with a shake of her head. "The woman is crazy. Let's let the case move forward."

"Still, it does need to be noted." Owen handed James to Hannah, then walked over and snapped a few pictures of the marks with his phone. "Sending these to the lawyer. I'm sure there is footage of the incident. Why didn't Brett tell us?"

"I'm sure he didn't want to disturb you. He told me he'd file a report and already took pictures of my arm last night. I was thankful I was behind the bar so she couldn't do too much damage to me."

"What did she say?" Hannah asked, shifting the baby in her arms.

"She warned me to drop the games. I think she attacked me because everyone else was here. I was the only one working last night that she knew."

"I'm going to have Brett send out a bulletin to all the employees to keep their eyes out for them and make sure neither of them is allowed on the grounds again," Owen said as he dialed his phone.

"Next time you see her, let me know," Damion said, helping Jules stand.

"We should let the family rest." Jules motioned as James started fussing.

"It's his lunchtime." Hannah smiled. "I'm a mom," she added with a giggle.

"Congratulations," Jules and he said at the same time.

After leaving the new family to rest, he drove them to one of their favorite beachfront restaurants. They were an hour early for lunch, which thankfully allowed them to beat most of the tourists.

They were seated at an outside table under large awnings. Jules ordered a fruity alcoholic drink and he stuck with an iced tea.

Jules took a picture of them holding up their drinks in front of the white sand and the teal waters and posted it.

"We're not official until we link ourselves in our accounts," he said, pulling out his phone. "There," he said after a switching his social media to show that he was in a relationship with Jules.

Jules laughed and did the same. "Making it official." She held up her glass.

He tapped his tea to her drink.

They had just gotten their appetizers when a crazed-looking Lisa came barging through the patio doors of the restaurant. Damion saw her first since Jules's back was to the door.

The woman glanced around and, upon spotting him, marched towards them.

Her normally sleek hair and clothing were in disarray. Her mass of wild curls flowed in the light breeze that was coming off the water, making her appear even crazier.

"You!" she screamed. "You ruined everything."

Damion stood, but it wasn't him she was talking to. It was Jules. Jules jerked around to see who was yelling at her.

It happened so quickly, Damion had no time to brace or to react.

Lisa raised her hand, and a glint of sun bouncing off the gun blinded him momentarily.

Then he moved without a single thought in his head. Gut reaction. Instinct.

Everyone around them gasped. Someone screamed. A loud bang echoed out over the white sands as happy people played in the surf and sun.

He was slightly surprised to hear several other shots ring out, after he and Jules hit the ground.

More screams. The sound of people running. Someone stepped on his leg. Kicked the chair. Tables were turned over as people ran.

He must have bumped his head at one point since his ears were ringing so loud that he couldn't hear anything.

Out of the corner of his eye, he watched a large man in a tank top tackle Lisa from behind. When their bodies hit the ground, Damion realized it was too late. The last bullet had been for herself. Her blue eyes stared back less than five feet away from him, unseeing, as blood oozed out of the missing back of her head.

"Damion?" Jules gasped. "You're bleeding."

He was shifted off Jules's body and pushed to lay with his shoulders against the wood planks of the deck. He started up at the sky-blue awning over them as his shirt was ripped away and clean rags were held against his chest. There were more screams to call for help.

It was all so... silly. Everyone was so panicked. They didn't have to be. This was peaceful. There was no pain. Just numbness.

Then Jules's face lowered to his. Her tear-filled eyes locked with his own.

Damn. He had something else to do. He couldn't go yet. The moment that realization hit him, so did the pain.

Every nerve in his body suddenly came alive. Shooting pain radiated from his armpit and chest area. His knee was throbbing as well as the back of his head.

"Jules, are you okay?" he asked through a cough.

"Don't move," she said, and suddenly everything was shifting. Gone was the blue awning, replaced by bright lights and a distant humming that sounded oddly familiar.

His only focus was to make sure Jules was okay. Her face came and went several times. He saw her mouth move, watched her eyes pool with tears.

He tried to reach out to her. To tell her what he needed to. To make her his forever. To link their lives together forever. But he kept slipping up. His mind kept getting fuzzy and then everything went dark.

# CHAPTER TWENTY-EIGHT

Jules paced in the lobby of the hospital. The very hospital they had just left over an hour ago. She was still covered in Damion's blood. The image of Lisa shooting at them and then turning the gun on herself and watching that pretty face, the one Jules had instantly been jealous of, explode was locked in her mind.

What the hell had happened? How had she known where they were? Had the woman seriously been stalking them on social media? Why? Why would she shoot at Jules and Damion?

It was obvious she was aiming for Jules. Damion hadn't been the target.

Jules closed her eyes and swayed slightly, remembering seeing the dark red blood ooze from his chest. "God," she cried out.

"Jules?" Someone's arms wrapped around her. Jules looked up into a face and it took her brain a moment to click into gear. It was Owen.

"What's happened?" Owen asked, moving her to a chair.

"Lisa... shot Damion," she cried out.

"Jesus," Owen gasped. "Is he..."

"Surgery." She buried her face into Owen's chest, gripping his shirt with her blood-soaked hands. "She shot him in the chest and then killed herself."

"Jesus Christ," Owen said softly. "Are you okay?"

She nodded, not trusting her voice. "I... have to call..." Who? She wasn't thinking clearly, couldn't think about anything beyond Damion.

"We got this Jules," Owen said. "Sit. Pray." Owen took her over and sat her in a chair. Then he pulled out his phone and started making calls.

Jules closed her eyes and started praying and didn't stop until she felt hands take her own.

"We're here." It was Zoey. She was kneeling in front of Jules, tears in her eyes. Everyone else she cared about, who cared about Damion, was gathered around her.

Jules jumped up and hugged her friends, holding on tight to them as if they could possibly will the last hours away.

"Why?" everyone asked.

She heard someone say it was all over the news, but she didn't care. All she cared about was Damion. All she could think about was him. Time passed so slowly. Each heartbeat, each breath, pained her.

Lea and Brett arrived, and Lea quickly disappeared down the long hallway. Brett came up to her, knelt in front of her, and handed her a cup of coffee.

"Your favorite," he said softly.

"Thanks." She took it and was shocked at how hot it was on her chilled fingers. She hadn't even realized she'd been cold.

"I know this is tough, but you might want to hear it, so..." he started.

"Lisa is dead," she said firmly.

"Yes." Brett sighed. "So is Joe, her husband. Shot by Lisa hours, possibly days, before."

Jules let that bit sink in. The man who had aggressively flirted with her. He hadn't deserved this. Jail. But not death.

Jules swallowed. "Why?"

Brett sighed. "There's a video going around. She posted a video of her husband's murder. We'll go into it later." He cupped her hands over the coffee. "This had nothing to do with you or Damion. It was just a very sick woman lashing out. The two of you just got in her way."

Jules nodded then looked up when Lea came back.

"He's just coming out of surgery," Lea said with a smile. "He has a very good chance."

Her words didn't make Jules relax. She needed to see him. Needed to hold him. Needed to look into his eyes and see his smile. To hear his laughter.

Tears rolled down her cheeks. Her coffee was taken from her and arms wrapped around her as she cried until everything went fuzzy.

She snapped back to attention when she heard his parents talking. When had they arrived?

Wiping her eyes, she saw them standing across from her, talking quietly with her own parents. Her mother had Jules's duffel bag in her arms.

When her mother noticed her looking at her, she rushed over.

"I brought you some clothes, sweetie." Her mother knelt next to her and hugged her. "They said..." Her mother took a deep breath. "Let's go get you cleaned up."

Jules moved as a child would, unsure of each step, her mother's arms wrapped around her, along with Aubrey's.

"We got you," Aubrey said with a smile.

Instead of leaving her alone in a massive bathroom, her

mother and Aubrey helped her clean up and change into clean jeans and a T-shirt and sweatshirt. Her mother had even brought her another pair of shoes.

When they stepped back out of the bathroom, a doctor was talking with Damion's parents. Jules rushed over.

"What?" she said eagerly. "What's happened?"

The doctor turned to her and smiled. "He's out of surgery and in the ICU. He'll be waking up soon and can have one visitor at a time."

Jules reached out and gripped the man's hand as if it was a lifeline. "Thank you," she said, tears rolling down her cheeks again. Then she burst forward and hugged the stranger as if he was her best friend.

The doctor smiled at her when she finally let him go. "He's a strong man," he said, and turned and left.

Jules turned and hugged both of his parents and the three of them cried together.

Almost an hour later, Jules was shown back to where Damion was lying on a huge bed hooked up to so many machines and tubes.

Jules rushed to his side and took his hand gently in her own. She watched his eyes flutter open. Even though they were unfocused, he looked at her.

"Jules?" he croaked out in a raspy voice.

"I'm here," she cried.

"Are you... did she get you?"

"No, I wasn't shot."

"She's dead?"

"Yes." Jules sighed and some of the worry she had for Damion slipped away. "How are you feeling?"

"Numb. Tired."

"Sleep. Your parents are here. They let me come back first," she said quickly. "Everyone's here. Sleep. I love you."

"Love too." He drifted off.

She sat there, listening to the machines, his heartbeat, and the quiet for a few moments. Then she got up and let his parents take turns going back to see him.

"Why don't we take you home for a few hours so you can rest. Dr. Val says they will move him into a private room in the morning. Until then, there's nothing you can do," her mother said when she sat down again.

"No, I'm going to wait right here." The thought of leaving Damion turned her stomach.

"At least let us get you some food," her mother suggested.

It was then that Jules realized they'd left the restaurant without eating. She wanted to tell her mother that she would eat when Damion did, but she knew better. Her mother probably wouldn't rest until she had something to eat.

"A salad would be fine," she suggested.

In the next hours, people came and went. Jules had three more short visits back to the ICU before they finally moved Damion to a private room. Here, she and his parents sat up all night, watching him sleep peacefully as the machines hummed around him. Nurses came and went each hour, checking on him.

She asked questions about what they were doing, what medicines he was on. What his recovery would look like. The nurses' answers gave her and his family more hope.

With the morning light came a visit from the doctor who had performed Damion's surgery.

While they were listening to the doctor talk, Damion's eyes opened, and he called out for Jules.

"I'm right here," she said softly. "Your parents are here too. They're talking to the doctor."

The doctor came over and asked Damion a few questions.

How did he feel? Was there any pain? The man had Damion wiggle his fingers and toes.

Jules watched everything as if her own life depended on it. She hung on every word as the doctor explained how he had removed the bullet that had shattered two of Damion's ribs and lodged in his muscles and fatty tissue.

"The ribs slowed the bullet down some," the doctor said. "The bullet entered just under his arm, here." He pointed to his own armpit area. "Then traveled sideways through his muscles, grazing and shattering two ribs." He motioned over his own right chest with his pen. "Which was extremely lucky for Damion. The bullet traveled through a lot of his flesh, fat, and muscle and finally came to rest just under his pectoral muscle." He pointed to his own chest area. "All in all, one of the easier scenarios. There is plenty of tissue and muscular damage. It may be a year or two before he's back to lifting weights like he used to."

"Thanks, doc," Damion said. "When can I have something to eat?"

"If you're hungry, now. I'm going to ask that you start off slow. No hamburgers just yet."

"How about brownies?" Damion asked. Jules smiled for the first time since yesterday.

"We'll hold off until later this evening for anything that heavy," the doctor answered with a chuckle.

"I can wait until later. For now, I'll take anything. Can I sit up?" Damion asked.

The doctor walked over and hit the button on the bed until Damion was sitting up slightly. "Better?"

Damion glanced around, reached for Jules's hand, and then nodded. "Thanks."

After the doctor left, his parents talked with him for a few moments, then decided to head home, shower, change and get some food of their own.

"Want us to bring you back anything?" they asked her.

"No, I'm good," she said, hugging them. "Thanks."

When they were alone, she sat on the edge of the bed and wished more than anything that she could hold him. Instead, she held his hand and looked deep into his eyes.

"I thought..." Her breath hitched. "I thought I'd lost you."

"Ditto," he said, his eyes running over her face. She could see they were still unfocussed from the drugs. "I thought she'd shot you." He lifted her hand to his lips and kissed her knuckles. "I love you. I don't want to go another day without you."

"Me either." She smiled as she wiped the tears from her eyes with her free hand.

"Does this mean you'll marry me?" he asked. "I could get down on one knee..."

She moved forward and very carefully kissed his lips. "No, you don't have to get down on a knee. Yes, of course I'll marry you," she said against his lips. "As long as you promise me that you're going to get better and never get shot again."

He chuckled, then winced and coughed a few times. "Damn, I might need some more drugs." He sighed when the slight fit was over. "Don't make me laugh again."

She smiled. "Not until you get better. Then, I make no promises."

He smiled up at her. "I love you."

"I love you too." She kissed him again.

The rest of the day visitors came and went. Flowers, balloons, and stuffed animals filled the hospital room.

Someone delivered food for Jules at each mealtime. Another bag of her clothes and toiletry items were brought for her.

She took a nap lying next to Damion shortly after lunch

and was woken when his parents returned. Then she sat with them, talking quietly as Damion rested some more.

After that, a large group filed into the room—Zoey, Dylan, Elle, Liam, Aubrey, Aiden, Scarlett, Levi, and Hannah and Owen, along with baby James. Seeing all of her friends, she knew something was up. Then Brett walked in, and her heart skipped. They were here with news. To be there for support for them when the shoe dropped.

"What is it?" she asked Brett as he stepped into the room.

Damion had woken with the sound of everyone else entering. Jules walked over and sat on the edge of the bed, holding his hand in hers.

"How are you feeling?" Brett asked Damion.

"Like I got shot," Damion answered.

Brett smiled. "I know the feeling."

"I'd sure like to know why," Damion said.

"And I think I might have the answer as to why." Brett moved a little closer and the entire room quieted. "What we know so far is that Lisa and Joe's relationship had turned rocky in the past year. They had married less than five years ago. Shortly after their marriage, they started going on these elaborate and extremely expensive trips. While Lisa claimed on her videos that all of the trips were comped by the resorts and hotels, they weren't. Joe was bleeding his bank accounts and his business accounts dry to please his new wife. Basically, they were ruined before they even stepped foot onto River Camps. After they lashed out at the camp, she posted several crazy videos, which we all saw on her social media accounts. Then we hit back with all the positive promotions you guys organized." Brett looked around the room at everyone. "After you contacted all the hotels and resorts, word spread fast through the industry. No one wanted to do business with them and their magazine any longer. The magazine had been suffering for a while now as it was. Joe had contacted their lawyer to file for divorce a few days ago."

"So, Lisa went on a killing spree?" Jules asked.

"It's just coming to light that she was bipolar. Nikki Fields, Lisa's sister, claims that she'd stopped taking her meds shortly after she married Joe. He didn't even know about her condition. Nikki watched her sister get worse and worse but stood by her since she was utilizing some of the travel and money perks coming her way from her sister. Nikki's the one that bought Lisa the gun. Lisa came to her one night claiming to have been jumped and robbed. She begged Nikki to buy a gun for her so she could feel like she could defend herself."

"But why go after Jules and Damion?" Elle asked.

"Because she could. The night Lisa showed up at the camp, she had already shot and killed Joe," Brett said. "He'd been dead for a few hours before she contacted Byron and his wife Edith to ask them if she and Joe could join them for dinner, knowing they were staying at the camp for the week. Then she made some excuse to them that Joe had grown sick. She most likely had plans to get to the rest of you." Brett motioned towards the group.

"But I went into labor, and everyone was at the hospital," Hannah said, holding James tighter.

"Exactly." Brett nodded. "The only one left there that evening that she knew was Jules. But we'd stepped up security. I don't know why she didn't do anything that night before I got to her, maybe she had a change of heart? Maybe she got spooked?" He shrugged. "Whatever the reason, she left and went back home and filmed several more videos she never published. Shortly before finding you at the restaurant, she posted the video of her killing Joe. While posting it, she found the image of the two of you at the restaurant, which was less than two blocks from their home."

"I should have never posted it." Jules groaned.

"You couldn't have known," Brett said at the same time Damion and a few others chimed in.

"The woman was on a downward spiral. Sooner or later, she was going to do something drastic. River Camps was just an excuse," Brett added. "Nikki is being charged for the purchase of the gun, since it was obtained illegally."

"That's it then?" Jules asked. "We're left to pick up the pieces?" She looked down at Damion.

"Yeah. I'd like to be able to tell you that she got what she deserved, but in truth, what she deserved was to rot in a jail cell or in a mental institution for the rest of her life." Brett sighed.

"Thanks," Damion said with a sigh. Jules could see he was tired again and knew that he needed his rest. "Thank you everyone for being here for us." She stood up and hugged everyone. Then she smiled down at baby James. "You don't know it, but you saved your mama's life. You saved a lot of lives by coming a week early." She leaned down and kissed the baby's forehead. A tear slipped down her nose and landed on the boy's cheek. She used a fingertip to wipe it away. Then she stepped back over to hold Damion's hand as she sat on the edge of the bed. "I think we're going to get some rest now," she said to the group. "Then, when we get out of here, after Damion is better, we're going to plan our wedding," Several people cheered. "Which will be held at River Camps. Then"—she looked down at Damion— "we're going to take a very long honeymoon and sail to Hawaii."

## EPILOGUE

Jules leaned her head back and soaked up the sun shining down on her face. For as far as the eye could see, there was only water around them.

The massive white and blue sails were full of wind, pushing them further west. With each day on the water, she grew more and more comfortable.

By this time, she knew every inch of the *Wind Chaser*. She knew what to do when the wind turned or died down. She knew what lines to pull to make the sails move where they needed to go.

She was a sailor.

She was a wife.

And in five months' time, she would be a mother. She reached up and ran her hand over her small belly.

"Slacking off?" Damion asked her.

She glanced over at her handsome husband. He was standing behind the wheel, his legs spread wide like a true sailor. Billy, their mutt dog, lay at his feet. The thing was so loyal to Damion and loved the water like a fish.

Damion's shirt was off, showcasing the new scars he carried that marked the horrors they had gone through in order to get where they were today.

"Just taking a moment to enjoy." She smiled.

Damion smiled back and motioned ahead of them. "I thought you'd like to see that."

She jerked her head up and around. There in the distance was land. Just a tiny dot of green on the horizon. Her family would be waiting for them there. They would remain there until they welcomed their daughter. Then they would turn around and make the journey back home with a newborn. How they would do it, she didn't know, but she had no doubt it would be an adventure. Nor did she doubt her husband's ability to protect his family at all costs.

Standing up, she walked over to him and wrapped her arms around him.

"We made it," she said with a sigh. "How does it feel?"

He smiled down at her and laughed. "The second best feeling in the world. Next to holding you." He leaned down and kissed her.

# ALSO BY JILL SANDERS

## The Pride Series

Finding Pride

Discovering Pride

Returning Pride

Lasting Pride

Serving Pride

Red Hot Christmas

My Sweet Valentine

Return To Me

Rescue Me

A Pride Christmas

## The Secret Series

Secret Seduction

Secret Pleasure

Secret Guardian

Secret Passions

Secret Identity

Secret Sauce

Secret Obsession

Secret Desire

Secret Charm

Secret Santa

**The West Series**

Loving Lauren

Taming Alex

Holding Haley

Missy's Moment

Breaking Travis

Roping Ryan

Wild Bride

Corey's Catch

Tessa's Turn

Saving Trace

Christmas Holly

**The Grayton Series**

Last Resort

Someday Beach

Rip Current

In Too Deep

Swept Away

High Tide

Sunset Dreams

**Lucky Series**

Unlucky In Love

Sweet Resolve

Best of Luck

A Little Luck

Christmas Wish

**Silver Cove Series**

Silver Lining

French Kiss

Happy Accident

Hidden Charm

A Silver Cove Christmas

Sweet Surrender

Second Chances

**Entangled Series – Paranormal Romance**

The Awakening

The Beckoning

The Ascension

The Presence

The Calling

The Chosen

The Beyond

**Haven, Montana Series**

Closer to You

Never Let Go

Holding On

Coming Home

The Hard Way

**Pride Oregon Series**

A Dash of Love

My Kind of Love

Season of Love

Tis the Season

Dare to Love

Where I Belong

Because of Love

A Thing Called Love

First Comes Love

Someone to Love

**Wildflowers Series**

Summer Nights

Summer Heat

Summer Secrets

Summer Fling

Summer's End

Summer Wish

Summer Breeze

**Distracted Series**

Wake Me

Tame Me

Save Me

Dare Me

**Stand Alone Books**

Twisted Rock

Hope Harbor

Raven Falls

Angel Bluff

For a complete list of books:

http://JillSanders.com

# ABOUT THE AUTHOR

*Jill Sanders is a New York Times, USA Today, and international bestselling author of Sweet Contemporary Romance, Romantic Suspense, Western Romance, and Paranormal Romance novels. With over 85 books in eleven series, translations into several different languages, and audiobooks there's plenty to choose from. Look for Jill's bestselling stories wherever romance books are sold or visit her at jillsanders.com*

*Jill comes from a large family with six siblings, including an identical twin. She was raised in the Pacific Northwest and later relocated to Colorado for college and a successful IT career before discovering her talent for writing sweet and sexy page-turners. After Colorado, she decided to move south, living in Texas and now making her home along the Emerald Coast of Florida. You will find that the settings of several of her series are inspired by her time spent living in these areas. She has two sons and off-set the testosterone in her house by adopting three furry little ladies that provide her company while she's locked in her writing cave. She enjoys heading to the beach, hiking, swim-*

*ming, wine-tasting, and pickleball with her husband, and of course writing. If you have read any of her books, you may also notice that there is a love of food, especially sweets! She has been blamed for a few added pounds by her assistant, editor, and fans... donuts or pie anyone?*

facebook.com/JillSandersBooks

twitter.com/JillMSanders

amazon.com/Jill-Sanders/e/B009M2NFD6?tag=jillmcom-20

bookbub.com/authors/jill-sanders

instagram.com/jillsandersauthor

tiktok.com/@jillsandersauthor